GREAT PERSONALITIES OF THE WORLD

Legends Who Inspire Us Forever

Tanvir Khan

V&S PUBLISHERS

Published by:

V&S PUBLISHERS

F-2/16, Ansari Road, Daryaganj, New Delhi-110002
011-23240026, 011-23240027 • *Fax:* 011-23240028
Email: info@vspublishers.com • *Website:* www.vspublishers.com

Branch : Hyderabad
5-1-707/1, Brij Bhawan (Beside Central Bank of India Lane)
Bank Street, Koti, Hyderabad - 500 095
040-24737290
E-mail: vspublishershyd@gmail.com

Branch Offi ce Mumbai
Godown # 34 at The Model Co-Operative Housing, Society Ltd.,
"Sahakar Niwas", Ground Floor, Next to Sobo Central, Mumbai - 400 034
022-23510736
E-mail vspublishersmum@gmail.com

Follow us on:

All books available at **www.vspublishers.com**

© **Copyright:** *V&S PUBLISHERS*
ISBN 978-93-815883-4-5
Edition 2014

Printed at : Param Offseters, Okhla, New Delhi-110020

Publisher's Note————————————

In keeping with the philosophy of bringing out books of immortal values, V&S Publishers has brought out this book, *Great Personalities of the World.* This information-packed book chronicles the lives of 250 of the most influential personalities whose achievements have helped shape the modern world.

The list includes famous statesmen and women, entrepreneurs, scientists, social reformers, film artists, sportsmen and women, among others. Also included in the book are eminent people that include those who have achieved distinction as writers, musicians, business persons, philanthropists, etc.

The selection has been made out of personalities from several countries across the globe. Enjoy reading about Mahatma Gandhi, Jawaharlal Nehru, Abraham Lincoln, John Kennedy, Albert Einstein, JRD Tata, Lata Mangeshkar, R.K. Laxman, Elvis Presley, Tom Cruise, Pele, Sachin Tendulkar, etc. These famous personalities have influenced our lives, and have become a source of constant inspiration and motivation for all of us.

The text is organised category-wise for easy access and reference.

Each biography includes a *trivia,* a *quote,* the successes, failures and awards associated with these great people to inspire the readers and satisfy their curious instincts.

So read on the success stories of each of these great men, and discover for yourself if you can imbibe their traits during your growing years to make it big in your life.

Contents

HISTORIANS/HISTORIC FIGURES

SINGERS/MUSICIANS

POLITICIANS/DIPLOMATS

PHYSICIANS

SCIENTISTS/INVENTORS

SOCIAL REFORMERS

SPORTSPERSONS

WRITERS/POETS/LYRICISTS

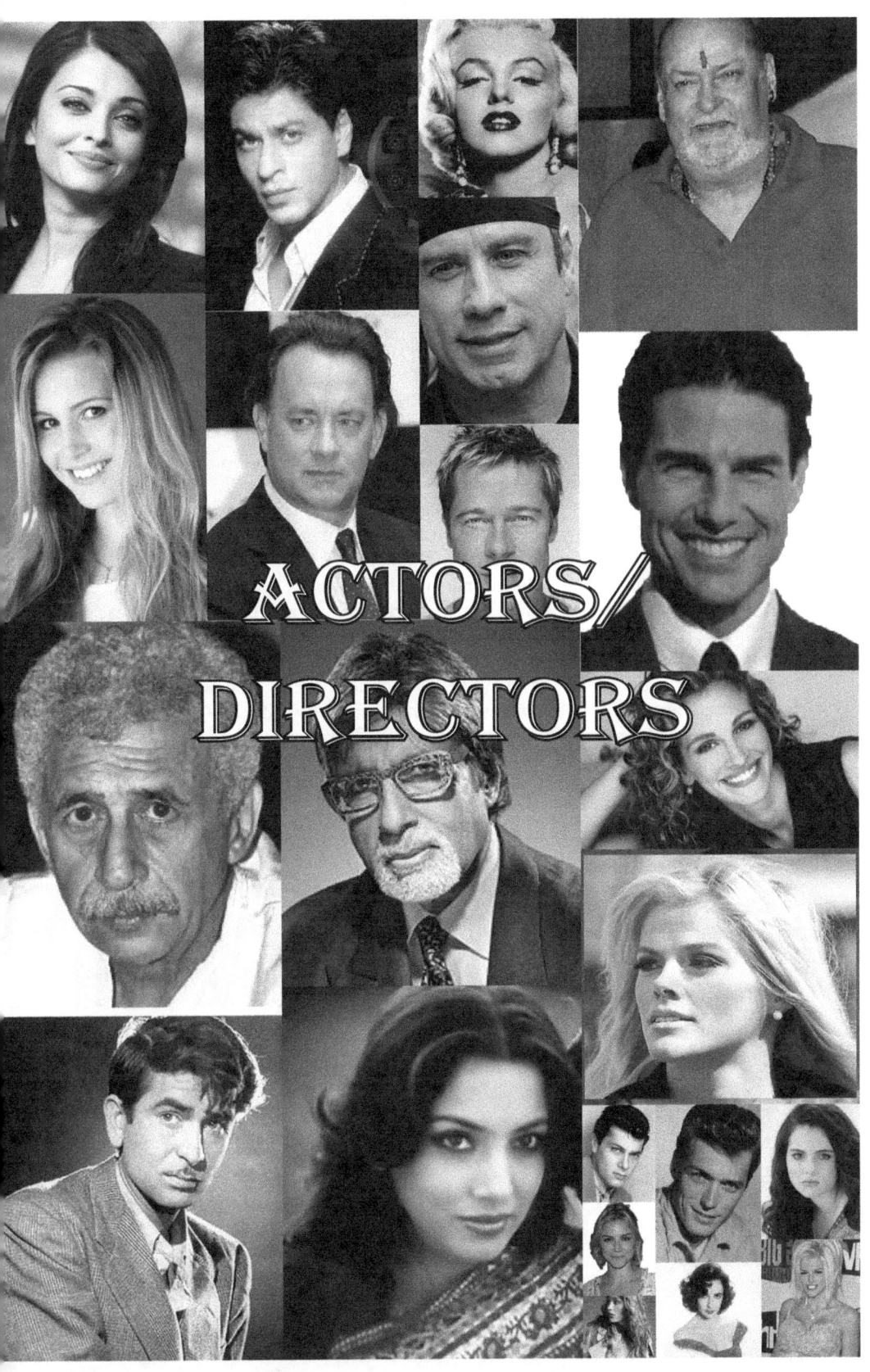

ACTORS/
DIRECTORS

AISHWARYA RAI

Aishwarya Rai was born on November 1, 1973 in Mangalore, Karnataka, India. Though born into a traditional south Indian family, Aishwarya started modelling at a young age. This green-blue-eyed beauty appeared in advertisements for many prestigious firms – the ones that brought her into the limelight were the Garden sari and the Pepsi ad.

Crowned Miss India 1994 runner-up, she was a hot favourite in the run for the **Miss World** title, which she won. Her beauty and charm made her India's darling. Ash stormed into the Indian film industry, where she has proven herself a brilliant and genuine actor.

Her performance in *The Duo* (1997) was critically acclaimed and she won the Screen best female debutant award for her role in *Aur Pyaar Ho Gaya* (1997). She was adored in movies like *Taal, Hum Dil De Chuke Sanam, Devdas*. Her item number in *Bunty Aur Babli* had sent waves of rhythm across the nation. With her successful Bollywood movies and prestigious Hollywood projects lined up for release, it is impossible to ignore this Indian diva in international scenes.

In Southern India, she was best known for her role as Madhumita/ Veishnavi in *Jeans* (1998) and as Meenakshi in *I Have Found It* (2000). She won the **Filmfare Award** for best actress for her performance in *Hum Dil De Chuke Sanam* (1999). She also won rave reviews for her performance as a rape victim in *Hamara Dil Aapke Paas Hai* (2000).

Aishwarya has got married to Abhishek Bachchan, the Bollywood Megastar, Amitabh Bachchan's son and is the proud mother of a beautiful baby girl.

Trivia

Aishwarya Wanted to study medicine, but circumstances prevented her.

Quote

"I always believed that my silence on several topics will be an advantage in the long run."

AMITABH BACHCHAN

Born on October 11, 1942 to well-known poet Harivansh Rai Bachchan and Teji Bachchan, Amitabh Bachchan is a famous Bollywood actor since 1969.

Known as the 'Angry Young Man' of Bollywood, he is popularly called Big B or Amitji. After studying at the Boys' High School, he took up arts as his subject in Sherwood College.

Amitabh Bachchan started his film career as a voice narrator in *Bhuvan Shome* in 1969. He got his first opportunity as an actor in *Saat Hindustani*.

Having starred in many films including *Parwaana, Reshma Aur Shera, Guddi* and many others during 1969-1972, he married Jaya Bhaduri after his first hit film, *Zanjeer* in 1973. The couple has a son and a daughter. His son, Abhishek Bachchan is also a popular Bollywood star.

The year 1975 had been a year of blockbuster hits for him, in which he gave films like *Deewar* and *Sholay*.

Some of the other films to his credit are *Amar Akbar Anthony, Kabhie Kabhie, Muqaddar Ka Sikandar, Trishul, Ram Balram, Mr. Natwarlal, Dostana, Silsila, Shaan, Lawaaris* and *Shakti*.

After an injury on the sets of a film, he had decided to quit films and enter politics but returned to films again in 1988 with *Shahenshah*.

He is conferred with **Padma Shri** in 1984 and **Padma Bhushan** in 2001. Having more than 100 films to his name, Amitabh Bachchan is still going strong.

In addition to acting, Bachchan or the Big B has also worked as a playback singer, a film producer and a television presenter in one of the most popular T.V. shows, *Kaun Banega Crorepati*. He was also an elected member of the Indian Parliament from 1984 to 1987.

Trivia

He was initially named *Inquilab* by his father, but later changed to his current name on the advice of a friend.

ANNA NICOLE SMITH

Anna Nicole Smith was born on November 28, 1967. She was an American model, actress and television personality. Smith fi rst gained popularity in Playboy, becoming the 1993 Playmate of the Year. She modelled for clothing companies, including Guess Jeans and Lane Bryant.

In 1992, Smith was chosen by Hugh Hefner to appear on the cover of the March issue of *Playboy*, where she was listed as Vickie Smith, wearing a low-cut evening gown. The centrefold was photographed by Stephen Wayda. Smith once said she planned to be "the next Marilyn Monroe". Becoming one of *Playboy's* most popular models, Smith was heavier and larger than the typical *Playboy* model. Smith was chosen to be the 1993 Playmate of the Year. By the time of her PMOY pictorial, she had settled on the name, Anna Nicole Smith.

Smith dropped out of high school and was married in 1985. Her highly publicised second marriage to oil business mogul J. Howard Marshall, 62 years her senior, resulted in speculation that she married such an elderly person for his money, which she denied. Following Marshall's death, Smith began a lengthy legal battle over a share of his estate; her case, Marshall v. Marshall, reached the U.S. Supreme Court on a question of federal jurisdiction.

She died on February 8, 2007 in a hotel room in Florida as a result of an overdose of prescription drugs. Within the final six months of her life, Smith was the focus of renewed press coverage surrounding the death of her son, Daniel and the paternity and custody battle over her biological daughter Dannielynn.

Trivia
Anna Nicole was ranked #1 on Entertainment Tonight's "Hot List of 2007".

Quote
"I never thought to ever ask for money. I was so stupid."

BRAD PITT

Born on December 18, 1963 at Shawnee Oklahoma, United States, William Bradley 'Brad' Pitt is an actor and film producer. Pitt has received two **Academy Award nominations** and four **Golden Globe Award nominations**, winning one Golden Globe. He has been described as one of the world's most attractive men, a label for which he has received substantial media attention.

Pitt began his acting career with television guest appearances, including a role on the CBS prime-time soap opera, *Dallas* in 1987. He later gained recognition as *cowboy hitchhiker* who seduces Geena Davis's character in the 1991 road movie, *Thelma & Louise.* He was cast opposite Anthony Hopkins in the 1994 drama, *Legends of the fall,* which earned him his first **Golden Globe nomination**.

In 1995, he gave critically acclaimed performances in the crime thriller *Seven* and the science fiction film, *12 Monkeys,* the latter securing him a *Golden Globe Award* for the Best Supporting Actor and an Academy Award nomination.

He gave some more successful movies in the coming years namely: *Ocean's Eleven, Ocean's Twelve, Ocean's Thirteen, Fight Club, Troy, Mr and Mrs Smith,* etc. Pitt received his second Academy Award nomination for his title role performance in the 2008 film, *The Curious Case of Benjamin Button.*

Pitt got married to famous Hollywood actress, Angelina Jolie that generated wide publicity. He and Jolie have six children – Maddox, Pax, Zahara, Shiloh, Knox and Vivienne. Pitt owns a production company named Plan B Entertainment, whose productions include the 2007 Academy Award winning Best Picture, *The Departed.*

Trivia
He was considered for the lead in The Matrix (1999).

Quote
"You must lose everything in order to gain anything."

13

Bruce Lee

Martial arts expert, Bruce Lee was born on November 27, 1940, in San Francisco, California. He began acting in 1946 and appeared in roughly 20 films as a child actor in Hong King. Young Bruce appeared in his first film at the age of three months, when he served as the stand-in for an American baby in the *Golden Gate Girl.*

Lee gained popularity with his role in the television series, 'The Green Hornet' from 1966 to 1967, and then went on to star in many films until 1973, before he died in Hong Kong at the age of 32.

His father was a Hong Kong opera singer and moved to the United States in 1939 with his family. Lee's mother called him 'Bruce', which means 'strong one in Gaelic'.

As a teenager, Lee became a member of a Hong Kong street gang and began studying kung-fu to sharpen his fighting skills in 1953. In 1959, after Lee got into trouble with the police for fighting, his mother sent him back to the US to live with family friends outside Seattle in Washington.

Though Lee is best known for his martial arts, he also studied drama and philosophy at the University of Washington. He had an extensive library.

His books on martial arts and fighting philosophy are known for their philosophical assertions.

Trivia
Bruce Lee also studied dance, once winning a 'cha–cha' competition.

Quote
"Do not deny the classical approach, simply as a reaction, or you will have created another pattern and trapped yourself there."

CHARLIE CHAPLIN

Born on April 16, 1889, in London to Charles and Hannah Chaplin, Sir Charles Spencer Chaplin was a British comedian, producer, writer, director and composer.

He is best known for his work during the silent film era. Famous for his *Little Tramp* character, the sweet little man with a bowler hat, moustache and cane, Chaplin was one of film's first superstars, elevating in a way one could have ever imagined.

Charlie Chaplin's rise was a true 'rags-to-riches' story. His father abandoned Chaplin, his mother and his brother, Sydney.

Chaplin began his official acting career at the age of eight, touring with The Eight Lancashire Lads. At 18, he began touring with Fred Karno's vaudeville troupe, joining them on the troupe's 1910 US tour.

After having made many films, Charlie Chaplin, Douglas Fairbanks, Mary Pickford and DW Griffith formed the United Artists (UA) in 1919.

He became the most famous film star before the end of World War I. Chaplin used slapstick, mime and other visual comedy routines and continued well into the era of the talkies, though his films decreased from the end of the 1920s.

Chaplin's life and career was full of scandals and controversy. Amid those controversies, Chaplin has seen a good career. Chaplin died of natural causes on December 25, 1977 at his home in Switzerland.

Trivia

Chaplin married four times and had a total of 11 children. In 1918, he married Mildred Harris. The couple had a son who just lived for three days. After their divorce in 1920, he married Lita Grey in 1924. The couple had two children. Then, he married Paulette Goddard in 1936 and his final marriage was to Oona O'Neill in 1943. Oona gave birth to eight children.

CHRIS COLUMBUS

Born in Pennsylvania and raised in Ohio, Chris Columbus was first inspired to make movies after seeing 'The Godfather' at the age of 15. After enrolling at the NYU film school, he sold his first screenplay (never produced) while a sophomore there.

After graduation, Columbus tried to sell his fourth script, "Gremlins", with no success, until Steven Spielberg optioned it. Columbus moved to Los Angeles for a year during working on the project in Spielberg's bungalow at Universal.

After writing two more scripts for Spielberg, *The Goonies* and *Young Sherlock Holmes*, Columbus own directing career was launched a few years later with *Adventures in Babysitting*. He is best known to audiences as the director of the runaway hit, *Home Alone*, written and produced by John Hughes, its sequel, *Home Alone 2*, and most recently, *Mrs. Doubtfire*.

He got the directing gig on Harry Potter after longtime front-runner Steven Spielberg passed on the project. He met author J.K. Rowling in England and won the job over several other candidates after promising her he would film entirely in the United Kingdom and use an all-British cast. Most of the crew was also British.

Trivia

At one time lived in River Forest, Illinois which shares a high school with the suburb, Oak Park, in which Adventures in Babysitting (1987) was based. Oak Park and River Forest High School's name was changed for the movie, however, they kept the style of the high school's jackets same for the film.

Quote

"By prevailing over all obstacles and distractions, one may unfailingly arrive at his chosen goal or destination." — Christopher Columbus

CHRISTIE HAYES

Christie Lynne Hayes was born on October 31, 1986. She is an Australian actress. Christie is the sister of actress Katherine Hayes.

In 2000, Hayes was cast as Maria in the family adventure series, *Search for Treasure Island.* Later that year, Hayes was cast in her biggest role to date as Kirsty Sutherland in the successful soap opera, *Home and Away.* She was the first person to be cast in her on screen "Sutherland" family. She played both Kirsty Phillips and Laura De Groot; the two characters were twin sisters separated at birth. Hayes, who was on the cover of the *TV Week,* more times in 2004 than any of her other castmates, left *Home and Away* in October 2004 in order to travel. Her final *Home and Away* appearance aired in February 2005.

She appeared in a Pepsi Light commercial in 2006 and made a guest appearance on the soap, *Blue Water High.* She was also involved in the making of various films and television shows, including *Room 101, Searching For Eva, The First Goodbye and Noir.*

Christie plays the lead in *I.D.* as Kate in 2011. Hayes returned to *Home and Away* in May 2008, as a series remaining regular until October 2009.

Christie has also done various television commercials, and at the age of nine was flown to New Zealand for a German yogurt commercial. She also did various Employment National ads, a P&O cruise ad and a Potato Nuggets ad.

She sang in her on-screen wedding on "Home And Away". Voted as the Youth Ambassador for Australia in 2003, she also sponsors children through the World Vision Australia. Christie also appears at the annual Teddy Bears Picnic for sick children.

CHUCK JONES

Born on September 21, 1912 in Spokane, Washington, Charles Martin 'Chuck' Jones was an American animator, cartoonist, producer, screen writer and director of animated films.

Jones had an interest in drawing from early childhood. After graduating from Chouinard Art Institute, Jones started looking for jobs in the animation industry.

He joined 'Leon Schlesinger Productions', which produced Looney Tunes and Merrie Melodies for Warner Bros. in 1933.

Jones' first cartoon was 'The Night Watchman' that featured a cute kitten. After having an extraordinary career at Warner Bros. till 1962, Jones started his independent animation studio with his business partner, Les Goldman by the name, 'Sib Tower 12 Productions'. Jones has the credit of producing the famous 'Tom and Jerry cartoons'.

Later, Sib Tower 12 Productions was absorbed by the MGM and renamed as the 'MGM Animation/Visual Arts'.

In a career of over 60 years, Jones made many classic short animated cartoons starring Sylvester, Daffy Duck, Bugs Bunny, the Road Runner and Wile E Coyote, Pepé Le Pew and a slew of other Warner characters.

Making more than 300 animated films, Jones won **three Oscars** as director and **an honorary Oscar for Lifetime Achievement in 1996**. Among the many awards and recognitions, one of those most valued was the honorary life membership from the 'Directors Guild of America'.

Jones' animated short film, *The Dot and the Line: A Romance in Lower Mathematics* won the **1965 Oscar for the Best Animated Short Films**.

Jones died of heart failure on February 22, 2002.

Trivia

Three of these short films, Duck Amuck, One Froggy Evening and What's Opera, Doc? – were later inducted into the National Film Registry.

CLINT EASTWOOD

Clinton 'Clint' Eastwood, Jr. was born on May 31, 1930 to Clinton, Sr. and Ruth Eastwood. He is an American film actor, director, producer, composer and a politician.

After graduating from high school, he moved to Seattle in 1951 and started working as a lifeguard and swim instructor for the military.

Eastwood first became popular as a supporting cast member in the TV series, *Rawhide* in 1959. He then rose to fame for playing the 'Man with No Name' in *A Fistful of Dollars, For A Few Dollars More,* and *The Good, the Bad and the Ugly* during the 1960s. He also worked as Inspector Harry Callahan in the film – *Magnum Force* by Dirty Harry. The other films he worked are *The Enforcer, Sudden Impact* and *The Dead Pool.*

Eastwood won Academy Awards for Best Director and Producer of the Best Picture. He also received nominations for Best Actor, for his work in films, *Unforgiven* and *Million Dollar Baby.*

Some of his other well-known films include *Play Misty for Me* (1971), *The Outlaw Josey Wales* (1976), *Pale Rider* (1985), *In the Line of Fire* (1993), *The Bridges of Madison County* (1995) and Gran Torino (2008).

He also directed films in which he did not appear, such as *Mystic River* (2003) and *Letters from Iwo Jima* (2006).

He was awarded two of France's highest honours – the Ordre des Arts et des Lettres medal in 1994 and the Légion d'honneur medal in 2007.

Since 1967, Eastwood has started his own production company, Malpaso films or Malpaso Productions. He also served as the non-partisan mayor of Carmel-by-the-Sea, California, from 1986 to 1988.

Trivia

Eastwood has seven children by five different women, and has married twice.

Quote

"If you want a guarantee, buy a toaster."

ELIZABETH TAYLOR

Born on February 27, 1932, Dame Elizabeth Rosemond 'Liz' Taylor was a British-American actress. As a child star with the Metro-Goldwyn-Mayer (MGM), she became a great screen actress of Hollywood's Golden Age.

Elizabeth lived in London until the age of seven, after which the family left for the United States when clouds of war began brewing in Europe in 1939.

Taylor was known for her acting ability, glamorous lifestyle, beauty and distinctive violet eyes. Her first venture on the screen was in *There's One Born Every Minute* in 1942. It was released when she was ten years old. Later, Elizabeth was picked up by the MGM.

She did many films with the studio, the first one being *Lassie Come Home* in 1943. She had minuscule parts in her next two films – *The White Cliffs of Dover* and *Jane Eyre*.

She gained widespread popularity with MGM's *National Velvet* in 1944. In 1947, she starred in *Life with Father* with popular actors like William Powell, Irene Dunne and Zasu Pitts.

Her busiest year was 1954, with roles in *Rhapsody, Beau Brummell, The Last Time I Saw Paris* and *Elephant Walk*. Some of her other successful films include *Raintree County, Cat on a Hot Tin Roof, Suddenly* and *Last Summer*. She also won an **Oscar** for *Butterfield 8*.

Taylor died of congestive heart failure in March 2011 at the age of 79, having suffered many years of ill health.

Trivia

She married eight times in her lifetime and has four children.

JACKIE CHAN

Born on April 7, 1954, Jackie Chan is an actor, comedian, director, martial artist, action choreographer, producer, entrepreneur, screenwriter, singer and stunt performer.

Chan has started acting at an early age at the school level and had joined a performance group, *Seven Little Fortunes*. Eventually, Chan appeared in the film, *Big and Little Wong Tin Bar* with others from the *Seven Little Fortunes*. He subsequently went on to appear in several more films as a child.

At the age of 17, Chan served as a stuntman in two Bruce Lee films – *Fist of Fury* and *Enter the Dragon*. His first adult starring role was in *Little Tiger of Canton*. It was in 1978 that Chan established himself as a comedy Kung Fu actor with Snake in the Eagle's Shadow.

Much of Chan's martial arts skills came from practising the arts while at the Chinese Opera Research Institute. He earned his blackbelt under Grandmaster Jin Pal Kim.

In his movies, he is known for his comic timing, acrobatic fighting style, use of improvised weapons, and innovative stunts. Since the 1960s, Jackie Chan has appeared in over 100 films.

He holds the **Guinness World Record** for 'Most Stunts by a Living Actor'. Chan is also a successful singer in Hong Kong and Asia with numerous albums to his credit.

In 1982, Jackie Chan married popular Taiwanese actress Lin Feng-Jiao (aka Joan Lin). The couple had a son.

Trivia

He also became friends with Sammo Hung and Yuen Biao in the group, a trio that became collectively known in Hong Kong as 'Three Brothers' or 'Three Dragons'.

JOHN TRAVOLTA

Born on February 2, 1954, John Travolta is an American actor who rose to fame with his lead role in the film, *Grease*.

Travolta had joined an area actors' group by the age of 12, and soon began appearing in local musicals and dinner-theatre performances.

By the age of 16, he dropped out of high school to take up acting full-time. He then earned himself a role in a touring version of *Grease*, as well as a part in *Over Here!* on Broadway.

One of Travolta's first TV acting jobs was with soap opera, *The Edge of Night*. In 1976, Travolta did his first notable movie role in *Carrie*.

Travolta's breakthrough role came around in the late 1970s, when he starred as Vinni Barbarino in the sitcom, *Welcome Back, Kotter*.

In 1977, Travolta appeared as Tony Manero in *Saturday Night Fever* and got the role of Danny Zuko in the film version of *Grease* in 1978. These two films are perhaps two of his best known. He was also nominated for the Best Actor for Oscar.

Some of his other known films were *Urban Cowboy, Staying Alive, Two of a kind, Pulp Fiction*.

John Travolta married actress Kelly Preston in 1991. The couple have a son, Jett and a daughter, Ella Bleu.

His more recent works were *Hairspray*, Adam Shankman's screen adaptation of the stage musical, which put Travolta in drag to play the heavy set; *The Taking of Pelham 13* and *From Paris with Love*, as well as a sequel to *Wild Hogs, 2009's Old Dogs*.

Trivia

He won the Golden Globe Award for Best Actor – Motion Picture Musical or Comedy for his performance in Get Shorty.

JULIA ROBERTS

Born in Smyrna, Georgia on October 28, 1967, Julia Fiona Roberts had never dreamt that she would become the most popular actress in America. As a child, due to her love of animals, Julia originally wanted to be a veterinarian but later studied journalism.

After her brother Eric Roberts achieved some success in Hollywood, Julia decided to try acting. Her first break came in 1988 youth-oriented movies, *Mystic Pizza* and *Satisfaction*. The movies introduced her to a new audience who instantly fell in love with this pretty woman.

Julia's biggest success was in the signature movie, *Pretty Woman*, for which Julia got an **Oscar nomination** and also won the **People's Choice Award** for Favourite Actress.

Audience would always love Julia best in romantic comedies. With *My Best Friend's Wedding* in 1997, Julia gave the genre fresh life that had been lacking in Hollywood for some time.

Off screen, after a brief marriage, Julia has been linked with several other actors. Julia also got involved with UNICEF charities and has made visits to many different countries, including Haiti and India in order to promote goodwill. Julia is one of the most popular and sought-after talents in Hollywood.

Trivia

She was chosen one of the '50 Most Beautiful People in the World' by the People magazine in 2000.

Quote

"Happiness isn't happiness unless there's a violin-playing goat."

MARILYN MONROE

Marilyn Monroe was born as Norma Jeane Mortenson on June 1, 1926, in Los Angeles General Hospital. Prior to her birth, Marilyn's father headed north to San Francisco, abandoning the family in Los Angeles. Marilyn grew up not knowing for sure who her father really was. Her mother, Gladys, had entered into several relationships, further confusing her daughter as to who it was who fathered her.

Her first film was in 1947 with a bit part in *The Shocking Miss Pilgrim*. Her next production was not much better, a bit in the eminently forgettable *Scudda Hoo! Scudda Hay!* (1948). Two of the three brief scenes she appeared wound up on the cutting room floor. Later, she was given a somewhat better role as waitress, Evie in *Dangerous Years*. However, Fox declined to renew her contract, so she went back to modelling and the acting school.

Columbia gave her a six-month contract in the B movie, *Ladies of the Chorus* (1948) in which she sang two numbers. Joseph L. Mankiewiez saw her in a small part in *The Asphalt Jungle* (1950) and put her in *All About Eve* (1950), resulting in resigning her to a seven-year contract with the *20th Century Fox Film Corporation*. *Niagara* (1953) and *Gentlemen Prefer Blondes* (1953) launched her as a sex symbol superstar.

The work on her last picture, *The Misfit* (1961), written for her by departing husband Miller was interrupted by exhaustion. She was dropped from the unfinished *Something's Got to Give* (1962) due to chronic lateness and drug dependency. Four months later, she was found dead in her Brentwood home of a drug overdose, adjudged "probable suicide".

Trivia
She has voted the 'Sexiest Woman of the Century' by the People magazine. [1999]

Quote
"A career is wonderful, but you can't curl up with it on a cold night."

NASEERUDDIN SHAH

Born on July 20, 1950, Naseeruddin Shah is a Bollywood film actor and director. Shah did his schooling at St. Anselm's, Ajmer and St. Joseph's College in Nainital. After his graduation, he attended the National School of Drama (NSD) in Delhi.

Naseeruddin Shah has been successful in both the mainstream and parallel cinema.

Shah has acted in movie like *Aakrosh, Nishant, Sparsh, Albert Pinto Ko Gussa Kyon Ata Hai, Mirch Masala, Trikal, Bhavni Bhavai, Junoon, Mandi, Ardh Satya, Jaane Bhi Do Yaaro* and many more.

Naseeruddin Shah was earlier married to Surekha Sikri's sister, who was a doctor working in Iran. He married actress Ratna Pathak after the demise of Sikri's sister. He has three children – a daughter, Heeba from his earlier marriage and two sons, Imaad and Irhaan from Ratna Pathak Shah.

He also starred in many international films, most notably playing the character of *Captain Nemo* in the Hollywood comic book adaptation, *The League of Extraordinary Gentlemen* in 2003.

Naseeruddin Shah has been giving performances with his theatre troupe in New Delhi, Mumbai, Bengaluru and Lahore. He has directed plays written by Lavender Kumar, Ismat Chughtai and Saadat Hasan Manto. His directorial debut in Bollywood was *Yun Hota To Kya Hota* in 2006.

He made his Pakistani film debut with the critically acclaimed and controversial film *Khuda Ke Liye,* where he also played a cameo.

More recently, he has worked in films like *Maqbool, Jaane Tu Ya Jaane Na, Ishqiya, Omkara* and many more.

Naseeruddin Shah is characterised by seamless and gripping performances in cinema and theatre for over thirty years now.

Trivia

His elder brother Lt General Zameeruddin Shah was in the Indian Army.

PIPER PERABO

Piper Perabo was born on October 31, 1976 to Mary Charlotte and George William Perabo in Dallas, Texas and grew up in Toms River, New Jersey. She is an American stage, film and TV actress. She is of Portuguese and Norwegian descent.

Piper graduated from the Ohio University in Athens, Ohio with a degree in theatre.

Piper was cast in *The Adventures of Rocky* and *Bullwinkle* as FBI agent Karen Sympathy in 2000. Next, she was cast in *Coyote Ugly* as Violet Jersey Sanford for which she won an MTV Movie Award for the Best Music Moment for One Way or Another. She was also nominated for Blockbuster Entertainment Award for Favourite Female – Newcomer and MTV Movie Award for Female Breakthrough Performance for the same film.

Piper starred in an independent Canadian movie called *Lost and Delirious* in 2001. The next year, she starred as a French exchange student in *Slap Her... She's French*. In 2003, she had a role as the eldest Baker child in *Cheaper by the Dozen*, a role also played in the 2005 sequel of the film.

She had also worked in *The I Inside* (2003), *Perfect Opposites* (2004), *George and the Dragon* (2004), *The Cave* (2005), *Imagine Me & You* (2005), *Edison* (2005), *The Prestige* (2006) and *Beverly Hills Chihuahua* (2008). She also appeared in the Fox TV Show House as a nutritionist.

Piper made her Broadway debut in 2009 in Neil LaBute play, *Reasons to Be Pretty*. Piper was also cast as the lead character, CIA agent Annie Walker in the television spy series, *Covert Affairs* on the USA Network. For her work in *Covert Affairs*, she received a nomination for the **2010 Golden Globe Award** for the Best Actress – Television Series Drama.

Trivia

Piper's mother is a physical therapist and her father is a professor of poetry at the Ocean County College. She has two brothers, Noah and Adam.

RAJ KAPOOR

A legendary actor, director, and producer of many Bollywood movies, Raj Kapoor was born on December 14, 1924 at Peshawar in the North-West Frontier Province of what is now Pakistan.

Raj Kapoor began his career as a clapper boy assisting director Kidar Sharma. He appeared in films for the first time in the film *Inquilab* in 1935 at the age of eleven.

The big break came to him when he played the main lead in *Neel Kamal* in 1947. He established his studio, **RK Films**, when he was 24 and became the youngest director of his era in the Hindi cinema.

His directorial debut in *Aag* was a thumping success. He directed many films that are still remembered and loved – *Barsaat* (1949), *Awaara* (1951), *Shri 420* (1955), and *Sangam* (1964). He also starred in a number of the films, he directed, often with his real-life love interest, actress, Nargis.

Films like *Mera Naam Joker, Bobby, Satyam Shivam Sundaram* and *Ram Teri Ganga Maili* are also to his credit.

At the age of 22, in 1946, Raj Kapoor was married to Krishna Malhotra in a traditional family-arranged wedding. The couple have five children – Randhir, Ritu, Rishi, Rima and Rajiv.

Raj Kapoor suffered from asthma in his later years and died of complications in 1988. He was working on the movie *Henna* when he died. The film was later completed by his son, Randhir Kapoor.

Noted film personalities of the present Bollywood, Karisma and Kareena Kapoor are the granddaughters of Raj and Krishna Kapoor, being the daughters of their eldest son, Randhir by his wife Babita. His younger brothers Shammi Kapoor and Shashi Kapoor were also actors. Rishi Kapoor, the younger son of Raj Kapoor, too is a great actor.

Trivia

Raj Kapoor's performance in Awaara, was ranked one of the "Top-Ten Performances of all time", by the Time magazine of the Indian Cinema.

RUSSELL PETERS

Born on September 29, 1970, Russell Peters is an Indo-Canadian. He is a comedian, actor and a disk jocky by profession. He started his career by performing first in Toronto in 1989 and has also been nominated for four Gemini Awards.

Russell Peters was born in Canada to Eric and Maureen Peters. His family is of Anglo-Indian ancestry and is a Catholic. His father was born in Pune, India and worked as a federal meat inspector and his mother was born in Calcutta (Kolkata), India. He has an elder brother named Clayton who was born in Calcutta.

Russell Peters' stand-up performances are mostly made up of observational comedy, where he uses humour to poke fun at the subjects of race, class and culture, often using his own life experiences as well as impersonations of different cultural accents to illustrate his act. Another well-known comedian like him is Carlos Mencia. Russell Peters uses his minority status to allow him to poke fun at different races in his performances, but according to an interview done for 'The National', he does not intend to put down or offend different races and cultures, but instead tries to raise them up through humour.

Trivia

Peters became the first comedian to sell out Toronto's Air Canada Center with more than 16,000 tickets in two days for the single show. He ended up selling over 30,000 tickets nationally over the two-day sales period. A total of over 60,000 tickets were sold across six cities.

SAMAIRE ARMSTRONG

Samaire Armstrong was born on October 31, 1980 in Tokyo to Hunter Armstrong and Sylvia Sepielli. Samaire lived in Tokyo for several years before moving to Hawaii and later Sedona, Arizona, where she grew up and attended Sedona Red Rock High School. She has also lived in Malaysia and China. She is an American actor, designer and model.

Samaire made her film debut as *Kara Fratelli*, one of the conjoined twins in the parody film, *Not Another Teen Movie* in 2001. Samaire has since appeared in small roles in films like *Would I Lie To You, Gramercy Park* and *Trash*. In 2006, Samaire co-starred alongside Lindsay Lohan in the film, *Just My Luck*. In 2005, she was offered the leading female protagonist role in the horror film, *Stay Alive*.

In 2006, Samaire played the role of Nell Bedworth in the Canadian comedy, *It's a Boy Girl Thing*. The film was released in 2006 and received positive reviews from critics. Samaire's performance in this film was praised by critics.

Samaire starred in a relatively small supporting role as Jenny in the horror film, *Rise: Blood Hunter* in 2007. She also had a leading role portraying *Caitlin Atwater* in the lifetime film, *The Staircase Murders*.

In 2008, Samaire starred in the independent romantic film, *Around June*. She has been cast in another independent film, a crime thriller, *The Last Harbor*. She will also star in another thriller, *5 Souls*.

Samaire made her television debut guest starring in an episode of the teen drama television series, *Party of Five* portraying Meredith in 2000. Throughout 2000 to 2001, she made guest roles in shows, such as *The X-Files, Judging Amy* and *Freaks and Geeks*.

In 2003, Samaire was cast in the role of Anna Stern on the Fox teen drama television series, *The O.C.* In 2004, she appeared on the HBO television series, *Entourage*, an assistant to Ari Gold and love interest for Eric Murphy. She went on to be a guest star in the television series, *CSI: Miami* and *Living with Fran*.

Samaire was cast in her first series regular role on the ABC drama/comedy television series, *Dirty Sexy Money* in 2007. The series was an instant success and premiered to about 10.44 million viewers. However in March 2008, she announced she would not return for the series second season as a series regular.

SATYAJIT RAY

Satyajit Ray was born on May 2, 1921 in Calcutta (now Kolkata). He joined Shantiniketan, Rabindranath Tagore's university to study art. Satyajit Ray began his career as a commercial artist. His father, Sukumar Ray, was an eminent poet and writer in the history of Bengali literature.

Satyajit Ray's first movie *Pather Panchali* was an immediate success and won the **Grand Prix** at the 'Cannes Festival'. *Pather Panchali* with his *Aparajito* and *Apur Sansar* are known as 'Apu Trilogy'.

In 1948, he married Bijoya Das, a former actress/singer who also happened to be his cousin. Their only offspring, Sandip, was born in 1953.

His later films include *Jalsaghar, Kanchenjunga, Charulata, Ashanti Sanket, The Chess Players, The Home and The World, Ganashatru,* and *Agantuk.* Ray also edited *Sandesh,* a children's magazine and wrote numerous fictions and non-fiction works. In 1992, he received an honorary Academy Award.

In 1983, Satyajit Ray suffered a massive heart attack. He died on April 23, 1992 in Calcutta after having some 40 films and documentaries and numerous books and articles to his credit.

Trivia

He was voted the 25th Greatest Director of all time by the Entertainment weekly.

In 1967, he wrote a script, 'The Alien'. Columbia Pictures was in talks to produce it. Peter Sellers and Marlon Brando were supposed to be up for the leading roles. However, Ray was surprised to find that the script he had co-written had already been copyrighted and the fee appropriated. Brando dropped out of the project and though an attempt was made to bring James Coburn in to replace him, Ray was disillusioned, had enough of Hollywood machinations and returned to Calcutta.

SHABANA AZMI

Born on September 18, 1950, Shabana Azmi is an Indian actress of film, television and theatre.

An alumna of the Film and Television Institute of India of Pune, she made her film debut in 1974 and soon became one of the leading actresses of parallel cinema, an Indian New Wave Movement known for its serious content and neo-realism.

Regarded as one of the finest actresses in India, Shabana's performances in films in a variety of genres have generally earned her praise and awards, which include a record of five wins of the National Film Award for Best Actress and several international honours. She has also received **four Filmfare Awards**.

Shabana has appeared in over 120 Hindi films in both mainstream and independent cinema, and since 1988 she has been acting in several foreign projects. In addition to acting, she is a social and women's rights activist, a Goodwill Ambassador of the United Nations Population Fund (UNFPA), and a member of the Rajya Sabha, the upper house of the Indian Parliament. She is married to the Indian poet and screenwriter, Javed Akhtar.

Trivia

In the initial stage of her career, she was linked to film director Shekhar Kapur. She later married Javed Akhtar, who is known worldwide for his lyrics, poetry and as a screenwriter. It was Akhtar's second marriage the first being with Bollywood scriptwriter Honey Irani. Indian actresses Farah, Naaz and Tabu are her nieces.

SHAHRUKH KHAN

Shahrukh Khan was born on November 2, 1965. Shahrukh started his career with a TV serial called *Fauji* in 1988 that won him instant recognition. He has also acted in another TV soap called 'Circus' in 1989.

Being equally brilliant in studies and sports, he completed his education from Delhi. He fell in love with Gauri Chibba, and after many objections from her parents, married her before he got his break in Bollywood. The couple has two children.

Often referred to as 'the King of Bollywood', Shahrukh has acted in over 70 Hindi films.

He made his film debut in *Deewana* in 1992. The Government of India honoured him with the **Padma Shri** for his contributions towards the Indian Cinema in 2005.

Since 1992, he has been part of numerous commercial successes as well as has delivered a variety of critically acclaimed performances.

Some of his successful films include *Dilwale Dulhaniya Le Jayenge* (1995), *Kuch Kuch Hota Hai* (1998), *Kabhi Khushi Kabhie Gham* (2001), *Kal Ho Naa Ho* (2003), *Veer-Zaara* (2004), *Kabhi Alvida Naa Kehna* (2006), *Chak De! India* (2007), *Om Shanti Om* (2007), *Rab Ne Bana Di Jodi* (2008), *My Name Is Khan* (2010).

Shahrukh also branched out into film production and television presenting. He is the co-owner of two production companies, Dreamz Unlimited and Red Chillies Entertainment. Shahrukh is also the owner of the IPL cricket team, 'Kolkata Knight Riders'.

Shahrukh and his wife, Gauri Khan, own the production company "Red Chillies Entertainments" which Shahrukh started for his friend and colleague – Farah Khan, director/choreographer, for her debut directorial film – *Main Hoon Na* (2004).

Trivia

Khan has won fourteen Filmfare Awards for his work in Indian films and out of which, eight are in the Best Actor category (a record).

SHAMMI KAPOOR

Born on October 21, 1931, Shammi Kapoor was a famous Indian actor and director. Shamsher Raj or 'Shammi' Kapoor, son of actor Prithviraj Kapoor and Ramsarni 'Rama' Mehra Kapoor, moved into filmmaking with his father's company, Prithvi Theatres.

He started his career in 1953, but his movies did not succeed at the box office. He worked in films like *Coffee House* and *Rangin Raaten* from 1955 to 1957 but could not make his name.

His film *Tumsa Nahin Dekha* in 1957 was a turning point in his career. The new look with short hair and no moustache created a different persona, all together. The film was followed with many more hits like *Junglee, Teesri Manzil, Brahmachari* and many more.

He had married actress Geeta Bali in 1955. She died of smallpox in 1965. Shammi Kapoor married again to Queen of Bhavanagar Neila Devi in 1969.

Andaz was his last film as a leading actor in 1971. However, he continued to do supporting roles in several films in later years. He also directed two films, *Manoranjan* and *Bundal Baaz*. Later, Shammi founded the *Internet Users Community of India,* where he used to speak directly to his fans and made online videos.

Many of his family members including his elder brother, Raj Kapoor and younger brother, Shashi Kapoor, their spouses, grandchildren, are or have been into the film industry.

His last film was *Rockstar* with his great-nephew, Ranbir Kapoor. Shammi Kapoor died on August 14, 2011 due to chronic renal failure.

Trivia

Shammi Kapoor was one of the first persons in India to contribute in the field of Internet. Shammi Kapoor has two children, Aditya Raj and Kanchan, both from his previous wife.

TOM CRUISE

If you had told a Franciscan seminary student, Thomas Cruise Mapother IV that one day he would be considered one of the top 100 movie stars of all time, he would have probably grinned and told you that his ambition was to become a priest.

Nonetheless, this deeply religious youngster who was born in July 1962 in Syracuse, New York, was destined to become Tom Cruise, one of the highest paid and most sought-after actors in film history.

At the age of 18, Tom Cruise headed for New York and a possible acting career. The next 15 years of his life are the stuff of legends. He made his film debut with a small role in *Endless Love* in 1981 and from the outset, exhibited an undeniable box office appeal to both male and female audiences.

Some of the blockbusters given by Tom Cruise were *The Color of Money, Top Gun, Rain Man and Born on the Fourth of July, Interview with the Vampire: The Vampire Chronicles, Mission Impossible, Mission Impossible II, Mission Impossible III, Vanilla Sky, Minority Report, The Last Samurai, Collateral, War of the Worlds,* and *Jerry Maguire.*

He was married to actress Nicole Kidman until 2001. Thomas Cruise Mapother IV has indeed come a long way from the lonely wanderings of his youth.

Trivia

He was chosen by the Empire magazine as one of the 100 Sexiest Stars in film history.

Quote

"I always look for a challenge and something that's different."

34

TOM HANKS

Thomas Jeffrey or 'Tom' Hanks was born on July 9, 1956. He is an American actor, writer, producer and director.

Tom Hanks did not have the happiest of childhoods, as his parents got divorced when he was only 5 years old.

After he settled down in Oakland, Tom began taking part in high school plays. He left California State University to pursue his acting career further.

He then got married in 1978 to actress/producer Samantha Lewes. The couple got divorced in 1987. Tom Hank's first break as an actor came in a low budget movie called *'He Knows You're Alone'* in 1980. He then acted in TV Sitcom, *Bosom Buddies* and in a number of comedy films like *Taxi, Family Ties, Splash.*

It was with the film *Big* in 1988 that he gained popularity. His other successful films include Penny Marshall's *A League of Their Own* in 1992, *Sleepless in Seattle* in 1993, *Philadelphia, Forrest Gump, Toy Story, Apollo 13.*

His movie, *Cast Away* got him an Oscar nomination.

Tom Hanks is a family man married to actress Rita Wilson, who he met on the sets of the movie, *'Volunteers'* in 1985.

Surely with the bundle of talent that this actor has and his selective approach to movies, there is no match to this actor.

Trivia

He was ranked 17th out of 'The Top 100 Movie Stars of All Time' by the Empire magazine in October 1997.

TONY CURTIS

Born in Bernard Schwart, Tony Curtis (June 3, 1925 – September 29, 2010) was an American film actor, whose career spanned six decades. He had his greatest popularity during the 1950s and the early 1960s.

He acted in over *100 films* in roles covering a wide range of genres, from light comedy to serious drama. Curtis made numerous television appearances in his later years. His early film roles were partly the result of his good looks. By the later half of the 1950s, he had a notable and strong screen presence. He proved himself to be a 'fine dramatic actor', having acted in numerous dramatic and comedy roles.

In the beginning, he acted in a string of 'mediocre' films, including swashbucklers, light comedies, sports films, and a musical. However, after this, he starred in *Houdini* in 1953 with his wife, Janet Leigh.

Critic David Thomson notes it to be 'his first clear success'. His acting progressed immensely after that.

He won his first serious recognition as a skilled dramatic actor in *Sweet Smell of Success* in 1957. In 1958, he was nominated for an Oscar for the Best Actor in another drama, *The Defiant Ones*.

Curtis then gave a performance, what many believe was his best acting, in the comedy film, *Some Like It Hot* in 1959. It was voted the funniest film in history from a survey done by the American Film Institute.

TRIVIA

Curtis was the father of actresses, Jamie Lee Curtis and Kelly Curtis by his first wife, actress Janet Leigh.

VANESSA MARANO

Vanessa Nicole Marano was born on October 31, 1992 in Los Angeles, California and the elder sister of Laura Marano. She is an American actress.

Vanessa began acting professionally when she was two years old. Since then, she worked for productions at the Stage Door Theater.

Vanessa Marano started acting in the theatre when she was seven years old, performing in numerous plays at A.C.T. in Agoura Hills, California. She began her professional career with several national commercials.

Her biggest roles on television have been as Jack Malone's elder daughter in *Without a Trace*, Valerie's stepdaughter in *The Comeback* and as April Nardini in *Gilmore Girls*. She also played Layne Abeley in *The Clique* based on the books by Lisi Harrison and Samantha Combs in *Dear Lemon Lima*.

Vanessa played 'Eden' on *The Young and the Restless* and 'Hope' on *Scoundrels*. She now stars as 'Bay Kennish' on the ABC Family show *Switched at Birth*.

Vanessa has starred in films like *Easy* (2003), *Dear Lemon Lima* (2009) and *The Secret Lives of Dorks* (2011).

Vanessa has also starred in various other TV shows like *Grounded For Life*, *Six Feet Under*, *Malcolm in the Middle*, *The Closer*, *Dexter*, *Past Life*, *Private Practice*, etc.

She starred as a young girl who becomes a quadriplegic in the critically acclaimed television movie, *The Brooke Ellison Story* directed by Christopher Reeve. Marano's first film was the animated hit, *Finding Nemo*.

Vanessa speaks Italian and is enrolled in her sophomore year in college. She is also one of the youngest members of the prestigious Academy of Television Arts and Sciences.

ARTISTS

Augeste Rodin

Born on November 12, 1840 to Jean-Baptiste Rodin and Marie Cheffer, François-Auguste-René Rodin was somewhat shy and his very nearsighted nature proved a hindrance in his early academic work.

Rodin took serious interest in drawing and had his first drawing lesson when he was ten years old. His father tried to help him academically by sending him to his uncle's boarding school in Beauvais in 1851. Rodin remained there for three years but still faced difficulty in reading and writing.

He completely devoted himself to drawing early on and enrolled at the École Impériale de Dessin, a government school for craft and design or 'Small School' to distinguish itself from the more prestigious École des Beaux-Arts, or 'School of Fine Arts'. Rodin kept himself busy, attending classes at La Petite École. He also visited museums to study antique sculpture and attended the Gobelins tapestry manufactory.

During these early years, he also found himself to be a very capable and promising sculptor. He was awarded two prizes for drawing and modelling at the age of seventeen. However, Rodin was unable to gain admittance to the conservative École des Beaux-Arts, which rejected him thrice.

Trivia

Rodin met his lifetime companion, Rose Beuret, while working on a decorative commission. Beuret became his model and mistress. She remained completely devoted to him throughout her life. She gave birth to their son in 1866, although Rodin did not legally acknowledge paternity.

CLAUDE MONET

Claude Monte is one of the most famous painters known in history. Claude Monet's painting 'Impression: Sunrise' brought a new trend termed 'Impressionism'. His paintings have been a source of inspiration for many since then.

The unusual loose brushstrokes used in his painting, 'Impression: Sunrise' displayed at an exhibition earned the title of being 'Impressionistic'. This term was coined by the critics for a technique quite different from what the Renaissance painters used then.

Monet was born on November 14, 1840 in Paris to a grocer Claude-Adolphe and Louise Justine Aubree, a singer.

While Adolphe was disappointed from Monet's decision to become an artist, Monet's mother supported him. Monet's father wanted him to become a grocer like him.

Monet developed a love for drawing at an early age. His passion found a new direction when he met Eugene Boudin, who taught him new techniques of painting with oil paints.

Monet married Camille Doncieux and had a son from her. In 1876, Camille suffered tuberculosis and died on September 5, 1879.

Monet paid a tribute to Camille by painting her during her last days. Grief-stricken after his wife's death, he kept painting masterpieces like his *water lilies* in his garden. He died on December 5, 1926 in Giverny.

Monet found pleasure in painting things as they were. He painted landscapes seen in different lights. His famous paintings, such as *Haystacks* and *Rouen Cathedral* are examples of such masterpieces.

Trivia

Monet developed cataract and underwent a surgery. Though it affected his eyesight, it did not stop him from adjusting the colours on his paintings.

Harry Houdini

Harry Houdini was born on March 24, 1874. He was a Hungarian-born American magician and escapologist, actor, stunt performer and film producer noted for his sensational escape acts.

He was also a sceptic who set out to expose frauds purporting to be supernatural phenomena.

His father was Mayer Samuel Weisz, a religious teacher. Houdini ran away from home by hopping a freight car at the age of 12, but later rejoined his family.

He started his professional career at the age of 17 doing magic shows before civic groups, in music halls. Harry and Bess married in 1894 and Bess joined the act as Harry's new partner. Later, in 1895, they joined *Welsh Brothers Circus*. Together they performed a trick called 'Metamorphosis', in which they switched places in a locked trunk.

Continuously trying for new tricks, he also became an expert at handcuffs. His easy escapes provided him tremendous publicity. The Houdinis went to England with not enough money to survive there. But his shows in London gained him popularity soon and he gained a lot of fame.

By 1905, he was an international celebrity. He also served as the president of the Society of American Magicians and founded the Magician's Club in London.

Houdini became an actor, appearing in a 13-part silent film serial called *The Master of Mystery*. Later, he started a production house and produced some movies.

He died of peritonitis on October 31, 1926.

Trivia

Houdini tried to enlist in the army when America entered the First World War in 1917 but was rejected as being too old at the age of 43. He then started performing free shows for servicemen.

JOHN LAWS

R ichard John Sinclair alias 'John' Laws was born on August 8, 1935. An Australian radio presenter, sometimes known as Lawsie, from the 1970s until his retirement in 2007, was the host of a hugely successful morning radio programme, which mixed music with interviews, opinion, live advertising readings and listener talkback. His distinctive voice earned him the nickname, *the Golden Tonsils.*

Despite retiring in 2007, Laws' management confirmed in November 2010 that he would be returning to radio in February 2011, as the host of a morning programme on 2SM and the Super Radio Network.

Born in Wau, Papua New Guinea, Laws was educated at Mosman Preparatory School and Knox Grammar School in Sydney, Australia.

He began his radio career in 1953 at 3BO in Bendigo before working at several rural radio stations prior to joining 2UE in 1957, the first of four terms at that Sydney radio station, during which time Laws, (along with Bob Rogers, Tony Withersand Stan Rofe) became prominent as one of the first Australian disc jockeys to play rock'n'roll music.

Laws is said to have pioneered the practice of using contacts in the airline industry to supply him with the latest pop releases from overseas, a facility which gave him an edge at a time when many pop records were not released in Australia until weeks or even months after being issued overseas.

Trivia

Laws was on Australian talk radio longer than any other broadcaster and as a result of his popularity, for many years, he has been cited as Australia's highest-paid radio personality.

Leonardo Da Vinci

Most people are known for mastering a specific field. But, such is not the case with Leonardo Da Vinci. He was a curious soul. His curiosity led him to explore everything that he came across. As a result, he was an expert in many fields unlike anyone before or after him.

Leonardo was born on April 15, 1452 in Anchiano, Republic of Florence (now in Italy). His father was a landlord and mother was a peasant woman.

Gradually recognising Leonardo's hidden artistic talent, his father introduced him to the renowned artist, Andrea del Verrocchio. Leonardo received training of painting, sculpting and mechanical arts. He got admitted into the painters' guild of Florence in 1472 as his artistic abilities flourished.

He continued learning at the workshop for five years after which he worked independently. He died on May 2, 1519 in Cloux, France.

Leonardo is known for his famous paintings – *The Last Supper, The Mona Lisa* and *The Vitruvian Man: The Proportions of the Human Figure.*

Besides being known as a painter, he is known as a sculptor, an architect, a scientist and an engineer. To name a few, he had also explored areas like Anatomy, Geology, Botany and Archaeology.

He had explained the fundamental theory of evolution, hundreds of years before Darwin and also of a flying machine. Many inventions and discoveries made after him seem to have been drawn from such fundamental theories of Leonardo.

Trivia
Leonardo da Vinci's famous painting, The Mona Lisa is of Lisa del Giocondo, the wife of a silk merchant. The husband had hired Leonardo to paint his wife's portrait. Today it is displayed in the Louvre Museum in Paris.

Quote
"Art is never finished, only abandoned."

M.F. HUSSAIN

Popularly known as the 'Picasso of India', celebrated painter Maqbool Fida Hussain earned both fame and wrath for his paintings. M.F. Hussain, who died in June 2011, was an accomplished painter mostly famous for his paintings on Indian women.

At the age of 20, he moved to Mumbai determined to become an artist. He started his career in 1937 by painting *cinema hoardings* to earn his livelihood. Hussain's painting, 'Sunhera Sansaar' in an annual exhibition of the Bombay Art Society in 1947 marked his entry as a known artist.

He became a popular artist through a series of his exhibitions since 1948. He organised his first solo exhibition in 1952 and then there was no looking back for him.

He attracted a lot of controversies for his nude paintings of Hindu gods and goddesses. He was arrested and charged with hurting sentiments of the people. Organisations like 'Shiv Sena' and 'Vishwa Hindu Parishad' opposed such paintings. Following his arrest, the court had ordered that an artist has freedom of expression but within the limit of not hurting the sentiments of people.

One of Hussain's films, *Meenaxi: A Tale of Three Cities* was also pulled out of theatres after some Muslim organisations claimed that one of the songs in the film contained words directly taken from the Quran.

His first film, *Through the Eyes of a Painter,* made in 1967 received recognition at the Berlin Film Festival.

M.F. Hussain was conferred with respectable awards like the **Padma Shri**, **Padma Bhushan** and **Padma Vibhushan**.

Trivia

Born in Pandharpur of Madhya Pradesh on September 17, 1915, M.F. Hussain got married to Fazila in 1941 and had two daughters, Raisa and Aqueela and three sons, Mustafa, Shamshad and Owais. His single canvases have fetched up about 2 million dollars.

MICHELANGELO BUONARROTI

Michelangelo Buonarroti was born on March 6, 1475 in Italy in a middle-class family. His father enjoyed a reputed position in the government and hence considered his son's desire to be an artist as disgraceful.

Earlier, Michelangelo started to learn grammar but hated it. He started working as an apprentice under painter Domenico Ghirlandaio in Florence at the age of thirteen.

During his apprenticeship, he got access to the antique collection of Lorenzo de' Medici. This acquaintance gave Michelangelo the opportunity to meet great scientist and even trained by Bertoldo di Giovanni, the resident sculptor of the Medici family. This arrangement enhanced the artistic skill possessed by Michelangelo.

His major works were mostly left unfinished on account of their scale. Pope Julius II assigned him the task to build his tomb, which was to include 40 life-size statues in 1505. The project took 40 long years of Michelangelo's life.

The Pope gave him another project in 1508 which was to paint the ceiling of the Sistine Chapel. He painted stories from Genesis on the ceiling, unlike using the traditional technique of painting a single figure. After completing the ceiling, he continued his work on the Pope's tomb.

However, the project came to a stop when Julius died in 1513. Three years later, he was commissioned to paint the back wall of the *Sistine Chapel with The Last Judgement*. In 1555, he started working on *Pieta* in St. Peter's church, Milan, during which he fell ill and passed away in 1564.

Trivia
Michelangelo built an 18 feet tall statue of David in Florence in 1501.

NICHOLAS ROERICH

Also known as Nikolai Konstantinovich Rerikh, Nicholas Roerich (September 27, 1874 to December 13, 1947), was a Russian mystic, painter, philosopher, scientist, writer, traveller and public figure.

From childhood, Nicholas Roerich was attracted to painting, archaeology, history and the abundant cultural heritage of the East.

He was a prolific artist. He created thousands of paintings and about 30 literary works. Many of his paintings are exhibited in well-known museums of the world.

Roerich was also an author and a founder of an international movement for the defence of culture. He was also the initiator of an international pact for the protection of artistic and academic institutions and historical sites called the 'Roerich's Pact'.

Roerich earned several nominations for the **Nobel Prize**.

Members of Roerich's family occupied prominent military and administrative posts in Russia since the reign of Peter I. Nicholas Roerich's father, Konstantin Fedorovich was a well-known notary, who was born in Courland.

Roerich's mother, Maria Vasil'evna Kalashnikova was descended from a long line of merchants and traders. Among the friends of the Roerich's family, were famous personalities, such as D Mendeleyev, N Kostomarov, M Mikeshin, L Ivanovsky and many others.

Trivia

Roerich in translation from the ancient Scandinavian means 'rich of fame'.

REMBRANDT VAN RIJN

A famous Dutch painter, teacher and art dealer, Rembrandt Harmenszoon van Rijn was a master of various forms of paintings.

On July 15, 1606 in Leiden, Netherlands, Rembrandt was born in a family of modest means. His father was a miller and hence could not afford a luxurious life for Rembrandt. Yet, his parents took great care with his education. He, at the age of 14, was enrolled at the University of Leiden.

The programme did not interest him and he left the university and studied art under two local masters – Jacon van Swanenburch and Pieter Lastma.

He painted landscapes, mythical figures and portraits in rich colours, exhibiting the movement of light in them.

He married the cousin of a successful art dealer Saskia van Uylenburgh, which helped him in enhancing his career. His acquaintances got him many deals and rich patrons.

He had three children, who passed away within a period of five years and Saskia also died at the age of 30 in 1642.

In 1649, he married his housekeeper, Hendrickje Stoffels, who became the subject of many of his paintings.

Despite Rembrandt's financial success as an artist, teacher and an art dealer, his fondness for ostentatious living forced him to bankruptcy in 1656 and had to auction most of his belongings.

He died on October 5, 1665.

Rembrandt is known for his works, such as *The Blinding of Samson*, and even his landscapes. His most well-known works include *The Jewish Bride*, *The Mill*, *Bathseba*, *The Return of the Prodigal Son*, and many more.

Trivia

The house in Amsterdam, in which Rembrandt lived and later sold, was converted into a museum in 1911 in the honour of the artist.

ROLF HARRIS

Born on March 30, 1930 in Perth, Western Australia, Rolf Harris is an Australian musician, composer, singer, songwriter, painter and a television personality.

Harris was a champion swimmer before studying art. He moved to England in 1952, where he started to appear on television programmes on which he drew the characters. He began a musical career initially with piano accordion.

He wrote the famous song, 'Tie Me Kangaroo Down, Sport' and while performing in Canada, he introduced his popular routine around his song, 'Jake the Peg'.

He often uses unusual instruments in his performances – plays the didgeridoo. He has been credited with the invention of the wobble board, which is a rhythmic percussion instrument. Harris was also associated with the Stylophone, a small electronic keyboard instrument.

He became a popular television personality from the 1960s, presenting shows including Rolf's Cartoon Club, Animal Hospital and various programmes about the serious art.

In late 2005, he painted an official portrait of Queen Elizabeth II.

Trivia

He illustrated magician Robert Harbin's Paper Magic. He also had a few acting roles in British television programmes and films as 'Harry' in The Vise and as 'Pte Proudfoot' in the 1955 Tommy Trinder film You Lucky People.

SALVADOR DALI

A Spanish painter, sculptor, graphic artist and designer, Salvador Dali was born on May 11, 1904.

Young Salvador was an intelligent child, who was prone to fits of anger against his parents and schoolmates.

He was a skilled draftsman. Best known for the striking and bizarre images in his surrealistic work, his painterly skills are often attributed to the influence of Renaissance masters.

Though Dali took over the surrealist theory of automatism, he transformed it into a more positive method, 'critical paranoia'. He claimed that this method should be used not only in artistic and poetical creation but also in the affairs of daily life.

Dali described his pictures as hand - painted dream photographs'. His best-known work, *The Persistence of Memory*, was completed in 1931. Dali's expansive artistic repertoire includes sculpture, film and photography, in collaboration with a range of artists in a variety of media.

In 1937, Dali visited Italy and later moved to the United States in 1940. During this period, he devoted his time largely in self-publicity. One of his most important works is *The Crucifixion of St John of the Cross* (1951).

He also made the first surrealist films – *Un chien andalou and L'Age d'or* and also contributed a dream sequence to Alfred Hitchcock's *Spellbound* (1945).

Dali died on January 23, 1989 of heart failure.

Trivia
Dali's full name was Salvador Domenec Felip Jacint Dali i Domenech, Marquis de Pubol.

Quote
"Don't bother about being modern. Unfortunately, it is the one thing that, whatever you do, you cannot avoid."

VAN GOGH

Vincent Willem Van Gogh (March 30, 1853 – July 29, 1890) was a Dutch post-Impressionist painter whose work was notable for its rough beauty, emotional honesty, and bold colour. His work had a far-reaching influence on the 20th-century art.

He developed interest in drawing as a child and continued making drawings throughout the years leading to his decision to become an artist.

His work was known to only a handful of people and appreciated by fewer still.

Though Van Gogh loved art from an early age, he did not begin painting until his late twenties. He completed many of his best-known works during his last two years.

In just over a decade, he produced more than 2,000 artworks, consisting of 860 oil paintings and more than 1,300 drawings, watercolours, sketches and prints.

His works included self-portraits, landscapes, still lives of flowers, portraits and paintings of cypresses, wheat fields and sunflowers.

He died very young, at the age of 37 after years of painful anxiety and frequent bouts of mental illness.

Trivia

The extent to which his condition health affected his paintings has been a subject of speculation since his death. Despite a widespread tendency to romanticize his ill health, modern critics see an artist deeply frustrated by the inactivity and incoherence brought about by his bouts of illness.

WALT DISNEY

Walt Disney was born on December 5, 1901 in Chicago Illinois. His father, Elias Disney and mother, Flora Call Disney had five children, four boys and a girl. His father, a strict and religious man, who often physically abused his children, was working as a building contractor when Walter was born.

Walt had very early interests in art. He used to sell his drawings to neighbours and make extra money. He pursued his arts, by studying art and photography at McKinley High School in Chicago. He had grown his love for nature and wildlife and family and community, which were a large part of agrarian living. Walt was encouraged by his mother and elder brother, Roy to pursue his talents.

On returning from France, he opened his own company which fell bankrupt and then, with twenty dollars in his hand, he headed towards Hollywood. Walt became a recognised Hollywood figure after making success of his 'Alice Comedies'. In 1925, he married Lillian Bounds, in Lewiston. Later on they were blessed with two daughters, Diane and Sharon.

And then his productions fetched him many awards till 1937. During the next five years, **Walt Disney Studios** completed other full-length animated classics, such as *Pinocchio*, *Fantasia*, *Dumbo* and *Bambi*.

Walt Disney's dream of a clean and organised amusement park, came true, as **Disneyland Park** opened in 1955.

Trivia

During the fall of 1918, Disney attempted to enlist for military service but got rejected because of being underage. Instead, he joined the Red Cross and spent a year driving an ambulance and chauffeuring Red Cross officials in France. His ambulance was covered with Disney cartoons.

BUSINESSMEN/
ENTREPRENEURS

ADI GODREJ

Born on April 3, 1942, Adi Godrej is an Indian industrialist and philanthropist. As of 2012, he is one of the **richest Indians with net worth of US$2.4 billion**. He is also the **second richest person of Parsi descent** in the world after Pallonji Mistry. He is the present **Chairman of the Godrej Group**, which includes many Indian companies. He is also the Chairman of two international companies; **Keyline Brands, U.K** and **Rapidol, South Africa**; as well as the Chairman of the Board of Trustees of the **Dadabhai Naoroji Memorial Prize Fund**.

Godrej received his undergraduate degree from MIT and his MBA from the MIT Sloan School of Management, and a member of Tau Beta Pi. After his return to India, he joined the family business. He modernised and systematised management structures and implemented process improvements. Adi Godrej took the Godrej Group to great heights. After the liberalisation process, Adi Godrej restructured the company's policies to meet the challenges of globalisation.

He is married to the famous socialite, **Parmeshwar Godrej** and the couple has two daughters and a son.

His son, Pirojsha Godrej fi nished his management studies from abroad and has now joined the Godrej Properties. The Godrej Group was started more than a century ago and since then it manufactured **locks** and **vegetable based soaps** displacing many foreign brands. Adi Godrej is a recipient of several awards including the **prestigious Rajiv Gandhi Award, 2002**.

Trivia

Under Adi Godrej's leadership, the group is also involved in philanthropic activities. Godrej is a major supporter of the World Wildlife Fund in India.

Quote

"I only use the email and occasionally access the internet."

ANDREW CARNEGIE

Andrew Carnegie, (November 25, 1835 – August 11, 1919) was a Scottish-American businessman, entrepreneur and philanthropist. He led the enormous expansion of the American steel industry in the late 19th century.

Carnegie was born in Scotland and migrated to the United States. He started working as a factory worker in a bobbin factory. Later, he became a bill logger for the owner of the company and then a messenger boy. Progressing up the ranks of a telegraph company, he built the Pittsburgh's Carnegie Steel Company, which was later merged with Elbert H Gary's Federal Steel Company. It further merged with several smaller companies to create the US Steel.

He built the *Carnegie Hall* and later turned to philanthropy and interests in education. He founded the 'Carnegie Corporation of New York', 'Carnegie Endowment for International Peace', 'Carnegie Institution of Washington', 'Carnegie Mellon University' and the 'Carnegie Museums of Pittsburgh'.

Carnegie devoted the remainder of his life to large-scale philanthropy, with special emphasis on local libraries, world peace, education and scientific research.

Trivia

He cemented his name as one of the 'Captains of Industry' after he founded the Carnegie Steel Company. By the 1890s, the company was the largest and most profitable industrial enterprise in the world. Carnegie, later, sold it for $480 million to JP Morgan, who then created the US Steel.

AZIM PREMJI

The third richest Indian and the 36th richest in the world, Azim Hashim Premji is a business tycoon and a philanthropist. Born on July 24, 1945, Azim Premji is the Chairman of one of the leading software companies, Wipro Ltd.

Azim Premji was born to M.H. Premji. After his father's death, Azim Premji took over the reins of family business in 1966 at the age of 21.

He is an icon among Indian businessmen and his success story is a truly source of inspiration to a number of budding entrepreneurs.

Azim Premji's leadership metamorphosed Wipro from a Rs 70 million company in hydrogenated cooking fats to a pioneer in providing integrated business, technology and process solutions on a global delivery platform today.

He is married to Yasmeen. The couple has two children – Rishad and Tariq. Rishad is currently the Chief Strategy Officer of IT Business, Wipro.

Besides being a successful businessman, Azim Premji believes in charity as well. He is known for his modesty even being a wealthy person. In 2001, Premji contributed a signifi cant amount of funding to initiate the set up of the Azim Premji Foundation, a non-profit organisation that focuses on improving education for children in India.

Then, he established the Azim Premji University under the Azim Premji University Act, 2010 of the Government of Karnataka to award degrees in teacher training.

Trivia

In 2005, the government of India honoured Azim Premji with Padma Bhushan.

BILL GATES

Born on October 28, 1955 in Seattle, **William Henry 'Bill' Gates III** is an American businessman, philanthropist, author, investor and current Chairman of Microsoft, the software company he founded with **Paul Allen**.

He had an early interest in software and began programming computers at the age of thirteen. Bill Gates became a student at the Harvard University in 1973. His life changed in January 1975 when a magazine carried a cover story on a $350 microcomputer, the Altair, made by a firm called the MITS.

He dropped out of the University and started working as a software designer. Allen and Gates planned to develop software for the newly emerging personal computer market.

The company, **Microsoft** became famous for their computer operating systems and business deals.

Gates proceeded to make a fortune from the licensing of an operating system, MS-DOS that IBM needed for their new personal computer.

On November 10, 1983, Microsoft Corporation was formally announced Microsoft Windows, a next-generation operating system.

Bill Gates married Melinda French Gates in January 1994. The couple has three children.

Besides being the most famous businessman of the late 1990s, Gates has also distinguished himself as a philanthropist.

Bill Gates and his wife Melinda have endowed the Bill and Melinda Gates Foundation with huge amounts of money to support philanthropic initiatives in the areas of global health and learning.

Trivia

The Gates's home is on a hill overlooking Lake Washington in Medina. According to sources in 2006, the total value of the propterty was 125 million dollars.

CHANDA KOCHHAR

Chanda Kochhar was born on November 17, 1961 in Jodhpur, Rajasthan and was raised in Jaipur. She then moved to Mumbai, where she joined the Jai Hind College for a Bachelor of Arts degree. After graduating in 1982, she then pursued Cost Accountancy or ICWAI. Later, she acquired the Masters Degree in Management Studies from Jamnalal Bajaj Institute of Management Studies in Mumbai.

Chanda Kochhar is married to Deepak Kochhar, a wind energy entrepreneur and her Business schoolmate. The have two children – a son and a daughter.

She joined ICICI as a Management trainee after her Masters in the year, 1984. After nine years of hard work, Kochhar was appointed as a part of the core team to set up the ICICI bank.

Chanda Kochhar is currently the Chief Executive Officer (CEO) and Managing Director (MD) of the ICICI bank from May 2009. She served as a Joint Managing Director and Chief Financial Officer of the ICICI Bank Ltd from October 2007 to April 2009. She was also the bank's Chief Financial Officer (CFO), official spokesperson and also heads the Corporate Centre of the ICICI Bank.

Kochhar personally was awarded the **Retail Banker of Year, 2004 (Asia-Pacific region)** by the Asian Banker and Business Woman of the Year, 2005 by 'The Economic Times'.

Kochhar has also consistently figured in *Fortune's* list of Most Powerful Women in Business since 2005. She is also at the top of the list of top 20 powerful women.

Trivia

Under her leadership, ICICI Bank won the Best Retail Bank in India Award in 2001, 2003, 2004 and 2005 and Excellence in Retail Banking Award in 2002 by the The Asian Banker.

DHIRUBHAI AMBANI

Dhirajlal Hirachand Ambani, popularly known as Dhirubhai Ambani was born on December 28, 1933 in Chorwad, Gujarat. He was an Indian business magnate and entrepreneur.

He founded the Reliance Industries, the Petrochemicals, the Communications, Power, and Textiles Corporation and the only privately owned Indian company in the *Fortune 500 list*.

Dhirubhai started off as a small time worker with Arab merchants in the 1950s. He moved to Mumbai in 1958 to start his own spice business. He moved into textiles and opened his mill near Ahmedabad, after making modest profits.

Dhirubhai founded the Reliance Industries in 1958. The company today has over 85,000 employees, providing almost 5 percent of the central government's total tax revenue.

Dhirubhai Ambani is credited with introducing the stock market to the average investor and thousands of investors attend the Reliance annual general meetings, which were sometimes held in a football stadium.

Dhirubhai has been one among the select 'Forbes' billionaires and has also figured in the 'Sunday Times' list of top 50 businessmen in Asia. His life is often referred to as a true 'rags to riches' story.

After a heart attack in 1986, he handed over the Reliance Group to his sons, Mukesh and Anil. After his death on July 6, 2002, the group was split into the Reliance Industries, headed by Mukesh Ambani and Reliance Anil Dhirubhai Ambani Group (Reliance ADAG) led by Anil Ambani.

Trivia
A poll conducted by 'The Times of India' in 2000 voted him the "Greatest Creator of Wealth in the Centuries".

Quote
"Think big, think fast, think ahead. Ideas are no one's monopoly."

G. D. BIRLA

Ghanshyam Das Birla was born on April 10, 1894. He was an Indian businessman and member of the influential Birla Family.

His grandfather, Shiv Narayan Birla was a traditional Marwari moneylender. Ghanshyam Das Birla entered the business arena during the time of the First World War. He established a cotton mill in Sabzi Mandi, Delhi and later on established the Keshoram Cotton Mills and also the jute business shifting his base to Calcutta (Kolkata), the capital city of Bengal, the world's largest jute producing region.

Ghanshyam Das Birla is considered as a doyen of Indian Industry. He was the founder of the **Federation of Indian Chambers of Commerce and Industry** (FICCI). He is also popularly known as the builder of **Birla Mandirs**. In 1919, the Birla Brothers Limited was formed and a mill was set up in Gwalior. In 1930s, G.D. Birla set up Sugar and Paper mills. In 1940s, he ventured into the territory of cars and established Hindustan Motors. After independence, Ghanshyam Das Birla invested in tea and textiles through a series of acquisitions of erstwhile European companies. He also expanded and diversified into cement, chemicals, rayon and steel tubes.

He was also the founder of various educational institutions. Pilani has today evolved into one of India's best engineering schools. He also established many temples, planetariums and hospitals. Ghanshyam Das Birla died in 1983 at the age of 90. In his honour, the G.D. Birla Award for scientific research has been established to encourage the scientists for their contribution in various fields of scientific research. In 1957, he was awarded India's second highest civilian honour, the **Padma Vibhushan** by the Government of India.

Trivia

There is a memorial to Ghanshyam Das Birla in the Golders Green Crematorium, Hoop Lane, London.

J.R.D. Tata

Jehangir Ratanji Dadabhoy Tata or JRD Tata (July 29, 1904 – November 29, 1993) was a pioneer aviator and important businessman of India.

Born in Paris, Tata was the second child of Ratanji Dadabhoy Tata and Suzanne Brière. His father was the first cousin of Jamsetji Tata, who was a pioneer industrialist in India. He spent much of his childhood in France.

JRD Tata was inspired early by aviation pioneer Louis Blériot and took to flying. On February 10, 1929, Tata got the first pilot licence in India.

Came to be known as the Father of Indian Civil Aviation, Tata founded India's first commercial airline, 'Tata Airlines', in 1932, which came to be known as Air India in 1946.

The assets of the Tata Group grew from US$100 million to over US$5 billion under Tata's chairmanship.

JRD Tata was awarded the **'Bharat Ratna'** in 1992 and the 'Legion of Honour' from the French government in 1954.

Starting with 14 enterprises, Tata & Sons became a conglomerate of 95 enterprises, half a century later in 1988.

Trivia

JRD Tata was famous for succeeding in business while maintaining high ethical standards, refusing to bribe politicians or use the black market.

LAKSHMI N. MITTAL

Lakshmi Niwas Mittal, born on June 15, 1950 is an **Indian steel magnate**. He was born in Sadulpur, Rajasthan but he presently resides in London. He is the Chairman and Chief Executive Offi cer (CEO) of Arcelor Mittal, the world's largest steelmaking company. **Mittal is the richest man in India, Asia and the United Kingdom** and **second in Europe**, and is presently the sixth richest individual in the world with a personal wealth of US$20.7 billion. He is the 44th "most powerful person" of the 68 individuals named in *Forbes's* Most Powerful People list. His daughter, Vanisha Mittal's wedding was the most expensive in the recorded history of the world. He has a net worth of about US $ 20.7 billion, as estimated by 2012. His son's name is Aditya Mittal.

Mittal is an independent director of Goldman Sachs, member of Board of Directors to Goldman Sachs Media/Film IP Group, member of the Board of Directors of European Aeronautic Defence and Space Company, the World Steel Association, Foreign Investment Council in Kazakhstan, the International Investment Council in South Africa, the Investors' Council to the Cabinet of Ministers of Ukraine, the World Economic Forum's International Business Council, the World Steel Association's Executive Committee, the Presidential International Advisory Board of Mozambique and the International Iron and Steel Institute's Executive Committee.

He also presently serves as a board council member of the **Prime Minister of India's Global Advisory Council of Overseas Indians**. Mr. Lakshmi Mittal was conferred with the **Padma Vibhushan** by the President of India in 2007. He has innumerable awards and honours to his credit.

Trivia

His residence at 18-19 Kensington Palace Gardens – which was purchased from Formula One boss Bernie Ecclestone in 2004 for £57 million (US$128 million), making it the world's most expensive house at the time.

Quote

"At the end of the day you have to keep emotions away."

LALIT SURI

L alit Suri is the Founder, Chairman and Managing Director of Bharat Hotels Ltd. and was a Member of Parliament, Rajya Sabha. A widely respected and highly regarded figure amongst the Indian and international business community, he was acknowledged for his dynamism, foresight and forward thinking.

He was a sitting Member of Parliament of the Rajya Sabha and was elected for the second term to the Upper House of the Indian Parliament in May, 2004.

Mr. Lalit Suri's contributions to the Indian Tourism Industry are well documented and he took it upon himself to further the cause of the industry, as a Global Executive Committee. He was the member of the renowned World Travel & Tourism Council (WTTC) and Honorary Chairman of the WTTC – India Initiative; the Chairman of the FICCI Tourism Committee (Federation of Indian Chambers of Commerce and Industry). He was also the founder member of Hotel Association of India, a premier Hotel body of the country and also its President. Under his stewardship, the Bharat Hotels became one of the country's largest privately owned and fastest growing chain of hotels.

He is survived by his wife, Jyotsna and their four children.

Trivia

Suri was also the owner of the 'Midday' newspaper in Delhi. An alumnus of Sri Ram College of Commerce, New Delhi, Suri also won a number of prestigious awards and has been responsible for pushing a number of policy recommendations on the tourism sector.

MUKESH AMBANI

Mukesh Ambani is the face of new emerging India. He is the Chairman and Managing Director of Reliance Industries Limited, India's largest private sector company. Born on April 19, 1957 in Mumbai, his father Dhirubhai Ambani was then a small businessman who later on rose to become one of the legends of the Indian industry. Mukesh also owns the Indian Premier League team, 'Mumbai Indians'. He was educated at Abaay Morischa School in Mumbai and completed his graduation with a bachelor`s degree in chemical engineering from the UDCT.

Mukesh Ambani joined the Reliance Industries in 1981 and initiated Reliance`s backward integration from textiles into polyester fibres and further into petrochemicals. In this process, he directed the creation of 60 new, world-class manufacturing facilities involving diverse technologies that have raised Reliance`s manufacturing capacities from less than a million tonnes to twelve million tonnes per year. He has created the world's largest petrol refinery at Jamnagar, Gujarat, India, with a present capacity of 660,000 barrels per day. He was chosen the **businessman of the year, 2007** by a public poll in India conducted by the NDTV. He was ranked 42nd among the World`s Most Respected Business Leaders and second among the four Indian CEOs featured in a survey conducted by Pricewaterhouse Coopers. Mukesh Ambani has many achievements and honours to his name. He was chosen as the ET Business Leader of the Year 2006 and was ranked 42nd among the World's Most Respected Business Leaders. He was conferred the World Communication Award for the Most Influential Person in Telecommunications in 2004 by Total Telecom.

Trivia
Mukesh got enrolled for an MBA from the Stanford University, but completed only one year of the two-year program.

Nagavara Ramarao Narayana Murthy

Nagavara Ramarao Narayana Murthy, better known as N. R. Narayana Murthy was born on August 20, 1946 in Mysore, Karnataka. He graduated with a degree in electrical engineering from the National Institute of Engineering, University of Mysore in 1967. He received his master's degree from IIT Kanpur in 1969.

Mr. Murthy's first job position was at IIM Ahmedabad, where he worked as the chief systems programmer. He developed a time-sharing system and designed and implemented a BASIC interpreter for ECIL (Electronics Corporation of India Limited). After IIM Ahmedabad, he started a company named *Softronics* in 1976. When that company failed, he joined the Patni Computer Systems in Pune. Mr. Murthy met his wife, Sudha Murthy in Pune who was an engineer working at Tata Engineering and Locomotive Co. Ltd. (Telco, now known as Tata Motors) at the time.

After settling down in Pune, Mr. Murthy founded *Infosys* in 1981 with an initial capital injection of Rs. 10,000, which was invested by his wife Sudha Murty. Murthy served as the CEO of Infosys for 21 years and was succeeded by co-founder Nandan Nilekani in 2002. At Infosys, he articulated, designed and implemented the Global Delivery Model which has become the foundation for the huge success in IT services outsourcing from India. He also lead the company through several key decisions including its listing on the Indian Stock Exchange and on the NASDAQ.

He held the executive position of the Chairman of the Board from 2002 to 2006, when he became the "non-executive" Chairman of the Board and Chief Mentor. In August 2011, he retired completely from the company and took the title, 'Chairman Emeritus'.

Trivia

Murthy is the brother-in-law of serial entrepreneur Gururaj "Desh" Deshpandey.

Quote

"The real power of money is the power to give it away."

OPRAH WINFREY

Oprah Winfrey, born on January 29, 1954, is an American businesswoman, media proprietor, talk show host, actress, producer and philanthropist. She is best known for her self-titled, multi-award-winning talk show, which has become the highest-rated program of its kind and was nationally syndicated from 1986 to 2011.

She has been ranked the **richest African American of the 20th century**, the greatest black philanthropist in American history. She was, for a time, world's only black billionaire. She is also been titled as the most influential woman in the world.

Winfrey was born into poverty in rural Mississippi to a teenage single mother. She experienced hardships during her childhood, claiming to be raped at the age of nine and becoming pregnant at 14, her son died in infancy.

Winfrey was sent to live with the man she calls her father, who is a barber in Tennessee. She started working in radio while still in high school and began co-anchoring the local evening news at the age of 19.

Her emotional delivery eventually got her transferred to the daytime-talk-show arena. After boosting a third-rated local Chicago talk show to first place, she launched her own production company and became internationally syndicated.

Trivia

Winfrey was originally named 'Orpah' after the Biblical character in the Book of Ruth but her family and friends didn't know how to pronounce it and started calling her, 'Oprah' instead.

STEVE JOBS

Born on February 24, 1955, Steven Paul 'Steve' Jobs was an American inventor and businessman. He was the Co-founder, Chairman, and Chief Executive Officer of Apple Inc.

In the late 1970s, Jobs, along with Apple co-founder Steve Wozniak, Mike Markkula and others designed, developed and marketed one of the first commercially successful lines of personal computers, the Apple II series.

In the early 1980s, Jobs was among the first to see the commercial potential of Xerox PARC's mouse-driven graphical user interface, which led to the creation of the Apple Lisa and, one year later, the Macintosh. After losing a power struggle with the board of directors in 1985, Jobs left Apple and founded a computer platform development company specialising in business markets, 'NeXT'.

Apple's 1996 buyout of 'NeXT' brought Jobs back to the company he co-founded and he served as its interim CEO from 1997, then becoming the permanent CEO in 2000, spearheading the advent of the iPod, iPhone and iPad.

From 2003, he was fighting an eight-year battle with cancer and eventually, resigned as CEO in August 2011, while on his third medical leave. He was then elected as Chairman of Apple's board of directors.

On October 5, 2011, around 3:00 p.m., Jobs died at his home in Palo Alto, California, aged 56, six weeks after resigning as CEO of Apple.

Trivia

Jobs was born in San Francisco and adopted at birth by Paul Jobs and Clara Jobs. When asked about his 'adoptive parents', Jobs replied emphatically that Paul and Clara Jobs 'were my parents'. He later stated in his authorised biography that they 'were my parents 1,000 percent".

SUNIL MITTAL

Born on October 23, 1957, Sunil Mittal is the Chairman and Managing Director of the Bharti group. The USD 5 billion turnover company runs India's largest GSM-based mobile phone service.

Making bicycle parts as a teenager, Sunil Bharti Mittal has come a long way. At the age of 43, he created a Telecom Giant in India. Sunil is an Alumnus of Harvard Business School and has been at the forefront of technology revolutionising telecommunications with its world-class brands, products and services. The company has grown by leaps and bounds from its humble beginnings in the 1970s.

In the future, his focus is on providing international mobile services, retail industry and agriculture. He recently struck a joint venture deal with the Wal-Mart, the retail giant, for starting retail stores across India.

Sunil has received several awards including the **Padma Bhushan** in 2007 from the President of India, Asia Businessman of the Year, Fortune Magazine 2006, Telecom Person of the Year, CEO of the year 2005, at the Frost and Sullivan Asia Pacific ICT awards 2006, Best Asian Telecom CEO, Telecom Asia Awards 2005, Best CEO, India, Institutional Investor, 2005 , Business Leader Of The Year, Economic Times, 2005, Ernst & Young Entrepreneur Of The Year 2004, Ernst & Young.

Trivia

His mantra says 'work is love not stress'. He is superstitious about the number, 23, as he was born on the 23rd and also got married on the 23rd.

SHAHNAZ HUSAIN

Shahnaz Husain was born in Pakistan and hails from a traditional royal Muslim family background. She got married at the age of 15 and has a son, Sameer.

She is the Chairperson of the Shahnaz Husain Group, a leading Indian company dealing with beauty and anti-ageing products. She also manages Shahnaz Husain's Beauty Institutes offering courses, such as diploma and post-graduate diploma in skin and beauty therapy as well as a number of short-term vocational courses.

After her marriage, she went off to Iran with her husband. She became interested in cosmetology. She soon realised the harmful effects of chemical cosmetics and turned her attention to herbals and Ayurveda.

Shahnaz Husain was a pioneer in the field of Ayurvedic and herbal cosmetics.

Her company 'Shahnaz Husain Herbals' witnessed tremendous growth throughout these years. She has launched more than 400 different kinds of beauty products.

People are becoming more and more conscious about the way they look in the contemporary times. It is here that Shahnaz Husain is playing a major role by providing people with products that can bring the glow back to their skin.

Shahnaz Husain received many awards including the **Padma Shri** in 2006 and the **Rajiv Gandhi Sadbhavana Award**. She was voted the **Woman of the Year** by the *Success* magazine in 1996.

Trivia

The products of Shahnaz Husain Group are sold through prestigious stores like Harrods and Selfridges in London, Galleries Lafayette in Paris, Bloomingdales in New York, the Seibu chain in Japan, and La Rinascente in Milan. Her clients include such names as Princess Diana, Madonna, the Clintons and Cherie Blair.

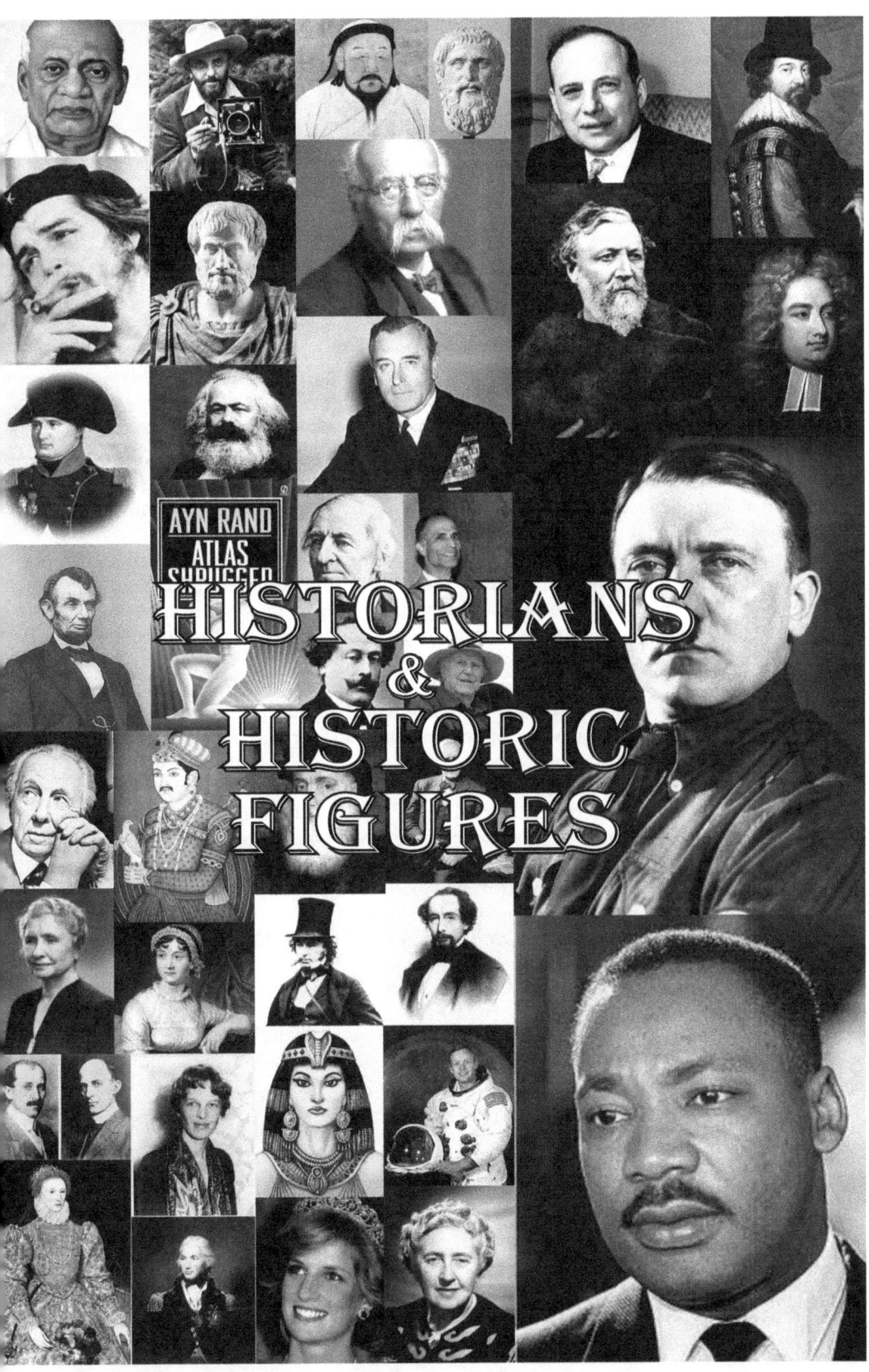

HISTORIANS
&
HISTORIC
FIGURES

ABRAHAM LINCOLN

An American hero, Abraham Lincoln is still remembered across the world as the one who rose from being ordinary to extraordinary. He was the President of the United States from 1861 to 1865 and a saviour of those enslaved.

Born in Hodgeville, Kentucky, Lincoln grew up on his father's farm. He used to help his father to look after the crops in the farm. He did meagre chores like splitting fence rails and working in a general store as a clerk. Whatever knowledge he acquired was from the books he read in the time he got between his chores.

This self-gathered education enabled him to become one of the finest lawyers of the world and the **President of The United States**.

In 1842, he married Mary Anne Todd and had four sons. However, only one of them survived.

An actor, John Wilkes Booth, shot Lincoln on April 14, 1865, while he was on a visit to the Ford's Theatre. He passed away after being in coma for long and became the first US President to be ever assassinated.

As the President of he guided the people during the Civil War. He issued the **Emancipation Proclamation** in 1863 to free people from slavery. His famous **Gettysburg Address** is still remembered and is quoted as the best speech in the history of America. He shed his views on the need for a free world with no bias towards any race.

Trivia

On Abraham Lincoln's 100th birthday in 1909, a penny was issued with his face on it to commemorate the occasion, becoming the first American coin to bear a president's image on it.

Quote

"As I would not be a slave, so I would not be a master. This expresses my idea of democracy."

ADOLF HITLER

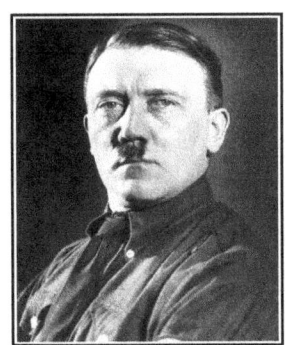

The German politician, Adolf Hitler was born on April 20, 1889. Commonly associated with the rise of Fascism in Europe, the World War II and the Holocaust, Hitler was the leader of the *National Socialist German Workers Party*, commonly referred to as the **'Nazi Party'**.

He left school at the age of 16 in 1905, intending to become a painter. He was rejected twice by the Academy of Fine Arts, Vienna because of his 'unfitness for painting'.

When the World War I touched off, Hitler's passion against foreigners, particularly Slavs was inflamed and he served as a soldier in the Bavarian Army. A decorated veteran of the World War I, Hitler joined the German Workers' Party, precursor of the Nazi Party in 1919, and became a leader of the party in 1921.

Gradually, he gained support by promoting Pan-Germanism and anti-communism with charismatic oratory and propaganda. He was appointed as Chancellor of Germany from 1933 to 1945 and head of the state from 1934 to 1945. He oversaw the rearmament of Germany and the invasion of Poland by the Wehrmacht in 1939, which led to the outbreak of World War II in Europe.

Under Hitler's direction, German forces occupied most of Europe and North Africa. These gains were reversed in 1945 when the Allied armies defeated the German army. Around six million Jews and 1,500,000 Roman people were targeted in the Holocaust.

During the Battle of Berlin in 1945, Hitler married his long-time mistress, Eva Braun. On April 30, 1945, less than two days of their marriage, the two committed suicide to avoid capture by the Red Army.

Trivia

In 1923, Hitler attempted a coup, known as the 'Beer Hall Putsch', at the Bürgerbräukeller beer hall in Munich. Hitler was imprisoned due to the failed coup. During his imprisonment, he wrote Mein Kampf (My Struggle).

AKBAR

T he third Mughal Emperor of India, Jalaluddin Muhammad Akbar is known for the rich cultural tradition India enjoys today.

Being forced into exile by the Afghan leader, Sher Shah Suri, Akbar's father, Emperor Humayun was on the run in 1540 when Akbar was born to him and his wife, Begum Hamida Banu on October 15, 1542, in Sind.

Therefore, Akbar spent most of his childhood running and fighting and hence, couldn't get any formal education. But, this did not hamper his interest in art, architecture, literature and music.

Humayun recaptured Delhi in 1555. Akbar was entitled to the throne after his sudden death. Akbar took full control as the King in 1560 and died on October17, 1605.

As an emperor, Akbar conquered the whole of Hindustan (India). He amalgamated the Hindus and Muslims by removing the *jizya* (tax) that the non-Muslims had to pay.

He married a Rajput princesses, making it possible for the Hindus to be a part of the ruling dynasty.

He banned cow slaughter and allowed the Jesuits to build a church in Agra. He built a place of worship in Fatehpur Sikri where people of all religions were invited.

He held an open court session every week to know about the problems faced by them. His court consisted of a group of 'nine extraordinary people' called the *Navratnas*, meaning 'nine jewels'.

Ain-i-Akbari and *Akbarnama*, the two very important historical works, were written by Abul Fazal in Akbar's honour.

Trivia

Akbar created a new religion called Din-i-Ilahi in 1581, as he believed that one religion did not had the sole authority over truth. The new religion promoted ethics, discouraged sins and held virtues, such as kindness and prudence as its core.

ALEXANDRE DUMAS

A lexandre Dumas was born on July 24, 1802 in Villers-Cotterêts in the department of Aisne, in Picardy, France, to Thomas-Alexandre Dumas and Marie-Louise Élisabeth Labouret. His mother's stories of his father's bravery during the years of Napoleon I of France inspired Dumas' vivid imagination for adventure. In 1822, after the restoration of the monarchy, 20-year-old Alexandre Dumas moved to Paris, where he worked at the Palais Royalin, the office of duc d'Orléans. On February 1, 1840, he married actress Ida Ferrier. He died on December 5, 1870.

His first play, *Henry III and His Court*, was produced in 1829, and was highly acclaimed with acclaim. The next year, his second play, *Christine*, was equally popular, and he was financially able to write full-time. In 1830, he participated in the Revolution which ousted Charles X.

After writing more successful plays, he turned his efforts to novels in 1838. Dumas rewrote one of his plays to create his first serial novel, titled *Le Capitaine Paul.*

From 1839 to 1841, Dumas, with the assistance of several friends, compiled *Celebrated Crimes*, an eight-volume collection of essays on famous criminals and crimes from the European history.

Dumas also collaborated with his fencing master, Augustin Grisier in his 1840 novel, *The Fencing Master.* Grisier is also mentioned with great respect in *The Count of Monte Cristo, The Corsican Brothers* and in *Dumas' memoirs.*

Auguste Maquet was the best known assistant of Dumas. He outlined the plot of *The Count of Monte Cristo* and made substantial contributions to *The Three Musketeers* and its sequels, as well as to several of Dumas' other novels.

In 1843, he wrote a short novel, *Georges*, that addressed some of the issues of race and the effects of colonialism.

In June 2005, Dumas' recently discovered last novel, *The Knight of Sainte-Hermine*, went on sale in France. The novel was nearly complete at the time of his death. A final two-and-a-half chapters were written by the modern-day Dumas scholar, Claude Schopp.

His stories have been translated into almost a hundred languages, and have inspired more than 200 motion pictures. Alexandre Dumas' home outside of Paris, the Château de Monte-Cristo, has been restored and is open to the public. The Alexandre Dumas Paris Métro station was named in his honour in 1970. Dumas appears as a character in the Kevin J. Anderson novel, *Captain Nemo: The Fantastic History of a Dark Genius.*

Trivia

Alexandre Dumas had three illegitimate children, all of whom he formally acknowledged, although he married none of the mothers.

Quote

"A person who doubts himself is like a man who would enlist in the ranks of his enemies and bear arms against himself. He makes his failure certain by himseelf being the first person to be convinced of it."

AMELIA EARHART

Born on July 24, 1897 in Atchison, The United States Amelia enjoyed a childhood which was a blend of luxuries and comfort as well as poverty and struggle.

Soon after her birth, she was sent to her grandparents' house, where she enjoyed all the comforts of life. Her father, Edwin Stanton Earhart did not earn enough to give Amelia and her sister, Muriel the same comforts.

Amelia acquired training as a nurse in 1917 and worked at a military hospital till 1918.

At the age of ten, Amelia saw plane for the first time and it was in around 1920 that she attended an aerial meet at Daugherty Field in Long Beach and developed an interest in flying. Her first tenminute flight as a passenger over Los Angeles made her realise that she had to fly.

Soon she purchased her own yellow Kinner Airster plane, which she called 'The Canary'. She worked hard to acquire the flying skills. She broke the women's altitude record in 1922.

She was chosen by 'George Putnam', the famous publicist, whom Amelia later married, to become the *first woman to fly across the Altantic*.

Her around-the-world flight on June 1, 1937 with her navigator, Fred Noonan from Miami, Florida proved to be fatal for her. After having flown 22,000 miles and 7,000 miles more to go, her flight disappeared.

The then President Roosevelt ordered a search that cost around $4 million, but her flight could not be traced ever.

Trivia
The letters she used to send to her husband on her journey was made into a book, 'The Last Flight'.

Quote
"Never do things others can do and will do if there are things others cannot do or will not do."

ANNIE BESANT

A nnie Besant (October 1, 1847 – September 20, 1933) was a prominent British women's rights activist, theosophist, writer and orator and supporter of Irish and Indian self-rule.

She was married at 19 to Frank Besant but soon separated from him over religious differences.

Annie Besant became a prominent speaker for the National Secular Society (NCS) and writer. During this time, she became good friends with Charles Bradlaugh.

They were prosecuted for publishing a book by birth control campaigner Charles Knowlton in 1877. The scandal made them famous and Bradlaugh was elected Member of Parliament for Northampton in 1880.

She became involved with Union organisers including the Bloody Sunday demonstration and the London matchgirls strike of 1888. She was a leading speaker for the Fabian Society and the Marxist Social Democratic Federation (SDF).

Besant was elected to the London School Board for Tower Hamlets, topping the poll.

Besant met Helena Blavatsky in 1890 and her interest in Theosophy grew gradually while her interest in secular matters waned. She, eventually, became a member of the Society and a highly successful lecturer in Theosophy. She travelled to India as part of her Theosophy-related work, where in 1898, she helped to establish the Central Hindu College. In 1902, she formed the International Order of Co-Freemasonry in England. She also established lodges in many parts of the British Empire. In 1907, she became the President of the Theosophical Society.

Trivia

Annie Besant also became involved in politics in India and joined the Indian National Congress (INC).

ANSEL ADAMS

Born on February 20, 1902 to Charles Hitchcock Adams and Olive Bray in San Francisco, Ansel Adams was one of the most well-known photographers of the 20th century.

Ansel Adams is known for the pictures of landscapes that he captured.

An unfortunate incident during his childhood left Adams with a broken nose. This made him very conscious about his appearance and hence, felt as a misfit in school. Therefore, he had to leave school midway. His father arranged for his education at home.

He married Virginia Best in 1928 and was blessed with two children. He died on April 22, 1984.

As a child, he loved to explore the outside world and was also interested in music. He learnt to play the piano when he was twelve. He wanted to become a musician until he took a trip to the 'Yosemite National Park' in 1916 and took his first set of photographs.

He joined the 'Sierra Club', which dealt with the protection of wildlife of Sierra Nevada in 1919 and later became the President of the club.

He wrote and clicked photographs for many publications by the Sierra Club. He, later, started his own gallery where he taught as well as worked. He learnt several new photographic techniques from renowned photographer Paul Strand during one of his working stints in New Mexico.

As a commercial photographer, he captured the wilderness, unexplored by mankind and American landscapes throughout his career.

Trivia

There may not be a photographer more famous than Ansel Adams in history, yet he was not financially sound.

ARISTOTLE

A ristotle, one of Plato's greatest disciples, was born in 384 BC. He was a Greek philosopher and a polymath.

Aristotle's father was a physician to the king of Macedonia. His father sent Aristotle to study at the academy when he was seven years old.

At the beginning, he was there as a student, then became a researcher and finally a teacher. He adopted and developed Platonic ideas there. When Plato died, Plato willed the Academy to his nephew, Speusippus and not to Aristotle.

Aristotle then went to Assos in Asia Minor to open a branch of the Academy. This particular Academy focused more on biology than its predecessor that relied on mathematics.

His writings covered many subjects – rhetoric, metaphysics, physics, poetry, music, theatre, politics, logic, linguistics, government, biology, ethics, and zoology.

He married the niece of another former student of Plato, Hermias. Pythias died after Pythias, ten years. During these years in Assos, Aristotle started to break away from Platonism and developed his own ideas.

Later, Aristotle was invited by King Philip of Macedonia in 343 BC to tutor his thirteen-ear-old don, Alexander.

King Philip was then murdered in 336 BC after which Alexander became the king. He mobilised his father's great army and subdued some city-states, thus becoming 'Alexander The Great'.

After Aristotle stopped teaching Alexander the Great, he returned to Athens in 335 BC.

Then, Aristotle founded his own school, which was named the Lyceum, named after the Greek God, Apollo Lyceus.

He died in Athens in 322 BC.

Trivia

Aristotle's works that have survived from antiquity through medieval manuscript transmission are collected in the Corpus Aristotelicum.

BENJAMIN GRAHAM

Benjamin Graham was born on May 8, 1894, in London to Jewish parents. He moved to New York City with his family when he was one year old. After the death of his father and experiencing poverty, he became a good student, graduating from Columbia University, as salutatorian of his class, at the age of 20. He received an invitation for employment as an instructor in English, Mathematics, and Philosophy, but took a job on Wall Street eventually starting the 'Graham-Newman Partnership'.

Graham is considered the first proponent of value investing, an investment approach he began teaching at the Columbia Business School in 1928 and subsequently refined with David Dodd through various editions of their famous book, *Security Analysis*. Graham's disciples include Warren Buffett, William J. Ruane, Irving Kahn, Walter J. Schloss and others. Buffett, who credits Graham as grounding him with a sound intellectual investment framework, described him as the second most influential person in his life after his own father. In fact, Graham had such an overwhelming influence on his students that two of them, Buffett and Kahn, named their sons, Howard Graham Buffett and Thomas Graham Kahn, after him.

According to *The Snowball* (a biography of Warren Buffett), Graham had an affair with his deceased son's girlfriend (Marie Louise Amingues) and used to travel to France frequently to visit her. He later separated from his wife, Estey in New York, after she refused his novel idea of living in New York for six months and France for six months. Marie Louise was content to live with Ben without marriage. Ben never officially divorced Estey.

Trivia
He is regarded by many as the "Father of Value Investing."

Quote
"Wall Street people learn nothing and forget everything."

CHE GUEVARA

Ernesto (Che) Guevara was born in Rosario in Argentina in 1928. He worked as a doctor after studying medicine at the University of Buenos Aires.

While in Guatemala in 1954, he witnessed the socialist government of President Jacobo Arbenz overthrown by an American-backed military coup. He was disgusted with what he saw and decided to join the Cuban revolutionary, Fidel Castro, in Mexico.

In 1956, Guevara, along with 80 other men and women arrived in Cuba in an attempt to overthrow the government of General Fulgencio Batista. This came to be known as the 'July 26 Movement'. Only sixteen men were left with twelve weapons by the time they reached the Sierra Maestra. Castro's guerrilla army raided the isolated army garrisons for the next few months and were gradually able to build up their stock of weapons.

The guerrillas redistributed the land amongst the peasants when they took control of the territory. The peasants helped the guerrillas against Batista's soldiers in return of the act.

Trivia

In 'Ultimate Sacrifice', which was published in 2006, Larmar Waldron and Thom Hartmann argued that Guevara was involved in a plot to overthrow Fidel Castro in 1963.

Quote

"Many will call me an adventurer and that I am, only one of a different sort: one of those who risks his skin to prove his platitudes."

CLEOPATRA

Cleopatra was born on 69 B.C. One of the most fascinating women in history was Cleopatra VII, daughter of Isis and King Ptolomy, the XII of Egypt. She has been portrayed as the Queen of Egypt in so many films, books, plays and is often a popular theme for *Halloween costumes*. She is noted for her great intelligence as well as beauty. Hollywood has often distorted many of the facts surrounding this remarkable woman and the history behind it.

It is said that Cleopatra and Caesar conceived a child near the Temple of Dendur. When the child was born, she named it Ptolemy Caesar, and soon it was known as Caesarion, meaning little Caesar.

When Caesar returned to Rome, she followed him with their baby and lived in Caesar's villa, where he visited her constantly, often feasting and making love until the early morning hours. Caesar was assassinated by members of the senate in Rome, who thought he was losing interest in the republic and spending too much time in Egypt. Cleopatra returned to Egypt and Ptolemy XIV died soon after, perhaps from poison by Cleopatra. She then named her son, Caesarion co-ruler.

Fortune turned against Cleopatra in 30 BC. Octavian was a man who was also in line for the throne of the Roman Empire. He was not fond of Mark Antony or Cleopatra, and he declared war on Egypt. He defeated Mark and then had Cleopatra arrested. At the age of 39, Cleopatra died in honour and was the last Pharaoh of Egypt.

Trivia
She became the Queen of Egypt at the age of 18.

Quote
"All strange and terrible events are welcome, but comforts we despise."

FRANK LLOYD WRIGHT

Born on June 8, 1867, Franklin Lloyd Wright was an American architect, interior designer, educator and writer, who designed more than 1,000 projects and completed 500 works. Wright believed in designing structures which were in harmony with humanity and its environment, a philosophy he called organic architecture, best exemplified by his design for Fallingwater (1935). He was a leader of the Prairie School Movement of architecture, and developed the concept of the Usonian home, his unique vision for urban planning in the United States.

His work includes original and innovative examples of many different building types, including offices, churches, schools, skyscrapers, hotels and museums. Wright also designed many of the interior elements of his buildings, such as the furniture and stained glass. Wright authored 20 books and many articles, and was a popular lecturer in the United States and in Europe. His colourful personal life often made headlines, most notably for the 1914 fire and murders at his Taliesin studio. Already well-known during his lifetime, Wright was recognised in 1991 by the American Institute of Architects as "the greatest American architect of all time".

In 1887, Wright arrived in Chicago in search of employment. As a result of the devastating Great Chicago Fire of 1871 and recent population boom, new development was plentiful in the city. He later recalled that his first impressions of Chicago were that of grimy neighbourhoods, crowded streets and disappointing architecture, yet he was determined to find work. Within days, and after interviews with several prominent firms, he was hired as a draftsman with the architectural firm of Joseph Lyman Silsbee.

He died on April 9, 1959.

Trivia

By 1901, Wright had completed about 50 projects, including many houses in Oak Park.

GENGHIS KHAN

enghis Khan was born in 1162. He was the founder and the Great Khan of the Mongol Empire. His father was Yesukhi and mother was Hoelun. Genghis Khan was earlier named Temujin. When Temujin was nine years old, he found his intended bride, Borje.

At the age of 27, Temujin held a *kuriltai* among the Mongols, who elected him *Khan.* The Mongols defeated the neighbouring Tatars and the Jurkins and assimilated their people. He united many of the tribes of North-East Asia. After founding the Mongol Empire, and being proclaimed Genghis Khan, he started the Mongol invasions.

The invasions were mostly in Eurasia. These were raids of the Kara-Khitan Khanate, Caucasus, Khwarezmid Empire, Western Xia and Jin dynasties. By the end of his life, the Mongol Empire occupied a substantial portion of Central Asia and China. Tribes from Kazakhstan and Kyrgyzstan heard about the Great Khan, and overthrew their Buddhist rulers to join his growing empire. By 1219, Genghis Khan ruled from northern China to the Afghan border, and Siberia to the border of Tibet.

By the end of that year, he had conquered every Khwarizm city, even lands from Turkey and Russia to his realm.

Genghis Khan assigned Ögedei Khan as his successor and split his empire into *khanates* among his sons and grandsons. He died in 1227 after defeating the Western Xia.

Genghis Khan promoted religious tolerance in the Mongol Empire. He guaranteed freedom of religion and protected the rights of Buddhists, Muslims, Christians and Hindus alike.

Trivia

Genghis Khan and his descendants made Mongolia the largest land empire in human history, but their story is often left out of textbooks.

Quote

"I will rule them by fixed laws [so] that rest and happiness shall prevail in the world."

HENRI LA FONTAINE

Henri La Fontaine was born on April 22, 1854 and studied law at the Free University of Brussels. He was admitted to the bar in 1877 and established a reputation as an authority on international law. He was an advocate for women, founding the Belgian League for the Rights of Women in 1890.

In 1893, he became the professor of international law at the Free University of Brussels and later, was elected to the Belgian Senate as a Member of the Socialist Party. He served as Vice-Chairman of the Senate from 1919 to 1932.

La Fontaine took an early interest in the International Peace Bureau and was influential in the Bureau's efforts to bring about 'The Hague Peace Conferences' of 1899 and 1907. He also served as 'President of the Bureau' from 1907 until his death in 1943.

In other efforts to foster world peace, he founded the *Centre Intellectual Mondial*, which was later merged into the 'League of Nations Institute for Intellectual Co-operation'. Fontaine proposed such organisations as a world school and university and a world Parliament.

La Fontaine is the co-founder of the Institute, *International de Bibliographie*, along with Paul Otlet. It was in this role that he and Otlet attended the World Congress of Universal Documentation in 1937.

He died on May 14, 1943.

Trivia
He was a Belgian international lawyer.

Karl Marx

A Philosopher, social scientist, historian and revolutionary, Karl Marx, is without a doubt the most influential socialist thinker to emerge in the 19th century. Born on May 5, 1818, Karl Marx developed the socio-political theory of Marxism.

Karl Heinrich Marx was born into a comfortable middle-class family in Trier on the river Moselle in Germany. At the age of 17, Marx enrolled in the Faculty of Law at the University of Bonn. Then, he went to the University of Berlin.

In 1836, he got engaged to Jenny von Westphalen and married her in 1843. Marx moved into journalism after his studies and in October 1842, became editor of the influential *Rheinische Zeitung*, which was a liberal newspaper backed by industrialists. The Prusssian government closed the paper due to his articles.

Moving to Paris in 1843, Karl Marx began writing for other radical newspapers including the *Deutsch-Französische Jahrbücher* and *Vorwärts*. He also wrote a series of books, several of which were co-written with his fellow German revolutionary socialist, Friedrich Engels. His most notable books were *The Communist Manifesto* and *Capital*.

After Marx was expelled from Paris at the end of 1844, he moved to Brussels. Marx became a communist and set down his views in his writings known as the **Economic and Philosophical Manuscripts** in 1844, which remained unpublished until the 1930s.

His other major contributions were *The German Ideology*, *The Communist Manifesto*, *The Class Struggles in France* and *The 18th Brumaire of Louis Bonaparte*.

Marx died on March 14, 1883 after prolonged illness.

Trivia

He was not a very well-known figure during his life, but his works became popular soon after his death.

LORD MOUNTBATTEN

L ouis Francis Albert Victor Nicholas Mountbatten or Lord Mountbatten was born on June 25, 1900. He was a British admiral and the first Earl Mountbatten of Burma. He was born in Windsor, London. He was the youngest child of Prince Louis of Battenberg and Princess Victoria of Hesse. Mountbatten attended Locker's Park Prep School and Naval Cadet School. He joined the Royal Navy during the World War I.

Before moving to India, he served as the First Sea Lord from 1954 to 1959. He was appointed as the last viceroy of the British Indian Empire in 1947.

In 1940, he invented the Mountbatten Pink naval camouflage pigment. During his career as a Supreme Allied Commander of South Asia, Mountbatten saw many high points and recapturing Burma from the Japanese after their surrender.

In India he made friends with many princes who had faith in him. During his tenure, he oversaw the partition of Pakistan and India. He remained in Delhi serving the viceroy till June 1948.

Soon after leaving India, Mountbatten served in the Mediterranean Fleet. He was honoured as the 'First Sea Lord'. Lord Mountbatten was appointed Chief of the Defence in1959. Mountbatten became the first Lord Lieutenant of the Isle of Wight, and kept the position until his death. During 1967-1978, he served as the president of the United World Colleges. During his presidency, he played a key role in the establishment of the United World College of South-east Asia in Singapore in 1974.

Mountbatten was married in 1922 to Edwina Cynthia Annette Ashley. They together has two daughters. Lady Mountbatten died in 1960. Mountbatten was a strong influence in the upbringing of his great-nephew, Prince Charles, the Prince of Wales.

Mountbatten was assassinated in a bomb blast by IRA in 1979. Mountbatten was buried in Romsey Abbey after a televised funeral. In 1979, Thomas McMahon was convicted of murder for his part in planning and was released in 1998.

MARTIN LUTHER KING

Martin Luther King Jr. was born on January 15, 1929 in Atlanta, Georgia. His father, Martin Luther King Sr., was a pastor of the Ebenezer Baptist Church in Atlanta. His mother was a schoolteacher.

After graduating from Morehouse College at the age of 19, he decided to enter Crozer Theological Seminary in Chester, Pennsylvania. He won the highest class ranking and a $1,200 fellowship for graduate school. In 1951, he entered the Boston University School of Theology to pursue his Ph.D.

He led the 1955 Montgomery Bus Boycott and helped found the Southern Christian Leadership Conference in 1957, serving as its first president. King's efforts led to the 1963 March on Washington, where King delivered his "I Have a Dream" speech. There, he expanded American values to include the vision of a colour blind society, and established his reputation as one of the greatest orators in American history.

Martin became the youngest person to receive the **Nobel Peace Prize** in 1964 for his work to end racial segregation and racial discrimination through civil disobedience and other non-violent means. By the time of his death in 1968, he had refocused his efforts on ending poverty and stopping the Vietnam War.

King was assassinated on April 4, 1968, in Memphis, Tennessee. He was posthumously awarded the 'Presidential Medal of Freedom' in 1977 and 'Congressional Gold Medal' in 2004. Martin Luther King. Jr. Day was established as a U.S. federal holiday in 1986.

Trivia
January 20, 1986 was the first national celebration of King's birthday as a holiday.

Quote
"Be a sinner and sin strongly, but more strongly have faith and rejoice in Christ."

NAPOLEON

Napoleon was born on August 15, 1769 in Corsica to parents of noble Genoese ancestry and trained as an artillery officer in mainland France. He rose to prominence under the French First Republic and led successful campaigns against the First and Second Coalitions arrayed against France. In 1799, he staged a coup d'état and installed himself as the First Consul; five years later the French Senate proclaimed him Emperor.

In the first decade of the 19th century, the French Empire under Napoleon engaged in a series of conflicts – *the Napoleonic Wars* – involving every major European power. After a streak of victories, France secured a dominant position in continental Europe, and Napoleon maintained the French sphere of influence through the formation of extensive alliances and the appointment of friends and family members to rule other European countries as French client states. Napoleon's campaigns are studied at military academies throughout the world.

The fight against the guerrilla in Spain and 1812 French invasion of Russia marked turning points in Napoleon's fortunes. His Grande Armée was badly damaged in the campaign and never fully recovered. Napoleon spent the last six years of his life in confinement by the British on the island of Saint Helena. An autopsy concluded that he died of stomach cancer, although this claim has sparked significant debate, and some scholars have held that he was a victim of arsenic poisoning.

Trivia
He is famed for his great military successes.

Quote
"A leader is a dealer in hope."

OLIVER CROMWELL

Oliver Cromwell was born on April 25, 1599 in Huntingdon, Cambridgeshire into a family of minor gentry. He studied at the Cambridge University.

He became a Member of Parliament for Huntingdon from 1628 to 1629. Cromwell experienced a religious crisis and became convinced that he would be guided to carry out God's purpose in the 1630s. In 1640, he was elected to represent Cambridge, first in the Short Parliament and then in the Long Parliament.

A Civil War broke out between Charles I and the Parliament in 1642. Even though lacking military experience, Cromwell created and led a superb force of cavalry, the 'Ironsides'. He rose from the rank of 'Captain' to that of 'Lieutenant-General' in three years. He convinced the Parliament to establish a professional army – the New Model Army. The Army won the decisive victory over the king's forces at Naseby in 1645.

Cromwell became the Army Commander and Lord Lieutenant of Ireland, where he crushed resistance with the massacres of the garrisons at Drogheda and Wexford in 1649.

After the restoration of the monarchy in 1660, he fled to Paris. He returned to England in 1680 and lived quietly under an assumed name until his death in 1712.

Trivia

The king's alliance with the Scots and his subsequent defeat in the Second Civil War convinced Cromwell that the king must be brought to justice. Cromwell was a prime mover in the trial and execution of Charles I.

PLATO

Born around 428 BCE in Athens, Plato was a Classical Greek philosopher, student of Socrates, mathematician, writer of philosophical dialogues and founder of the Academy in Athens.

Plato's father died while he was very young and his mother remarried to Pyrilampes.

He studied music and poetry at a very young age. Plato developed the foundations of his metaphysics and epistemology by studying the doctrines of Cratylus, and the work of Pythagoras and Parmenides, according to Aristotle.

Later, Plato adopted his philosophy and style of debate as Socrates' disciple. Plato was in military service from 409 BC to 404 BC. Socrates' execution in 399 BC had a profound effect on Plato.

Plato began to write extensively after 399 BC. Most scholars agree to divide Plato's major work into three distinct groups. The first of these is known as the *Socratic Dialogues* because of how close he stays within the text to Socrates' teachings.

Other texts relegated to this group include the Crito, Laches, Lysis, Charmides, Euthyphro, and Hippias Minor and Major.

The period from 387 to 361 BC is often called Plato's 'middle' or transitional period. It is thought that he may have written the Meno, Menexenus, Cratylus, Euthydemus, Phaedrus, Repuglic, Syposium and Phaedo during this time.

Plato's most influential work, *The Republic*, is also a part of his middle dialogues.

Plato died in 347 BC, leaving his school of learning Academy to his sister's son, Speusippus. The Academy remained a model for institutions of higher learning until it was closed in 529 CE.

Trivia

Plato's birth name was Aristocles, and he gained the nickname, Platon, meaning broad, because of his broad build.

PRINCESS DIANA

Born on July 1, 1961, Princess of Wales Diana was the first wife of Charles, Prince of Wales. The couple got married on July 29, 1981. She has been an international charity and fund-raising figure as well as a pre-eminent celebrity of the late 20th century.

Her wedding to the Prince of Wales was televised and watched by a global audience of over 750 million people. After the marriage, she was given courtesy titles, such as the Duchess of Cornwall, Duchess of Roth's and Countess of Chester. The couple had two children – Prince William and Prince Harry. A public figure since the announcement of her engagement to the Prince of Wales, Diana was born into an aristocratic English family with royal ancestry.

The marriage ended in divorce on August 28, 1996. The divorce was followed by her death in a car crash in Paris on August 31, 1997. There was subsequent display of public mourning a week later.

Diana, in her lifetime, also received recognition for her charity work and for her support of the 'International Campaign to Ban Landmines'. She was the president of 'Great Orion Street Hospital' for children since 1989.

Trivia

Although in 1983, she confided in the then-Premier of Newfoundland, Brian Peck ford, "I am finding it very difficult to cope with the pressures of being the Princess of Wales, but I am learning to cope," from the mid-1980s, the Princess of Wales became increasingly associated with numerous charities.

QUEEN ELIZABETH

Born on September 7, 1533, Elizabeth I is considered to be one of the greatest monarchs of England and Ireland from November 17, 1558 until her death.

Sometimes called Gloriana, The Virgin Queen, Elizabeth was the fifth and last monarch of the Tudor dynasty. Daughter of Henry VIII, she was born a princess. Her mother, Anne Boleyn was executed two and a half years after her birth and Elizabeth was declared illegitimate.

In 1558, Elizabeth succeeded the Catholic Mary I, during whose reign she had been imprisoned for nearly a year on suspicion of supporting protestant rebels.

Elizabeth was more moderate than her father, brother and sister had been, in her government. One of her mottoes was 'video et taceo' (I see, and say nothing). After 1570, when the pope declared her illegitimate, several conspiracies threatened her life. However, all plots were defeated with the help of her ministers' secret service.

Elizabeth was cautious in foreign affairs, moving between the major powers of France and Spain. The defeat of the Spanish Armada in the mid 1580s, when they tried to conquer England, associated her with what is popularly viewed as one of the greatest victories in English history.

She died on March 24, 1603.

Trivia

It was expected that Elizabeth would marry and produce an heir so as to continue the Tudor line. But not doing so, as she grew older, Elizabeth became famous for her virginity and a cult grew up around her which was celebrated in the portraits, pageants and literature of the day.

Sir Edmund Percival Hillary

Sir Edmund Percival Hillary born on July 20, 1919 was a New Zealand mountaineer, explorer and a philanthropist.

On May 29, 1953, at the age of 33, he and Sherpa mountaineer, Tenzing Norgay became the first climbers to have reached the summit of Mount Everest. Hillary and Norgay were part of the ninth British expedition to Everest, led by John Hunt.

Hillary was named as one of the 100 most influential people of the 20th century by the 'Time' magazine.

Hillary became interested in mountaineering at a young age, making his first major climb in 1939, reaching the summit of Mount Ollivier.

He served in the Royal New Zealand Air Force as a navigator during the World War II. He had been part of a reconnaissance expedition to the mountain in 1951 and an unsuccessful attempt to climb Cho Oyu in 1952 before the successful expedition in 1953 to Everest. As part of the Commonwealth Trans-Antarctic Expedition, he reached the 'South Pole' overland in 1958.

After he had successfully climbed Everest, he devoted much of his life to helping the Sherpa people of Nepal through the Himalayan Trust, which he founded. Through his efforts, many schools and hospitals were built in this remote region of Nepal.

He died on January 11, 2008 of heart failure.

Trivia

Upon the outbreak of World War II, Hillary applied to join the air force, but had earlier withdrawn the application before it was considered because he was harassed by his religious conscience.

SUBHAS CHANDRA BOSE

Subhas Chandra Bose was born on January 23, 1897 in Cuttack, Orissa to Janakinath Bose and Prabhabati Devi.

Known by the name, Netaji, Subhas Chandra Bose was an Indian revolutionary, who led an Indian national political and military force against Britain and the Western powers during the World War II.

Being one of the most prominent leaders in the Indian independence movement, he is a legendary figure in India.

He is presumed to have died on August 18, 1945, from injuries sustained in an alleged aircraft crash in Taihoku Taipei. However, no actual evidence of his death on that day has been authenticated. Many committees were set up by the government of India to investigate the mystery of his presumed death.

Subhas Chandra Bose advocated complete unconditional independence for India, whereas, the All-India Congress Committee wanted it in phases. Later, at the historic Lahore Congress convention, the Congress adopted *Purna Swaraj* (complete independence) as its motto. Subhas Chandra Bose later wrote that the great enthusiasm he saw among the people enthused him tremendously and that he doubted if any other leader anywhere in the world received such a reception as Gandhi did during these travels across the country.

Trivia

He was imprisoned and expelled from India. He came back to India and was imprisoned again for defying the ban.

Vallabhbhai Patel

Vallabhbhai Jhaverbhai Patel (October 31, 1875 – December 15, 1950) was an Indian barrister and statesman.

Known to be a social leader of India, Vallabhbhai played a major role in the country's struggle for independence. Oftenly called as the 'Iron Man of India', he was often addressed as *Sardar* which means Chief in many languages of India.

He was raised in the countryside of Gujarat in Leva-Gujjar Patidar community. Vallabhbhai Patel was practising as a lawyer when he was first inspired by the work and philosophy of Mahatma Gandhi.

Patel organised the peasants of Gujarat for non-violent civil disobedience against oppressive policies imposed by the British Raj. Subsequently, he became one of the most influential leaders in Gujarat.

He rose to the leadership of the Indian National Congress (INC). He was at the forefront of rebellions and all the political events in 1934 and 1937, promoting the Quit India Movement.

He was the first 'Home Minister' and 'Deputy Prime Minister' of India.

Trivia

Patel is remembered as the 'Patron Saint' of India's civil servants for establishing the modern all-India services.

Quote

"There is something unique in this soil, which despite many obstacles has always remained the abode of great souls."

VASCO DA GAMA

Born in 1460, Vasco da Gama was a Portuguese navigator and acquired a reputation as a brave and able sea commander. When the king of Portugal decided to send an expedition in search of a passage south of Africa to India, Vasco da Gama was selected to command.

After confessing and receiving absolution after the manner of those going to their death, Vasco and his companions set out with four ships. In spite of storms and tempests, they reached Calicut, and set up a marble pillar in evidence of their arrival in the country.

A fleet of 13 ships was sent out at once to establish a factory for trade with India. The ships returned in due time, heavily laden with rich shawls, silks, spices and precious gems bringing great gain into the king's coffers.

In 1502, he was sent accordingly with a fleet to the coast of India. He bombarded Calicut and treated the inhabitants with great cruelty.

He was made the Portuguese Viceroy of India.

He died in India on December 24, 1524 and was buried in a monastery, but his remains were brought home and buried with pomp and ceremony.

Trivia
He was instrumental in making Portugal for a time the leading commercial nation of Europe.

Quote
"May God our Lord allow us to complete our journey in His service, Amen."

SINGERS/
MUSICIANS

A.R. RAHMAN

Allah Rakha Rahman (A.R. Rahman) was born on January 6, 1966 in Madras, presently Chennai as A.S. Dileep Kumar. He is an Indian music composer, record producer, musician, singer and philanthropist. Rahman started learning piano at the age of four. His father passed away when he was nine years old.

He accompanied the great tabla maestro, Zakir Hussain on a few world tours and also won a scholarship at the 'Trinity College of Music' at Oxford University.

Then he moved to advertising and composed more than 300 jingles over five years. In 1989, he started a small studio called the Panchathan Record Inn that was one of the most well-equipped and advanced sound recording studios in India.

Rahman played a few of his music samples to famous director Mani Ratnam at an award function and Mani Ratnam took him as a music composer in his next film – *Roja*. The enormous success of his first Hindi venture was followed by the chart-topping soundtrack albums.

A.R. Rahman now is popularly known as the man who has redefined contemporary Indian music. Hailed by the *Time* magazine as the 'Mozart of Madras', Rahman, according to a BBC estimate, has sold more than 150 million copies of his work comprising music from more than 100 film soundtracks and albums across over half a dozen languages, including landmark scores, such as 'Roja', 'Bombay', 'Dil Se', 'Taal', 'Lagaan', 'Vandemataram' and more recently, 'Jodhaa Akbar', 'Delhi 6' and 'Slumdog Millionaire'.

In 2009, Rahman bagged two Occars for his work in *Slumdog Millionaire*.

Trivia

In 1989, Rahman converted to Islam, the religion of his mother's family.

ASHA BHOSLE

Asha Bhosle was born on September 8, 1933 in a Marathi family. She is one of the best-known and most highly-regarded Hindi playback singers in India. She is sister of another legendary singer, Lata Mangeshkar.

Her career started in 1943 and spanned over six decades. She has sung songs for a number of Bollywod movies. Bhosle has sung over **12,000** songs, including pop music, ghazals, bhajans, traditional Indian classical music, folk songs and others.

She was conferred with the **Dadasaheb Phalke Award** in 2000 and the **Padma Vibhushan** in 2008. 'The World Records Academy' recognised her as the 'Most Recorded Artist' in 2009. In 2011, she was officially acknowledged by the Guinness Book of World Records as the most recorded artist.

She has been a versatile singer throughout her career. Be it the romantic, 'Oh Mere Sona Re' or the sensuous, 'Aaiye Meherban' or the peppy, 'Kambakth Ishq', Asha Bhosle has been adding life to every song.

Being a renowned singer and actor, her father, Dinanath Mangeshkar, trained her in classical music at a very young age.

Asha got a chance to sing in a Marathi film at the age of ten. After a lot of struggle, Asha did playback singing for Hindi movie, *Chunariya* in 1948.

She eloped with her sister, Lata Mangeshkar's Personal Secretary Ganpatrao Bhosle at the age of 16 and married him. The marriage didn't work and she came back to her maternal house with her children. In 1980, she married music director RD Burman.

The movie, *Teesri Manzil* released in 1966 gave her enormous fame and she was acclaimed all over India and abroad as well.

Trivia

Asha Bhosle is a successful restaurateur and runs a chain of restaurants in Dubai and Kuwait, called the Asha's.

Bhimsen Gururaj Joshi

Pandit Bhimsen Gururaj Joshi, from February 4, 1922 - January 24, 2011, was an Indian vocalist in the Hindustani classical tradition. A member of the *Kirana Gharana*, he is renowned for the *khayal* form of singing, as well as for his popular renditions of devotional music, *bhajans* and *abhangs*. He was the most recent recipient of the **Bharat Ratna**, India's highest civilian honour, awarded in 2008.

Joshi was born into a *Kannada Madhwa Brahmin* family in the town of Ron, now in the Gadag district of northern Karnataka. His father, Gururaj Joshi, was a school teacher.

Bhimsen was the eldest in a family of '16 siblings'. Some of the siblings still live in their ancestral home in Gadag. Bhimsen lost his mother when he was young, and his stepmother then raised him. His parents lived initially with his grandfather as tenants of a Kulkarni household, but then moved to Gadag District.

As a child, Pandit Bhimsen Joshi's craving for music was evident to his family as he managed to lay his hands on a 'tanpura' used by his 'Kirtankar' grandfather, which had been kept away from his gaze at home. Music had such a magnetic pull over him that a 'bhajan singing' procession or just 'azaan' from a nearby mosque was said to draw him out of house.

Trivia

Until the first half of the 20th century, khayal was principally taught in the Guru Shishya (master-disciple) tradition.

BISMILLAH KHAN

Ustad Bismillah Khan was born on March 21, 1916 in Dumraon, Bihar. He was the second son of Paigambar Khan and Mitthan. The *shehnai* maestro was a **Bharat Ratna** Awardee and has been also awarded other three top Civilian Awards – **Padma Shri**, **Padma Bhushan** and **Padma Vibhushan**.

He gained worldwide acclaim for playing the shehnai for more than eight decades. He was named Qamaruddin to sound like his elder brother's name Shamsuddin. But, when his grandfather Rasool Baksh Khan saw him as a baby, he uttered the word 'Bismillah' and hence he came to be known as Bismillah Khan.

He moved to Varanasi at the age of six. He received his training under his uncle, late Ali Baksh 'Vilayatu', who was also a shehnai player. He mastered the art soon and is credited for making shehnai as one of the Indian classical instruments.

His concert in All India Music Conference in 1937 in Calcutta (Kolkata) brought shehnai into limelight and was hugely appreciated by music lovers.

Bismillah Khan had the rare honour of playing his shehnai on the eve of India's independence in 1947 and has been performing at the Red Fort since that year on August 15. He has a huge fan following across the world.

Ustaad Sahab Bismillah Khan died on August 21, 2006 at the age of 90 due to a cardiac arrest. His shehnai was buried with him in his grave.

Trivia

He started calling his Shehnai as 'Begum' after his wife died.

ELVIS PRESLEY

Elvis Presley (January 8, 1935 – August 16, 1977) was one of the most popular singers of the 20th century. He is widely known by the single name, Elvis. He is often referred to as the 'King of Rock and Roll' or simply 'the King'.

Born in Tupelo Mississippi, Presley moved to Memphis Tennessee with his family at the age of 13.

He began his career in Mississippi in 1954 when Sun Records owner, Sam Philips, eager to bring the sound of African American music to a wider audience, saw in Presley the means to realise his ambition.

Accompanied by guitarist Scotty Moore and bassist Bill Black, Presley was one of the originators of rock ability, an up-tempo, backbeat-driven fusion of Country and Rhythm and Blues. RCA victor acquired his contract in a deal arranged by colonel Tom Parker, who would manage the singer for over two decades. Presley's first RCA single, *Heartbreak Hotel*, released in January 1956, was a number one hit. He became the leading figure of the newly popular sound of Rock-n-Roll with a series of network television appearances and chart-topping records. His energised interpretations of songs, many from African American sources, and his uninhibited performance style made him enormously popular and controversial. In November 1956, he made his film debut in Love Me Tender.

Trivia

Presley is regarded as one of the most important figures of the 20th century popular culture. He is the best-selling solo artist in the history of popular music. Nominated for 14 competitive Grammys, he won three, and received the Grammy Lifetime Achievement Award at the age of 36. He has been inducted into four music halls of fame.

FRYDERYK FRANÇOIS CHOPIN

Born on March 1, 1810, Fryderyk François Chopin is a Polish composer, virtuoso pianist and a music teacher of French paternity.

Considered to be one of the masters of romantic music, Chopin has been called the 'poet of the piano'. A renowned child-prodigy pianist, he grew up in Warsaw and completed his music education there.

Fryderyk was the author of two polonaises - in *G minor* and *B flat major* – at the age of seven. He way first was published in the engraving workshop of Father Cybulski.

Eighteen-year-old Chopin struck out for the wider world in the company of a family friend, Feliks Jarocki in 1828.

In 1829, Chopin gave a brilliant debut in Vienna, giving two piano concerts. He left Poland for Vienna in 1831 before settling in Paris where he spent much of his life.

The 1830s were a productive time for the composer. Chopin completed several of his most famous works and also performed regular concerts, becoming a famous figure in Paris by 1838.

Chopin's larger scale works, such as the *scherzos, ballades, the barcarolle* and *sonatas* have paved a solid place within the repertoire. Some of his other works include *mazurkas, nocturnes, impromptus, waltzes* and *polonaises*.

Two important collections are the *24 Preludes Op. 28,* based loosely on Bach's Well-Tempered Clavier and the *Etudes*. They were a staple of that genre for pianists.

By the 1840s, his health started deteriorating. His last work was a *mazurka* in F minor. Chopin suffered from poor health for most of his life and died in Paris in 1849 at the age of 39.

Trivia

In 2010, the BBC TV made a 90-min documentary on Chopin's life titled 'Chopin – The Women Behind The Music explores Chopin's life'.

JAGJIT SINGH

Popularly known as 'the Ghazal King', Jagjit Singh was born on February 8, 1941.

He was a prominent Indian Ghazal singer, composer, music director, activist and entrepreneur.

He gained acclaim together with his wife, another renowned Indian ghazal singer, Chitra Singh in the 1970s and 1980s, as the first ever successful duo act.

He sung songs in Punjabi, Hindi, Urdu, Bengali, Gujarati, Sindhi and Nepali languages. He was also awarded India's third highest civilian honour, the **Padma Bhushan**, in 2003. He also received the 'Teacher's Lifetime Achievement Award' in 2006.

Singh is credited for the revival and popularity of ghazal by choosing poetry that was relevant to the masses and composing them in a way that laid more emphasis on the meaning of words and melody evoked by them.

He has composed music for many Bollywood movies including *Prem Geet*, *Arth* and *Saath Saath*, and also for TV serials *Mirza Ghalib* and *Kahkashan*.

He is the only composer and singer to have composed and recorded songs written by a Prime Minister, Atal Behari Vajpayee.

He expired on October 10, 2011 due to *cerebral haemorrhage*. The singer is survived by wife Chitra Singh. Their only son Vivek died in a car accident in the 1990s.

Trivia

He lent active support to several philanthropic endeavours, such as the library at St. Mary's School, Mumbai, Bombay Hospital, CRY, Save the Children and the ALMA.

JOHANN SEBASTIAN BACH

Johann Sebastian Bach (March 21, 1685 – July 28, 1750) was a German composer, organist, harpsichordist and violinist whose sacred and secular works for choir, orchestra, and solo instruments drew together the strands of the Baroque period and brought it to its ultimate maturity.

Although he did not introduce new forms, he enriched the prevailing German style with a robust contrapuntal technique, an unrivalled control of harmonic and motivic organisation, and the adaptation of rhythms, forms and textures from abroad, particularly from Italy and France.

Revered for their intellectual depth, technical command and artistic beauty, Bach's works include the Brandenburg Concertos, the Goldberg Variations, the Partitas, The Well-Tempered Clavier, the Mass in B minor, the St Matthew Passion, the St John Passion, the Magnificat, the Musical Offering, The Art of Fugue, the English and French Suites, the Sonatas and the Partitas for solo violin, the Cello Suites, more than 200 surviving cantatas, and a similar number of organ works, including the famous Toccata and Fugue in D minor and Passacaglia and Fugue in C minor, and the Great Eighteen Chorale Preludes and Organ Mass.

Trivia

Bach's abilities as an organist were highly respected throughout Europe during his lifetime, although he was not widely recognised as a great composer until a revival of interest and performances of his music in the first half of the 19th century. He is now generally regarded as one of the main composers of the Baroque style, and as one of the greatest composers of all time.

JOHNNY CASH

John R or 'Johnny' Cash (February 26, 1932 – September 12, 2003) was an American singer-songwriter, actor and author, who has been called one of the most influential musicians of the 20th century.

Although he is primarily remembered as a *country music artist*, his songs and sounds spanned many other genres including rockabilly and rock and roll – especially early in his career – as well as blues, folk and gospel. This crossover appeal led to Cash being inducted in the Country Music Hall of Fame, the Rock and Roll Hall of Fame, and Gospel Music Hall of Fame. Later in his career, Cash covered songs by several rock artists.

Cash was known for his deep, distinctive bass-baritone voice; for the 'boom-chicka-boom' sound of his Tennessee Three backing band; for his rebelliousness, coupled with an increasingly somber and humble demeanour; for providing free concerts inside prison walls; and for his dark performance clothing, which earned him the nickname, 'The Man in Black'.

He traditionally started his concerts by saying, "Hello, I'm Johnny Cash".

Trivia

Cash declared that he was 'the biggest singer of all', and viewed himself overall as a complicated and contradictory man.

JOHN LENNON

John Winston Lennon (October 9, 1940 – December 8, 1980) was an English musician and singer-songwriter.

Lenon rose to worldwide fame being among the founding members of one of the most commercially successful and critically acclaimed acts in the history of popular music, *The Beatles.*

He and **Paul McCartney** formed one of the most successful song-writing partnerships of the 20th century.

Born and raised in Liverpool, Lennon's first band The Quarrymen evolved into The Beatles in 1960.

After the group disintegrated towards the end of the decade, Lennon embarked on a solo career that produced the critically acclaimed albums 'John Lennon/Plastic Ono Band' and 'Imagine' and iconic songs, such as 'Give Peace a Chance' and 'Imagine'. He married Yoko Ono in 1969 and changed his name to John Ono Lennon.

In 1975, Lennon disengaged himself from the music business to devote time to his son, Sean but re-emerged in 1980s with a new album, 'Double Fantasy'.

Lenon was murdered three weeks after the album was released.

Lennon gave a sense of a rebellious nature in his music, his drawing, his writing, on film, and in interviews, which made him controversial. He moved to New York City in 1971, where his criticism of the Vietnam War resulted in a lengthy attempt by Richard Nixon's administration to deport him, but his songs were adopted as *anthems* by the anti-war movement.

Trivia

As of 2010 data, Lennon's solo album sales in the US exceed 14 million units. As a writer, co-writer or performer, he is responsible for 25 number–one singles on the US Hot 100 chart.

JUSTIN TIMBERLAKE

Justin Randall Timberlake was born to Lynn Harless and Randy Timberlake on January 31, 1981 in Memphis, Tennessee.

Timberlake grew up singing in the church choir. From 1993 to 1995, he performed with The Mickey Mouse Club along with pop stars, Britney Spears, Christina Aguilera and JC Chasez.

At the age of 14, Justin became a member of the boy band, *NSYNC. The group released their self-titled debut album in 1998. They became popular with fans and made a place for themselves in the music industry with a succession of big-selling albums.

Justin usually spent time working on and writing songs for his debut solo album in the beginning of 2002. During this time, he broke up with his longtime girlfriend, Britney Spears. His first solo album titled 'Justified' was released in 2002. His songs from his solo album debuting at number one of the music charts include 'SexyBack', 'My Love', and 'What Goes Around, Comes Around' from his second successful album, 'Future Sex/Love Sounds' in 2006.

He also has an acting career having starred in films, such as *The Social Network*, *Bad Teacher* and *Friends with Benefits*.

His other ventures include record label, Tennman Records, fashion label William Rast and the restaurants, Destino and Southern Hospitality.

Timberlake has won **six Grammy Awards** and **four Emmy Awards**.

Trivia
When he is not able to fall asleep, he sings himself to sleep.

Quote
"I'm a perfectionist. I can't help it, I get really upset with myself if I fail in the least."

KISHORE KUMAR

Born as Abhas Kumar Ganguly on August 4, 1929, the great singer, popularly known as Kishore Kumar and affectionately called Kishore Da, was one of those very few singers who took risks and experimented with different styles of music.

Kishore was the youngest in the Ganguly family and preferred singing and mimicking, Kundanlal Saigal. Once SD Burman had come to Ashok Kumar's house to meet him when he heard Kishore Kumar singing. He actually thought it was Saigal singing and inquired if he was there too. When he came to know that it was Kishore singing, he appreciated and encouraged young Kishore to continue refining his voice but at the same time, develop a style of his own. He, then, developed his own *signature style*.

He perfected *yodelling*. In Hindi film industry, his yodelling turned out to be widely popular and became a trademark of Kishore Kumar. His songs sounded absolutely natural, like laughter.

Kishore Kumar used to incorporate non-sensical terms into his songs that gave it an entirely a new feel. The ability to transform his voice according to not just the scene, but also the actor is something that was truly incredible of Kishore. He has sung many songs for Bollywood films. He has sung soulful songs for Dev Anand and also fun-filled songs for Rajesh Khanna, the yesteryear superstar.

Kishore Da has given some timeless classics, such as 'Chalte Chalte Mere Yeh Geet', 'Ek Ladki Bhigi Bhagi Si', 'Koi Humdum Na Raha', 'Yeh Jeevan Hai' and many others till his last song, 'Guru Guru Aajao Sanam'.

He was at the peak of his filmi career in 70's and 80's and died on October 13, 1987.

Trivia

Kishore Kumar had put a sign of 'Beware of Kishore' outside one of his flats, where he stayed for some time while his bungalow was made up.

LATA MANGESHKAR

Popularly known as the 'Nightingale of India', Lata Mangeshkar is the most versatile and popular playback singer of Hindi cinema, and was a theatre artist as well.

Born on September 28, 1929 in Indore, she started working as a theatre artist in *sangeet nataks* at the age of fi ve. Being the fi rst child of Dinanath Mangeshkar, she is the elder sister of singer Asha Bhosle.

She started learning music from her father Dinanath. Lata Mangeshkar began her career in 1942 which spanned over six and a half decades.

She sang songs in Hindi and about thirty-six other regional Indian languages and foreign languages.

After the sudden death of her father Dinanath, she decided to play small roles in various Hindi and Marathi fi lms due to unsound fi nancial condition of the house.

Lata got her biggest break when she was given a chance to sing the song 'Aayega Aanewaala' for the movie, *Mahal.* Her career saw a tremendous growth in the 1950s. She has worked with all the renowned music composers of her time like Shankar Jaikishan, SD Burman, Salil Chowdhury, Naushad, Hemant Kumar, etc.

She has sung songs for popular fi lms like *Lamhe, Diwale Dulhaniya Le Jayenge, Darr, Yeh Dillagi, Dil toh Pagal Hai,* etc.

She has won several awards including the **Padma Bhushan**, **Dada Saheb Phalke Award**, **Padma Vibhushna** for her singing. She is also been conferred with India's highest civilian award, the **Bharat Ratna**.

Trivia

Lata Mangeshkar has composed music and also produced movies under the name of 'Anand Ghan'. She is very fond of cooking. She always sings barefoot, in studies or on the stage.

LEONARD
BERNSTEIN

L eonard Bernstein (August 25, 1918 – October 14, 1990) was an American conductor, composer, author, music lecturer and pianist. He was among the first conductors born and educated in the United States of America to receive worldwide acclaim. According to *The New York Times*, he was "one of the most prodigiously talented and successful musicians in American history".

He derived fame through his long tenure as the music director of the New York Philharmonic, from his conducting of concerts with most of the world's leading orchestras and his music for West Side Story, as well as Candide, Wonderful Town, On the Town and his own Mass.

Bernstein was also the first conductor to give numerous television lectures on classical music, starting in 1954, continuing the same until his death. In addition, he was a skilled pianist, often conducting piano concertos from the keyboard.

As a composer he was prolific, writing symphonies, ballet music, operas, chamber music, pieces for the piano, other orchestral and choral works, and other concert and incidental music, but the tremendous success of *West Side Story* remained unequalled by his other compositions.

Trivia

While Bernstein is very well known for his music compositions and conducting, he is also known for his outspoken political views and his strong desire to further social change. His first aspirations for social change were made apparent in his producing (as a student) of a banned opera, The Cradle Will Rock, about disparagement between the working and upper class. As he went on in his career, Bernstein would go on to fight for everything from the influences of 'American Music' to the disarming of nuclear weapons.

LUCIANO

Luciano was born on October 12, 1935, in Modena, Emilia-Romagna, in Northern Italy. His father, Fernando Pavarotti, was a gifted amateur tenor, who instilled a love for music and singing in young Luciano. His mother, Adele Venturi, worked at the local cigar factory. Young Pavarotti showed many talents. He first sang with his father in the Corale Rossi, a male choir in Modena, and won the first prize in an international choir competition in Wales, UK. He also played soccer as a goalkeeper for his town's junior team.

Pavarotti made his operatic debut on April 29, 1961, as Rodolfo in La Boheme by Giacomo Puccini, at the opera house in Reggio, Emilia. Eventually, Pavarotti stepped in for Di Stefano in 1963, at the Royal Opera House in London as 'Rodolfo' in La Boheme by Giacomo Puccini, making his international debut. Pavarotti made his American debut opposite Sutherland in February of 1965, in Miami Opera. In March 2004, Pavarotti gave his last performance in an opera as painter Mario Cavaradossi in Giacomo Puccini's 'Tosca' at the New York Metropolitan Opera.

Luciano Pavarotti died of kidney failure on September 6, 2007, at home in Modena, Italy, where he was surrounded by his family. He was laid to eternal rest with his parents in the family tomb in Montale Rangone cemetery near Modena. His funeral ceremony in Modena was an international event attended by celebrities and over fifty thousand music lovers from all over the world.

Trivia

He was a recipient of the 'John F. Kennedy Center Honors' in 2001.

Quote

"Above all, I am an opera singer. This is how people will remember me."

Ludwig Van Beethoven

One of the most famous musicians of the Western Classical era, Beethoven was a pianist and a composer from Germany. His music and compositions have influenced many after his time.

Baptised on December 17, 1770 at Bonn in Germany, Beethoven is known to be one of the most popular music composers. He played at the Court of Bonn.

Being a musician himself, Beethoven's father realised the gift of God in the form of music and made him practise a lot. He wanted him to be a child prodigy like Mozart.

Beethoven's talent was discovered by renowned musician, Gottlob Neefe, who decided to teach him music. Neefe even placed him as an organist at the Court of Maximilian Franz, Elector of Cologne when Beethoven was 14 years old. Impressed with Beethoven, Prince Maximilian Franz sent him to Vienna to meet Mozart for further musical education.

Beethoven made extraordinary music in Vienna and toured a lot. Admiration for him grew and so did his supporters.

Beethoven started developing hearing problems by 1801. But his deafness didn't stop him from composing music. He indulged himself in creating exceptional symphonies and his one and only opera.

On March 26, 1827 the artist passed away, leaving behind music that inspired many.

Trivia

Beethoven's father claimed his age to be six on his first public performance when he was actually seven-and-a-half years old, to make him look like an extraordinary child prodigy.

Quote

"Beethoven can write music, thank God, but he can do nothing else on earth."

MADONNA

Madonna was born on August 16, 1958. She is an American singer-songwriter, actress and entrepreneur. Throughout her career, many of her songs have hit number one on the record charts, including "Like a Virgin", "Papa Don't Preach", "Like a Prayer", "Vogue", "Frozen", "Music", "Hung Up", and "4 Minutes". Critics have praised Madonna for her diverse musical productions, while at the same time serving as a lightning rod for religious controversy.

She won critical acclaim and a **Golden Globe** Award for Best Actress in Motion Picture Musical or Comedy for her role in *Evita* (1996), but has received harsh feedback for her other film roles. Madonna's other ventures include being a fashion designer, children's book author, film director and producer. Madonna has been acclaimed as a businesswoman. In 1992, she founded the entertainment company *Maverick* as a joint venture with the 'Time Warner'. In 2007, she signed an unprecedented US $120 million contract with Live Nation.

Madonna has sold more than 300 million records worldwide and is recognised as the world's top-selling female recording artist of all time by the 'Guinness World Records', according to the Recording Industry Association of America (RIAA),

In 2008, *Billboard* magazine ranked Madonna at number two, behind only The Beatles, on the Billboard Hot 100 All-Time Top Artists, making her the most successful solo artist in the history of the Billboard chart. She was also inducted into the Rock and Roll Hall of Fame in the same year.

Trivia

Madonna owns a chihuahua named Chiquita.

Quote

"Poor is the man whose pleasures depend on the permission of another."

MICHAEL JACKSON

R eferred to as the 'King of Pop', American superstar Michael Jackson was born in Gary, Indiana, on August 29, 1958.

Popularly known as MJ, Jackson is recognised as the most successful entertainer of all time by the 'Guinness World Records'.

Michael Jackson started his career as a singer along with his brothers as a member of 'The Jackson 5'. Soon he became a well-known figure in the music industry due to his mature dance moves and voice.

The five brothers, Jackie, Tito, Jermaine, Michael and Marlon gave many chart-busting hits including 'I Want You Back', 'Never Can Say Goodbye', 'Got to Be There' and many others.

He started his inevitable solo career in 1971. He uneasily ventured into films like 'The Wiz' in 1978 but was more successful with his music videos.

Michael had two brief marriages. In May 1994, Jackson married Elvis Presley's daughter, Lisa Marie Presley and they got divorced in less than two years of their marriage.

Jackson, then, got married to his long-time friend, Deborah Jeanne Rowe. They had two children – Michael Joseph Jackson Jr (commonly known as Prince) and Paris-Michael Katherine Jackson. The couple divorced in 1999 and Jackson got full custody of the children.

Jackson's life has been full of controversies. He was accused of child sexual abuse in 1993 but the case was settled out of court. In 2005, he was tried and acquitted of other sexual abuse allegations after the jury ruled him not guilty.

For all it to end, he died of drug-induced cardiac arrest on June 25, 2009 when he was preparing for his concert in London.

Trivia

His 1982 album, 'Thriller' is the biggest selling album of all time with confirmed sales of over 47 million, and over an estimated 100 million copies worldwide.

MICK JAGGER

Sir Michael Philip 'Mick' Jagger was born on July 26, 1943. He is an English musician, singer and songwriter. Best known as the lead vocalist of rock band, 'The Rolling Stones', Jagger gained much press notoriety for admitted drug use and romantic involvements.

He met Keith Richards when he was four and were friends until they went into secondary schools and lost touch. But they accidentally met in 1960 and realised that they had an interest in Rock n Roll combined with blues. This led to the formation of the 'Rolling Stones'.

With Richards, Brian Jones, Ian Stewart, Bill Wyman and Charlie Watts, Jagger was a key ingredient in attracting the audiences towards the group. The Rolling Stones first made the British charts in 1964 with a cover version of Bobby Womack's 'It's All Over Now'.

In the late 1960s, Jagger began acting in fi lms. Jagger released his fi rst solo album, *She's the Boss* in 1985.

He and his girlfriend singer, Marianne Faithfull were caught during police raids in 1967 with drugs and illegal substances.

The Rolling Stones had several hit albums in the 1970s Sticky Fingers, Exile on Main Street, and Some Girls.

The Rolling Stones made thousands of live performances and achieved endless record sales throughout the 70s with hits like 'Angie', 'It's Only Rock and Roll', 'Hot Stuff' and 'Respectable'.

In the late 1980s, the Rolling Stones were inducted into the Rock and Roll Hall of Fame. Jagger and Richards decided to work together again around this time.

In early 2009, he joined the eclectic super group, *Super Heavy*. Jagger's career has spanned over 50 years.

Trivia

Allmusic has described Jagger as 'one of the most popular and influential frontmen in the history of Rock-n-Roll.

MOHAMMED RAFI

Born on December 24, 1924, Mohammed Rafi was an Indian playback singer whose career spanned over four decades.

He made his singing debut in the Punjabi film, *Gul baloch* by rendering a duet with Zeenat Begum, 'Soniye Ni Heeriye Ni' composed by Shyamsunder.

Rafi has sung as many as 4,516 Hindi film songs, 112 non-Hindi film songs and 328 non-film songs from 1945 to 1980. Having a strong command over Hindu and Urdu, his songs ranged from classical numbers sad lamentations to highly romantic numbers, to patriotic songs, *qawwalis* to *ghazals* and *bhajans*.

While he was primarily noted for his Hindi-Urdu songs, he also sang in other Indian languages including Bhojpuri, Konkani, Oriya, Bengali, Punjabi, Sindhi, Marathi, Kannada, Gujarati, Telugu, Maithili, Assamese, etc.

He had been conferred with many awards for his contributions to the industry including a **National Award** and many **Filmfare Awards**. He was also honoured with the **Padma Shri** in 1967.

Best known for romantic and duet songs, he had sung most of his songs with famous singer, Asha Bhosle.

Some of the notable Films he sang for are *Aar Paar, Baiju Bawra, Barsat Ki Raat, Ek Musafir Ek Haseena, Dosti, Hum Dono, Teesri Manzil, Pyasa, Shaheed.*

He died on July 31, 1980, after he suffered a heart attack.

Trivia

His birth name was Mohammed Haji Ali Mohammed Rafi. An article in 'Times of India', published on July 24, 2010 sums up his voice as, "If there are 101 ways of saying, 'I love you' in a song, Mohammed Rafi knew them all".

MOZART

Mozart was born on January 27, 1756 in Salzburg, Austria. He grew up in Salzburg under the regulation of his strict father, Leopold who also was a famous composer of his time.

His abilities in music were obvious even when Mozart was still young so that in 1762 at the age of six, his father took him with his elder sister on a concert tour to Munich and Vienna and a second one from 1763-66 through the south of Germany, Paris and London. Mozart was celebrated as a wonder child everywhere because of his excellent piano playing and his improvisations.

In 1769, he became the concertmaster of the Archbishop and was knighted by the Pope in Rome. Working in Salzburg, he nevertheless travelled around Europe to meet other composers and orchestras. But in 1781, after a dispute with the Archbishop, he left Salzburg and went to Vienna, where he married Constanze Weber from Mannheim.

In Vienna, he also started his friendship with Joseph Haydn and a time of many work pieces. In the last year of his life, for example, he wrote one of his masterpieces, "Die Zauberflöte". Although some of his operas were successful, he could not make money from this and died in poverty at the age of 36, having even on his last day worked on a "Requiem". He was buried in a communal grave which could not be precisely identified years later.

Quote

"People are wrong who think my art comes easily to me. I assure you, nobody has devoted so much time and thought to composition as I."

NUSRAT FATEH ALI KHAN

Born on October 13, 1948, Nusrat Fateh Ali Khan was a world-renowned Pakistani musician. He was primarily a singer of *Qawwali*, the devotional music of the *Sufis*.

Considered one of the greatest singers ever recorded, he possessed a six-octave vocal range and could perform at a high level of intensity for several hours.

Nusrat Fateh Ali Khan extended the 600-year old Qawwali tradition of his family and is widely credited with introducing Sufi music to international audiences.

He was popularly known as Shahenshah-e-Qawwali, which means 'The King of Kings of Qawwali'.

Nusrat had his first public performance at the age of 16 at his father's *chelum*.

In subsequent years, Khan released movie scores and albums for various labels in Pakistan, Europe, Japan and the United States. He was engaged in collaborations and experiments with Western artists, becoming a well-known world music artist in the process. He toured extensively, performing in over 40 countries.

Khan was taken to London on August 11, 1997 for a kidney transplant due to illness with kidney and liver failure. He died of a sudden cardiac arrest at the age of 48. His body was returned to Faisalabad, Pakistan and his funeral was attended by the public and his fans.

Trivia

He officially became the head of the family qawwali party in 1971. He was signed by the Oriental Star Agencies (OSA), Birmingham, United Kingdom in the early 1980s.

PANDIT HARIPRASAD CHAURASIA

Pandit Hariprasad Chaurasia was born on July 1, 1938. A player of the *bansuri*, he is an Indian classical instrumentalist. Pandit Chaurasia has made a conscious effort to reach out and expand the audience for classical music.

His father was a wrestler and his mother died when he was four. Born in Varanasi, he had to learn music without his father's knowledge, as his father wanted him to become a wrestler.

Though he started going to the *akhada* for training with his father, he also started learning music and practising at his friend's house. Pandit Chaurasia often credits his wrestling training for giving him the immense stamina and lung power that helps him in his flute playing.

Hariprasad Chaurasia started learning vocal music from his neighbour, Pandit Rajaram at the age of 15. He switched to playing the flute under Pandit Bholanath Prasanna. Later, he received guidance from the reclusive Annapurna Devi, daughter of Baba Allaudin Khan, while he was working for the All India Radio.

Chaurasia is considered a rare combination of innovator and traditionalist. Apart from classical music, he has made a mark as a music director for Indian films along with Pandit Shivkumar Sharma. He formed a group called *Shiv-Hari*. Chaurasia also collaborated with various world musicians in experimental cross-cultural performances, including the fusion group, *Shakti*.

Trivia

He serves as the Artistic Director of the World Music Department at the Rotterdam Music Conservatory in the Netherlands.

PAUL MCCARTNEY

He was born as James Paul McCartney on June 18, 1942, in Liverpool General Hospital.

Sir Paul McCartney is a key figure in contemporary culture as a singer, composer, poet, writer, artist, humanitarian, entrepreneur, and holder of more than three thousand copyrights. He is in the **Guinness Book of World Records** for most records sold, most #1s (shared), most covered song, "Yesterday," largest paid audience for a solo concert (350,000+ people, in 1989, in Brazil). He is considered one of the most successful entertainers of all time.

After the death of his mother at the age of 14, he wrote his first song. In July 1957, he met John Lennon during their performances at a local church fête (festival). McCartney impressed Lennon with his mastery of guitar and singing in a variety of styles. He soon joined Lennon's band, *The Quarrymen*, and eventually became the founding member of *The Beatles*, with the addition of George Harrison and Pete Best.

McCartney received the 2002 Academy Award Nomination for the title song to the movie, *Vanilla Sky* (2001), and also went on his first concert tour in several years. In June, 2002, Sir Paul McCartney and Heather Mills married in a castle in Monaghan, Ireland.

In 2005, the *Entertainment* magazine poll named *The Beatles* the most iconic entertainers of the 20th Century. In 2006, the guitar on which Paul McCartney played his first chords and impressed John Lennon was sold at an auction for over $600,000.

Trivia

He is one of Britain's wealthiest men: according to the High Court judgment. Sir Paul's total fortune comes to about £387,012,000.

Quote

"I don't work at being ordinary."

USTAD AMJAD ALI KHAN

Born on October 9, 1945 in Gwalior, Ustad Amjad Ali Khan is a noted *sarod* player.

He belongs to the Bangash lineage and is the sixth generation sarod player in his family. He learnt sarod under his father, Haafiz Ali Khan's tutelage, who was also a musician to the royal family of Gwalior.

Amjad Ali Khan got the opportunity of his first solo recital at the age of 12 in 1958. Having developed a unique style of playing the sarod, he is considered one of the foremost classical musicians. The key innovations in his style are compositions based on vocal music, the technical ability to play highly complex phrases (ekhara taans) on the sarod spanning three octaves and the emphasis on simple and elegant compositions.

He has simplified the instrument by removing some strings and has also removed the resonant gourd (tumba) which is in use by the other sarod schools.

Amjad Ali Khan founded the Ustad Hafiz Ali Khan Memorial Society in 1977, which organises concerts and bestows an annual 'Hafiz Ali Khan Award'.

Ustad Amjad Ali Khan has performed in different parts of the world at various national and international festivals.

His family arranged a marriage for him, but that failed, and Khan got married second time to Bharatanatyam dancer Subhalakshmi in 1976. The couple has two sons – Amaan and Ayaan – who were taught music by their father.

He is the recipient of many awards and honours. These include: The **Padma Shri** (1975), **Sangeet Natak Academy Award** (1989), the **Tansen Award** (1989), the **Padma Bhushan** (1991) and the **International Music Forum Award**, UNESCO in 1970.

Trivia

Amjad Ali Khan is a Muslim and his wife, Subhalakshmi is a Hindu. Their family home in Gwalior was made into a musical centre and they live in New Delhi.

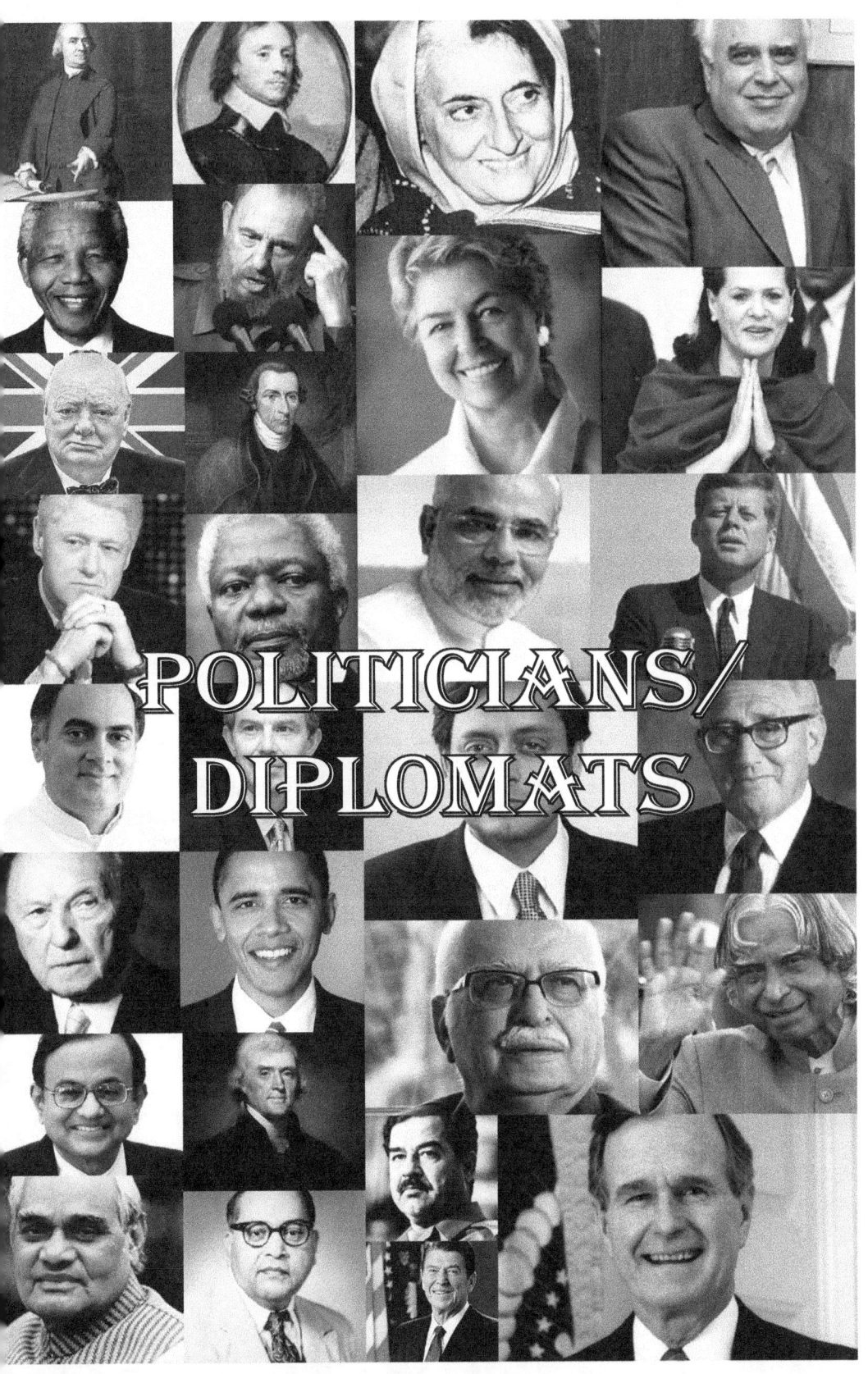

POLITICIANS/
DIPLOMATS

ANNA ELEANOR ROOSEVELT

Anna Eleanor Roosevelt was born on October 11, 1884. She was the First Lady of the United States from 1933 to 1945. She supported the New Deal policies of her husband, distant cousin, Franklin Delano Roosevelt, and became an advocate for civil rights.

After her husband's death in 1945, Roosevelt continued to be an international author, speaker, politician, and activist for the 'New Deal Coalition'. She worked to enhance the status of working women, although she opposed the Equal Rights Amendment because she believed it would adversely affect women.

In the 1940s, Roosevelt was one of the co-founders of 'Freedom House' and supported the formation of the United Nations. Roosevelt founded the UN Association of the United States in 1943 to advance support for the formation of the UN. She was a delegate to the UN General Assembly from 1945 and 1952, a job for which she was appointed by President Harry S. Truman and confirmed by the United States Senate. During her time at the United Nations, she chaired the committee that drafted and approved the Universal Declaration of Human Rights. President Truman called her the "First Lady of the World" in tribute to her human rights achievements.

Active in politics for the rest of her life, Roosevelt chaired the John F. Kennedy administration's ground-breaking committee which helped start second-wave feminism, the Presidential Commission on the Status of Women. In 1999, she was ranked in the top ten of Gallup's List of Most Widely Admired People of the 20th Century.

Trivia
Roosevelt received 48 honorary degrees during her life.

Quote
"A little simplification would be the first step toward rational living, I think."

ANTHONY CHARLES LYNTON BLAIR

Born on May 6, 1953, Anthony Charles Lynton Blair is a former British Labour Party politician, who served as the Prime Minister of the United Kingdom from May 2, 1997 to June 27, 2007.

He was the Sedgefield MP from 1983 to 2007 and Leader of the Labour Party from 1994 to 2007. He resigned from all of these positions in June 2007.

He became the youngest Prime Minister since Lord Liverpool in 1812 at the age of 43. Blair strongly supported the foreign policy of US President George W Bush, notably by participating in the 2001 invasion of Afghanistan and 2003 invasion of Iraq.

Blair is the Labour Party's longest-serving Prime Minister, the only person to have led the Labour Party to three consecutive general election victories and the only Labour Prime Minister to serve consecutive terms more than one of which was at least four years long.

On the day he resigned as Prime Minister, he was appointed the official Envoy of the Quartet on the Middle East. In May 2008, Blair launched his 'Tony Blair Faith Foundation'. This was followed by the launching of the Faith and Globalisation Initiative with Yale University in the United States, Durham University in the United Kingdom and the National University of Singapore in Asia in July 2009 to deliver a postgraduate programme in partnership with the Foundation.

Trivia
He was converted to Catholicism in December 2007.

Quote
"I feel like everyone else in this country today. I am utterly devastated."

ARIEL SHARON

Also known by the name of Ariel Scheinermann, Sharon was born in Kfar Malal to a family of Lithuanian Jews.

He is an Israeli statesman and a retired general. He served as Israel's 11th Prime Minister. Ariel has been in a permanent vegetative state since he suffered a stroke on January 4, 2006.

Sharon was a commander in the Israeli Army since its inception in 1948. He participated in the 1948 War of Independence as an Army officer, the Qibya massacre of 1953, the 1956 Suez War, the Six-Day War of 1967, and the Yom-Kippur War of 1973.

After retiring from the army, Sharon joined the right-wing Likud party. He then became the leader of the Likud in 2000 and served as Israel's Prime Minister from 2001 to 2006. He left Likud to form new Kadima Party in November 2005.

On January 4, 2006, Sharon suffered a severe stroke that left him in a persistent vegetative state.

In March 2006 elections, Kadima was led by Ehud Olmert following Sharon's stroke. It went on to win plurality of Knesset seats, becoming the senior coalition partner in Israel's 31st government.

Trivia

Sharon lost his son, Goor (from his first wife, Margalit) in a shooting accident in 1968.

Quote

"Iran, Libya and Syria are irresponsible states, which must be disarmed of weapons of mass destruction, and a successful American move in Iraq as a model will make that easier to achieve".

ATAL BIHARI VAJPAYEE

A tal Bihari Vajpayee was born to Krishna Devi and Krishna Bihari Vajpayee on December 25, 1924 in a Brahmin family in a town in Gwalior. Vajpayee's father Krishna Bihari was a poet and schoolmaster in his hometown.

Atal Bihari Vajpayee attended Gwalior's Victoria College, the present Laxmi Bai College, and graduated with distinctions in Hindi, English and Sanskrit. He did his Post Graduation in Political Science from the DAV College in Kanpur.

He started his career with joining the Rashtriya Swayamsevak Sangh (RSS), and served the *Rashtradharma*, *Veer Arjun* and *Panchjanya* newspapers as a journalist and poet.

Vajpayee never married, becoming the first and, till date, only bachelor Prime Minister of India.

After his first brief period as Prime Minister in 1996, Vajpayee headed a coalition government from March 19, 1998 till May 19, 2004.

Vajpaaye has been a parliamentarian for over four decades. He was elected to the Lok Sabha a record nine times and to the Rajya Sabha twice.

He was the Member of Parliament for Lucknow until 2009, when he retired from active politics due to health constraints.

Trivia

Vajpayee was referred to as 'The Bhishma Pitamah' of Indian Politics by Prime Minister Dr Manmohan Singh in one of his speeches.

Quote

"Global interdependence today means that economic disasters in developing countries could create a backlash on developed countries."

BAL GANGADHAR TILAK

Born on July 22, 1856, Bal Gangadhar Tilak was universally recognised as the 'Father of Indian Unrest'. One of the prime architects of modern India, he heralded Asian nationalism. However, his philosophy could not survive after his death as India came under sway of Mahatma Gandhi.

Bal Gangadhar Tilak was a brilliant politician as well as a profound scholar. He believed that independence is the foremost necessity for the well being of a nation. He was the first intellectual leader to understand the importance of mass support and subsequently became the first mass leader of India.

Tilak realised that the constitutional agitation in itself was futile against the British. He soon realised that India was ill-prepared for an armed revolt.

Tilak is often misinterpreted; perhaps, it is so because of his style of operation. His way of doing things raised bitter controversies. Many blame Tilak for opposing the Age of Consent Bill, which raised the age limit for marriage of girls to 12 from ten years. But at the same time, he had signed a counter-proposal where in one of the clauses was that the girls should not be married until they are 16 and boys until they are 20.

Trivia

He educated all his daughters and did not marry them till they were over 16. There are instances when he privately paid for the education of women. Still it remains true that he was a reactionary and did not use his considerable influence to give a much-needed support to the social reformists.

BARACK OBAMA

Barack Obama was born on August 4, 1961. Some of the nicknames given to him are 'Barry', 'Bama', 'Rock', 'The One', 'No drama Obama'. He was born to a white American mother, Ann Dunham and a black Kenyan father, Barack Obama Sr., who were both young college students at the University of Hawaii.

Obama attended the Columbia University but found New York's racial tension inescapable. He became a community organiser for a small Chicago church-based group for three years, helping poor South Side residents cope with a wave of plant closings. He then attended Harvard Law School, and in 1990 became the first African-American editor of the 'Harvard Law Review'.

He also began teaching at the University of Chicago Law School, and married Michelle Robinson, a fellow attorney. Eventually, he was elected to the Illinois state senate.

In 2004, Obama was elected to the US Senate as a Democrat, representing Illinois and he gained national attention by giving a rousing and well-received keynote speech at the Democratic National Convention in Boston. In 2008, he ran for President and despite having only four years of national political experience, he won. In January 2009, he was sworn in as the **44th President of the United States**, and *the first African-American* ever elected to that position. Obama was awarded the Nobel Peace Prize in 2009.

Trivia

He has won a Grammy for Best Spoken Word for the CD version of his autobiography, 'Dreams From My Father' (2006).

Quote

"Change will not come if we wait for some other person or some other time. We are the ones we've been waiting for. We are the change that we seek."

BILL CLINTON

Born on August 19, 1946, William Jefferson 'Bill' Clinton is an American politician who served as the 42nd President of the United States from 1993 to 2001.

Bill Clinton was the third-youngest President. He took office as the President at the end of the Cold War. Bill Clinton was the first President of the baby boomer generation. Often described as a New Democrat, many of his policies have been attributed to a centrist, *Third Way philosophy of governance.*

Clinton became both a student leader and a skilled musician. An alumnus of Georgetown University, he earned a Rhodes scholarship to attend the University of Oxford. He is married to Hillary Rodham Clinton. Hillary Clinton was the Senator from New York from 2001 to 2009 and has been serving as the United States Secretary of State since 2009. Both Clintons received law degrees from Yale Law School, where they met and began dating.

Clinton was elected as the President in 1992, defeating incumbent President George HW Bush. As President, Clinton presided over the longest period of peacetime economic expansion in the history of America. He implemented Don't ask, don't tell, a controversial intermediate step to full gay military integration.

After a failed health care reform attempt, Republicans won control of Congress in 1994, for the first time in forty years. Two years later, the re-elected Clinton became the first member of the Democratic Party since Franklin D Roosevelt to win a second full term as President.

Trivia

As Governor of Arkansas, Bill Clinton overhauled the State's education system and served as Chair of the National Governors Association.

FIDEL CASTRO

Fidel Castro was born on August 13, 1926 in Birab, Cuba. Some of the nicknames given to Fidel Castro were 'El Comandante', 'El Caballo' and 'El Jefe Maximo'.

Known as a rebellious, loud, and troublesome child, Fidel was sent to a Jesuit boarding school in Santiago de Cuba, where he was often teased by his wealthier classmates who called him a 'peasant'.

He later attended Belen College and the University of Havana, and earned a law degree.

After graduating from the university, Castro briefly practised law before he went on to marry a wealthy philosophy student, Mirta Diaz-Balart. The couple had one child and they divorced five years after their marriage.

After several years in prison and exile (he lived in Mexico and New York City before starting the revolution), Castro led an attack on the Moncada barracks on July 26, 1953. This was a major attack on Batista's hold of Cuba. Castro once again was imprisoned before he was released.

After his release, he went to the Yucatan, where he organised a rebel force that landed in Cuba in 1958 and after many successful battles, Castro rode triumphantly into Havana in 1959.

Trivia

He rarely sleeps more than three or four hours a day.

GEORGE H. W. BUSH

Born on June 12, 1924, George Herbert Walker Bush is an American politician who served as the 41st President of the United States (989–93). He had previously served as the 43rd Vice President of the United States from 1981 to 1989, a congressman, an ambassador and the Director of Central Intelligence.

Bush was born in Milton, Massachusetts, to Senator Prescott Bush and Dorothy Walker Bush. Following the attacks on Pearl Harbor in 1941, at the age of 18, Bush postponed going to college and became the youngest aviator in the US Navy at the time. He served until the end of the war, then attended the Yale University. Graduating in 1948, he moved his family to West Texas and entered the oil business, becoming a millionaire by the age of 40.

He became involved in politics soon after founding his own oil company, serving as a member of House of Representatives, among other positions. He ran unsuccessfully for president of the United States in 1980, but was chosen by party nominee Ronald Reagan to be the vice presidential nominee, and the two were subsequently elected. During his tenure, Bush headed administration task forces on deregulation and fighting drug abuse.

Trivia

During the World War II, following the attack on Pearl Harbor in December 1941, Bush decided to join the US navy. So after graduating from the Phillips Academy, he became a naval aviator at the age of just 18!

HENRY KISSINGER

Henry Alfred Kissinger was born in Fürth, Germany in 1923 to a family of German Jews. He is an American academic, political scientist, businessman and a diplomat.

Kissinger is the recipient of the Nobel Peace Prize. He served as National Security Advisor and later, as Secretary of State in the administrations of Presidents Richard Nixon and Gerald Ford.

Even after his term, Kissinger's opinion was still sought by many following Presidents and many world leaders.

Kissinger spent his high school years in the Washington Heights section of upper Manhattan. Later, he began attending school at night and worked in a shave brush factory during the day. Henry Kissinger played a dominant role in US foreign policy between 1969 and 1977. It was during this period that he pioneered the policy of détente with the Soviet Union, orchestrated the opening of relations with the People's Republic of China. Various American policies including the bombing of Cambodia, remained controversial.

Kissinger is still a controversial figure today. He was honoured as the first recipient of the Ewald von Kleist Award of the Munich Conference on Security Policy. He is the founder and chairman of Kissinger Associates, an international consulting firm.

Trivia

Although Kissinger assimilated quickly into American culture, he never lost his pronounced Frankish accent, due to childhood shyness that made him hesitant to speak.

Quote

"Ninety percent of the politicians give the other ten percent a bad reputation."

INDIRA GANDHI

Indira Priyadarshini Gandhi, known as Indira Gandhi, was born on November 19, 1917. She was an Indian politician who served as the Prime Minister of India for three consecutive terms – from 1966 to 1977 and a fourth term – 1980-1984.

Indira Gandhi was born to Jawaharlal and Kamala Nehru and spent her childhood in Allahabad. She received her college education at Somerville College, Oxford.

She married Feroze Gandhi in 1942 whom she knew from Allahabad and who died in 1960 before he could consolidate his own political force. The couple had two sons – **Rajiv Gandhi** and **Sanjay Gandhi**.

After the death of her father, Pt. Jawaharlal Nehru in 1964, Indira Gandhi was elected to Parliament and she was the Minister of Information and Broadcasting in Lal Bahadur Shastri's government. As Shastri died unexpectedly of a heart attack less than two years after assuming office, the numerous contenders for the position of the Prime Ministership picked Indira Gandhi as a compromise candidate. She showed extraordinary political skills and became the world's second longest serving female Prime Minister.

She was assassinated by her bodyguards as she garnered the undying hatred of Sikhs after she ordered an assault upon the Sikh shrine, the Golden Temple in Amritsar to crush the secessionist movement of Sikh militants, led by Jarnail Singh Bindranwale. The name of the operations was 'Operation Bluestar'.

Trivia

She was also the only Indian Prime Minister to have declared a state of emergency in order to 'rule by decree' and the only Indian Prime Minister to have been imprisoned after holding that office.

JAWAHARLAL NEHRU

Son of Swaroop Rani and Motilal Nehru, Jawaharlal Nehru was born on November 14, 1889, in Allahabad. Motilal Nehru was a wealthy lawyer and a prominent leader of the Indian independence movement.

Often referred as Panditji or affectionately *Chacha Nehru* by children, Nehru was the first Prime Minister of independent India from 1947 until he died on May 27, 1964.

He established the parliamentary government and became noted for his 'neutralist' policies in foreign affairs. He was also one of the principal leaders of India's independence movement in the 1930s and 1940s.

The Nehru family belonged to the saraswat Brahmin caste. Nehru graduated from Trinity College, Cambridge University and came back to India in 1912.

In 1916, by his parents' arrangement, he married seventeen-year-old Kamala.

He became the top political leader of the Indian National Congress Party along with his associate Mahatma Gandhi.

Nehru and his family followed Gandhi and abandoned fashionable British clothes and expensive possessions. Nehru and his family adopted the native language of Hindu or Hindustani for their common use.

Nehru used to wear a *khadi kurta* and a *Gandhi* cap as an Indian nationalist uniform. When Nehru's father joined the Swaraj Party in opposition to Gandhi, Jawaharlal Nehru did not join his father and stayed with Mahatma Gandhi. Together they led the nation of India to independence in 1947.

Nehru signed the first constitution of independent India in 1949. He was an outstanding public speaker.

Trivia

He was one of the founders of the international Non-Aligned Movement.

Quote

"A moment comes, which comes but rarely in history, when we step out from the old to the new; when an age ends; and when the soul of a nation long suppressed finds utterance."

JAYAPRAKASH NARAYAN

Popularly known as JP Narayan, Jayaprakash or Loknayak, Jayaprakash Narayan was born on October 11, 1902 in Sitabdiara, Saran in Bihar.

He was an Indian independence activist and political leader, remembered especially for leading the opposition to Indira Gandhi in the 1970s and for giving a call for peaceful Total Revolution.

J.P. Narayan was born in a Kayastha Family. His father Harsudayal was a junior official in the canal department of the State government and was often touring the region. Affectionately called *Baul*, Jayaprakash was left with his grandmother for studies.

His biography, *Jayaprakash*, was written by his nationalist friend and an eminent writer of Hindi literature, Ramavriksha Benipuri. He was posthumously awarded the **Bharat Ratna**, India's highest civilian award, in recognition of his social work in 1998.

He was also conferred with other awards including the 'Magsaysay Award' for Public Service in 1965. The airport of Patna is also named after him.

He died at the age of 79 on October 8, 1979 in Patna, Bihar.

Trivia

The then Prime Minister of India, Shri Charan Singh declared seven days mourning on the death of Shri J.P. Narayan calling him, 'the conscience of the nation'.

Quote

"If you really care for freedom, liberty, there cannot be any democracy or liberal institution without politics. The only true antidote to the perversions of politics is more politics and better politics. Not negation of politics."

JOHN F KENNEDY

John Fitzgerald Kennedy with the nicknames like 'JFK', 'JACK' and "CRASH KENNEDY" was born on May 29, 1917 to Rose Kennedy and Joseph P Kennedy. John was named after his maternal grandfather, John 'HoneyFitz' Fitzgerald, the mayor of Boston. John kept on getting ill as a child and was given the last rites five times, the first one being when he was a newborn.

He was the second of four boys born to an Irish Catholic family with nine children: Joseph Jr., John, Robert F Kennedy (called Bobby), and Ted Kennedy (born Edward). Because Rose made Joe and Jack (the name his family called him) wear matching clothes, they fought a lot for attention.

John went to Choate, a private school. John went to Princeton, then Harvard, and for his senior thesis he wrote a piece about why England refused to get into the war until late. It was published in 1940 and called "Why England Slept".

John ran for Congress in Massachusetts in the early 1950's and won. He married Jacqueline Kennedy on September 12 1953. He became a father rather late in life. Their first child, Caroline Kennedy, was born on November 27, 1957 when John was 40 and their son, John Kennedy Jr., was born on November 25, 1960 when JFK was 43. They had a son named Patrick Bouvier, but he died a few days after birth.

On November 22, 1963, John was to give a speech in Dallas, but on his way an assassin hidden on the sixth floor of the Texas School Book Depository opened fire at Kennedy, who was riding in an open car. Hit twice and severely wounded, Kennedy died in a local hospital at 1:00 pm. Lee Harvey Oswald, the assassin was captured after a short period of time for interrogation.

Trivia

He was the youngest elected US President.

Quote

"Ask not what your country can do for you; ask what you can do for your country."

KAPIL SIBAL

Born on August 8, 1948, in Jalandhar city, Kapil Sibal is an Indian politician and a lawyer. Presently, he holds the portfolio of the Minister of Communications and Information Technology, Telecom Minister and the Human Resource Development Minister in the present Prime Minister Manmohan Singh cabinet.

He has been a Member of Parliament for over ten years – first in 1998 as Member of the Rajya Sabha, and then in 2004, elected to the Lok Sabha from the Chandni Chowk Parliamentary Constituency.

He moved to Delhi in 1962 and qualified for the IAS in 1973 but instead chose to set up his own law practice.

Sibal has held several important positions in the government and the society, such as Additional Solicitor General of India (December 1989-1990); Member, Board of Management, Indira Gandhi National Open University (1993); President, Supreme Court Bar Association (1995-96, 1997-98 and 2001-2002); Member, Rajya Sabha (July 1998); Member, Executive Council, Institute of Constitutional and Parliamentary Studies (July, 2001); Member, Business Advisory Committee (August, 2001); Member, Committee on Home Affairs (January, 2002); Co-chairman, Indo-US Parliamentary Forum (2002); Member, Board of International AIDS Vaccine Initiative (2002); Member, Programme Board of the Bill and Melinda Gates Foundation's Indian AIDS initiative (2003); Member, Working Group on Arbitrary Detention set up by the Human Rights Commission, Geneva.

Trivia

Kapil Sibal was the first Indian Minister to have travelled to Antarctica and stayed at the Maitri base in sub-zero temperatures for getting a first hand experience about the hardships being faced by the Indian scientists.

KOFI ANNAN

Kofi Atta Annan was born on 8th April, 1938. He is a Ghanaian diplomat who served as the seventh Secretary-General of the UN from January 1997 to December 2006.

Since 1960, Ghana has been a republic within the British Commonwealth, a group of nations dependent on Great Britain.

Following his graduate studies in Geneva, Annan joined the World Health Organisation (WHO) Later, The UN posts took him to Addis Ababa, Ethiopia, and New York City.

Annan always assumed that he would return to his native land after college, although he was disturbed by the unrest and numerous changes of government that occurred there during the 1970s.

He moved to Cairo, Egypt, as the chief civilian personnel officer in the UN Emergency Force in 1974. Annan returned to international diplomacy and the UN in 1976. Remaining associated with the UN for many years, he filled the post of assistant secretary-general in the Office of Human Resources Management and served as security coordinator for the UN in the 1980s.

Annan was appointed secretary-general, the top post of the UN, by the UN General Assembly in December 1996.

Annan and the United Nations were the co-recipients of the **2001 Nobel Peace Prize** for founding the *Global AIDS and Health Fund* to support developing countries in their struggle to care for their people.

Trivia

He is the first African to head the UN and was awarded the 'Nobel Prize'. Noted for his cautious style of diplomacy, Annan is sometimes criticised for his soft-spokenness.

KONRAD ADENAUER

Konrad Hermann Joseph Adenauer was born on January 5, 1876 in Cologne to Catholic lawyer Konrad Adenauer and Helene. He studied law in Freiburg, Munich and Bonn. He married Emma Weyer in 1904. The couple had three children.

He was elected to the Cologne city council in 1906. He was elected as the Mayor of Cologne in 1917. In 1944, after they attempted Hitler's assassination, Adenauer was arrested and was put in a concentration camp.

In 1945, he restored as Cologne Mayor by the Americans. However, he was removed from office by the British in October 1945.

In 1949, Adenauer was elected as a representative in the German Bundestag (Parliament).

He became Germany's first Federal Chancellor, winning office by just one vote. He remained as the Chancellor for 14 years and died on April 19, 1967.

Trivia

In February 1933, Adenauer refused to receive Hitler during a campaign visit to Cologne and got Nazi flags removed from the Deutzer bridge.

In 1934, they arrested Adenauer but released him after two days.

Quote

"We all live under the same sky, but we don't all have the same horizon."

L.K. Advani

Lal Kishanchand Advani, popularly known as Lal Krishna Advani or L.K. Advani, was born on November 8, 1927 in Karachi, Pakistan (then, British India). He is a veteran Indian politician and a former president of the Bharatiya Janata Party (BJP). The BJP is currently the major opposition party in the country.

L.K. Advani has served as the Deputy Prime Minister of India from 2002 to 2004 and was the Leader of the Opposition in the tenth and the 14th Lok Sabha.

Advani began his political career as a worker of the Rashtriya Swayamsevak Sangh (RSS) and is often credited with having made the BJP an alarming force in Indian politics. He was elected as the Secretary of the RSS in 1947.

Advani has seen the formation of the BJP – from Jana Sangh to Janata Party and then the Bharatiya Janata Party. The unpopularity of the emergency called by the then Prime Minister Indira Gandhi in 1975 helped the BJP to get a landslide victory. Adavni served as the Minister of Information and Broadcasting in the Morarji Desai government.

In the 1990s, Advani took the party to new heights. BJP became the single largest party, thus forming the government with Atal Bihari Vajpayee as its Prime Minister in 1996. However, Vajpayee resigned after 13 days. The BJP again came into power under the umbrella of 'National Democratic Alliance' in 1998. He was also projected as Prime Ministerial candidate in 2009 elections.

The Congress emerged victorious in 2009 general elections while the BJP holds position of the main opposition. Mr. L.K. Advani has taken six major *yatras* throughout India, like the *Ram Rath Yatra, Janadesh Yatra, Swarna Jayanti Rath Yatra, Uday Yatra and Jan Chetna Yatra*. The most recent one is the *Jan Chetna Yatra* against corruption.

Trivia

He is married to Kamla Advani and has two children, Pratibha and Jayant.

NARENDRA MODI

Narendra Modi is the current Chief Minister of Gujarat. He was born on September 17, 1950 in a middle class family in Vadnagar.

Known to be a workaholic, he is an introvert. Modi has been trying to change his image from a Hindu nationalist to that of an able administrator.

He was elected as the student leader of the Akhil Bharatiya Vidhyarthi Parishad (All India Students' Council) and played a vital role in the socio-political developments in Gujarat. He then joined Rashtriya Swayamsevak Sangh (RSS).

It was in 1978 that he joined the mainstream politics by joining the Bharatiya Janata Party (BJP). He was appointed as the National Secretary of the party and promoted to the position of General Secretary in 1998. He held this position till 2001, when he was chosen as the Chief Minister.

The biggest challenge that Modi faced as he took over as the Chief Minister, was the reconstruction and rehabilitation of the areas affected by the massive earthquake of January 2001 in Bhuj.

The Modi government was accused of inaction for stopping the post-Godhra-riots that took place in Gujarat in 2002 that left many people dead. After being pressurised to submit his resignation, Modi resigned but won the next state elections with a majority.

He was sworn-in as the Chief Minister of Gujarat for the second time on December 22, 2002 and for the third time on December 23, 2007.

He became the longest serving Chief Minister in 2007.

Under his leadership, Gujarat is witnessing massive transformation in several sectors including education, agriculture and healthcare. He launched policy-driven reform programmes, reoriented government's administrative structure and successfully put Gujarat on the road to prosperity.

Trivia

During the Indo-Pak war in the mid sixties, even as a young boy, he volunteered to serve the soldiers in transit at the railway stations.

Nelson Mandela

Nelson Mandela alias Rolihlahla was born on the July 18, 1918 in a small village of Mvezo, in Umtata, South Africa. He became actively involved in the Anti-apartheid Movement and joined the African National Congress (ANC) in 1942.

He directed a campaign of peaceful, non-violent defiance against the South African government and its racist policies for 20 years.

Following the suggestion of one of Rolihlahla's father's friends, he was baptised into the Methodist Church and became the first in his family to attend school. As was the custom at the time and probably due to the bias of the British educational system in South Africa, his teacher told him that his new first name would be 'Nelson'.

Nelson Mandela is known as the leader of the African National Congress (ANC) and for his lifelong struggle against Apartheid (enforced racial separation), which was instituted in South Africa in 1948. The ANC was soon declared a terrorist organisation and banned by the South African government.

Mandela was arrested in 1962 and imprisoned for life on 'terrorist' charges, but in 1990, he was freed by South African President FW de Klerk. In 1994, he was elected President of South Africa. Two biographical movies were made, and the latest, *Mandela and de Klerk* (1997), focused on his life's struggles. He died on April 1, 2010 at Cape Town, South Africa.

Trivia
He was first Black President of the Republic of South Africa from 1994 to 1999.

Quote
"A good head and a good heart are always a formidable combination."

PATRICK HENRY

Henry was born in Studley, Hanover County, Virginia on May 29, 1736. His father was John Henry, an immigrant from Aberdeenshire, Scotland, who had attended King's College, Aberdeen before immigrating to the Colony of Virginia in the 1720s. Settling in Hanover County in about 1732, John Henry married Sarah Winston Syme, a wealthy widow from a prominent Hanover County family of English ancestry. Patrick Henry was once thought to have been of humble origin, but he was actually born into the middle rank of the Virginia gentry.

He was an orator and politician who led the movement for independence in Virginia in the 1770s. A Founding Father, he served as the first and sixth post-colonial Governor of Virginia from 1776 to 1779 and subsequently, from 1784 to 1786.

Henry led the opposition to the 'Stamp Act of 1765' and is well remembered for his "Give me Liberty, or give me Death!" speech. Along with Samuel Adams and Thomas Paine, he is remembered as one of the most influential exponents of Republicanism, promoters of the American Revolution and Independence, especially in his denunciations of corruption in government officials and his defence of historic rights. After the Revolution, Henry was a leader of the anti-federalists in Virginia who opposed the United States Constitution, fearing that it endangered the rights of the States, as well as the freedom of individuals. He died on June 6, 1799.

Trivia
Patrick Henry was elected from Louisa County to the House of Burgesses, the legislative body of the Virginia colony, in 1765 to fill a vacated seat in the assembly.

Quote
"Fear is the passion of slaves."

P. CHIDAMBARAM

Palaniappan Chidambaram was born on September 16, 1945 in Kanadukathan in Tamil Nadu. He is an Indian politician and presently serving as the Union Minister of Home Affairs in the Manmohan Singh cabinet. He has served as the Finance Minister of India from May 2004 to November 2008. He was made the Home Minister after Shivraj Patil resigned.

He started his career in 1969 as a lawyer in the Madras High Court. He then served as a Senior Advocate in 1984.

His political career started in 1984 when he was first elected for the Indian National Congress (INC) as a Lok Sabha Member from the 'Sivaganga' Constituency. He was re-elected from the same constituency in the years, 1989, 1991, 1996, 1998, 2004 and 2009.

He then got a chance to serve as a Minister of State in Commerce Ministry in the Rajiv Gandhi government. In 1986, he served as a 'Minister of State' in the Ministry of Personnel, Public Grievances and Pensions. Chidambaram got an additional responsibility as a Minister of State for Internal Security in the Ministry of Home Affairs in the same year.

After having resigned as the Minister of State (Independent) in Commerce Ministry in 1992 due to some controversies, he regained the portfolio in 1995.

Chidambaram formed the Tamil Maanila Congress (TMC) and went to the Lok Sabha as a TMC's MP in 1996. He was appointed as a Union Minister of Finance by the then Prime Minister HD Deva Gowda. Later, he formed his own party, 'Congress Jananayaka Peravaiand' and merged it with the Indian National Congress (INC) in 2004.

Trivia

He is married to Nalini Chidambaram, a Senior Advocate and a tax lawyer practising in the Madras High Court and the Supreme Court. The couple has a son Karti P Chidambaram, who is also a lawyer and a politician.

RAJIV GANDHI

The youngest Prime Minister of India, Rajiv Gandhi was born on August 20, 1944. He was the eldest son of Indira and Feroze Gandhi. He was the 9th Prime Minister of India since his mother's death on October 31, 1984.

As Prime Minister, Rajiv Gandhi endeavoured to eliminate the corrupt and criminal faces within the Indian National Congress (INC) party. To deal with the anti-Sikh agitation that followed the death of his mother Indira, Rajiv Gandhi signed an accord with Akali Dal President Sant Harchand Singh Longowal on July 24, 1985.

Rajiv Gandhi married Sonia Gandhi in 1968 after three years of courtship. They have two children – Rahul Gandhi and Priyanka Gandhi. While Rahul Gandhi is an active politician of the Congress, Priyanka Gandhi is married to businessman Robert Wadhera.

Going against the traditional socialism, Rajiv Gandhi decided to improve the bilateral relationships with the United States and subsequently, expanded the economic and scientific cooperation with it. His statement 'When a giant tree falls, the earth below shakes', during the anti-Sikh riots was widely criticised. Besides, Rajiv Gandhi's name had also surfaced in the major controversies like Bofors and the formation of Indian Peace Keeping Force (IPKF).

He died on May 21, 1991, while he was on his way towards the dais at a public gathering. The assassin greeted him and bent down to touch his feet. She then exploded an RDX explosive laden belt attached to her waist belt. The act of violence was reportedly carried out by the Liberation Tigers of Tamil Eelam (LTTE) expressing their resentment over the formation of the Indian Peace Keeping Force (IPKF).

Trivia

The economic policies adopted by Rajiv Gandhi were different from his precursors like Indira Gandhi and Jawaharlal Nehru.

RONALD REAGAN

R onald Reagan was born on February 6, 1911 in Illinois. He was the 40th President of the United States.

Reagan worked as a radio sports announcer for WOC radio in Davenport after graduating from the Eureka College in 1932. Before entering politics, Reagan was an actor. His started when his acting career he was asked to play a radio announcer in 'Love is on the air' in 1937.

Reagan became a famous actor by the time he did his last film, 'The Killers' in 1964.

He married actress Jane Wyman in 1940. The couple got divorced in 1948 during the time when Reagan was becoming politically active. Then, in 1952, he married actress Nancy Davis. The couple had two children.

Reagan switched political parties after actively supporting Nixon's campaign for President in 1960 and officially became a Republican in 1962.

In 1966, Reagan successfully ran for the 'Governor of California' and served two consecutive terms. He then won the Presidential elections for the United States in 1980.

He made the first major move forward in the Cold War when he and Russian leader Mikhail Gorbachev agreed to jointly eliminate some of their nuclear weapons.

After serving two consecutive terms as President, Reagan retired. He was soon officially diagnosed with Alzheimer's disease and decided to tell the American people in an open letter on November 5, 1994.

Reagan's health continued to deteriorate and on June 5, 2004, Reagan passed away at the age of 93.

Trivia

Republican Ronald Reagan became the 'oldest President elected' when he took office as the 40th President of the United States.

SAMUEL ADAMS

Samuel Adams was born on September 27, 1722. He was an American statesman, political philosopher and one of the Founding Fathers of the United States. As a politician in colonial Massachusetts, Adams was a leader of the movement that became the American Revolution, and was one of the architects of the principles of American republicanism that shaped the political culture of the United States. He was a second cousin to President John Adams.

A graduate of Harvard College, he was an unsuccessful businessman and tax collector before concentrating on politics.

After Parliament passed the 'Coercive Acts' in 1774, Adams attended the Continental Congress in Philadelphia, which was convened to coordinate a colonial response. He helped to guide the Congress towards issuing the Declaration of Independence in 1776, and helped draft the Articles of Confederation and the Massachusetts Constitution. Adams returned to Massachusetts after the American Revolution, where he served in the state senate and was eventually elected the governor.

Samuel Adams is a controversial figure in American history. Accounts written in the 19th century praised him as someone who had been steering his fellow colonists towards independence long before the outbreak of the Revolutionary War. This view gave way to negative assessments of Adams in the first half of the 20th century, in which he was portrayed as a master of propaganda who provoked mob violence to achieve his goals. Both of these interpretations have been challenged by some modern scholars, who argue that these traditional depictions of Adams are myths contradicted by the historical record.

Trivia

The younger Samuel Adams attended the Boston Latin School.

Quote

"How strangely will the Tools of a Tyrant pervert the plain Meaning of Words!"

SHASHI THAROOR

Born on March 9, 1956, Shashi Tharoor is an Indian politician and a Member of Parliament (MP) from the Thiruvananthapuram constituency in Kerala. He previously served as the United Nations Under-Secretary General for Communications and Public Information and as the Minister of State for the Ministry of External Affairs.

He resigned as Minister of State for External Affairs, following a controversy over his association with the bid for the Kochi IPL team.

He is also a prolific author, columnist, journalist and a human rights advocate.

He is the managing trustee of the 'Chandran Tharoor Foundation' which he founded with his family and friends in the name of his late father, Chandran Tharoor.

Shashi Tharoor was born in London to Lily and Chandran Tharoor, both Malayalis, hailing from the state of Kerala.

Tharoor studied at Montfort School in Yercaud and Campion School in Mumbai. He attended the high school at St. Xavier's Collegiate School in Kolkata and obtained his Bachelor of Arts degree in history from St. Stephen's College, Delhi.

He married Dubai-based entrepreneur Sunanda Pushkar in 2010.

Trivia

He also likes writing from the age of six and his first published story appeared in the "Bharat Jyoti", the Sunday edition of the "Free Press Journal", in Mumbai, when he was ten years old. Each of his books has been a best-seller in India. The Great Indian Novel is currently in its 28th edition in India along with his newest volume. The Elephant, the Tiger and the Cellphone have undergone seven hardback reprintings there.

SONIA GANDHI

Sonia Maino, now Sonia Gandhi, was born in an Italian family in a village called Ovassanjo on December 9, 1946. She weaved a dramatic way to politics. The Italy-born Indian politician was elected as President of the Indian National Congress by overwhelming support from across the country in 2005.

Rajiv Gandhi married Sonia Gandhi in 1968 after three years of courtship.

Though she had refused to enter politics after the assassination of her husband, Rajiv Gandhi in 1991, but agreed to join in 1997.

Married into India's best known family of Nehru-Gandhi, Sonia Gandhi became a primary member of the Congress before the Calcutta Congress Plenary Session in August 1997.

Sonia is the fifth foreign-born person to be a leader of the Congress Party. However, she is the first one since independence.

Sonia Gandhi became a full-fledged Indian citizen after the assassination of her mother-in-law and the then Prime Minister, Indira Gandhi in 1984.

She has served as the Chairperson of the ruling United Progressive Alliance (UPA) in the Lok Sabha and the National Advisory Council (NAC) since 2004. Sonia Gandhi became the longest serving President in the 125-year history of the Congress party in September 2010 when she was re-elected for the fourth time.

Sonia Gandhi had resigned from the chairmanship of the NAC in 2006 over the Office of 'Profit Controversy' but became the chairperson again in 2010.

Trivia

Sonia Gandhi was named the third most powerful woman in the world by the Forbes magazine in the year, 2004 and was ranked 6th in 2007. In 2010, Gandhi was ranked as the ninth most powerful person on the planet by the Forbes magazine. She was also named among the 'Time 100 most influential people in the world' for 2007 and 2008.

THOMAS JEFFERSON

Thomas Jefferson born on April 13, 1743. He was the principal author of the United States Declaration of Independence (1776) and the Statute of Virginia for Religious Freedom (1777), the third President of the United States (1801–1809) and founder of the University of Virginia (1819). He was an influential Founding Father and an exponent of Jeffersonian democracy.

Elected president in what he called the Revolution of 1800, he oversaw a peaceful transition in power, purchased the vast Louisiana Territory from France (1803), and sent the Lewis and Clark Expedition (1804–1806) to explore the new west. He decided to allow slavery in the acquired territory, which laid the foundation for the crisis of the Union, a half century later.

His second term was beset with troubles at home, such as the failed treason trial of his former Vice President Aaron Burr and escalating trouble with Britain. Jefferson always distrusted Britain as a threat to American values. With Britain at war with Napoleon, he tried aggressive economic warfare, however his embargo laws topped the American trade, hurt the economy, and provoked a furious reaction in the North-east.

He was a leading American opponent of the international slave trade, and presided over its abolition in 1807. Jefferson has often been rated by historians as one of the greatest U.S. presidents, though in recent decades scholars have tended to be more negative. He died on July 4, 1826

Trivia
He was elected as governor from 1779 to 1781.

Quote
"A coward is much more exposed to quarrels than a man of spirit."

WINSTON CHURCHILL

Popularly known by the name 'Winnie' and 'The British Bulldog', Winston Churchill was born in Blenheim Palace, England. His mother's name was Lady Randolph Churchill who had American lineage. He was the grandson of the seventh Duke of Marlborough from his father's side.

After completing his education from famous English public schools, such as Harrow, he went on to fulfil his ambition for a life in the army. He fought in various parts of the British Empire until in 1900 when he won the Conservative seat in Oldham in the general election. From here until 1929, he held various offices in the British Parliament.

Winston Churchill, the First Lord of the Admiralty, was chosen to become Prime Minister at the age of 65. It could be said that Churchill's fiery energy had never been experienced before in British politics and suddenly, it seemed as though Britain could face the Nazi giant.

He was re-elected as Prime Minister in 1951 but because of deteriorating health, he left the public scene. He died at Hyde Park Gate, London, on January 24, 1965 at the age of 90. His daughter Mary wrote to him on his deathbed. 'I owe you what every Englishman, woman and child owes you – liberty itself'.

Trivia

He is buried in a modest churchyard in Bladon, not far from his birthplace at Blenheim Palace. Chartwell, his countryhouse, is open to the public. Much of his paintings were done there.

Quote

"History will be kind to me for I intend to write it."

PHYSICIANS

CHRISTIAAN BARNARD

The South African surgeon, Christiaan N Barnard performed the world's first human heart transplant operation in 1967 and the first double-heart transplant in 1974. Born on November 8, 1922 in Beaufort West, South Africa, Christiaan N Barnard received his early education in Beaufort West and later went on to the University of Cape Town, where he received an MD (Doctor of Medicine) in 1953.

Barnard worked for a short time as a general practitioner before he joined the Cape Town Medical School staff as a research fellow in surgery. He then enrolled at the University of Minnesota Medical School in 1955 with the hope of pursuing his research interests and gain experience.

After two years of study with Dr Owen H Wangensteen, he received his PhD from Minnesota. Then he returned to his native country to embark upon a career as a *cardiothoracic surgeon.*

Among some of his known findings, he proved that the fatal birth defect known as congenital intestinal atresia was due to the fetus receiving an inadequate supply of blood during pregnancy and gave the surgical procedure for its remedy.

As he returned to South Africa, he introduced the **open-heart surgery** to the country. He designed **artificial valves** for the human heart and experimented with the transplantation of the *hearts of dogs.* And eventually, these experiments served as preparation for his 1967 human heart transplant.

Barnard died on September 2, 2001 in Paphos, Cyprus at the age of 78.

TRIVIA

Barnard, eventually, gained recognition for research in gastrointestinal pathology.

NARESH TREHAN

Dr. Naresh Trehan is an Indian surgeon and medical administrator. Born on August 12, 1946, Trehan is the CEO and Managing Director of 'Medanta' – the Medicity and is one of the leading cardiologists of the country.

Trehan's parents were well known doctors in Pakistan.

He holds the credit for being a personal surgeon to the President of India and has received numerous awards for his contributions in the field of healthcare.

He is considered as one of India's most successful cardiac surgeons. He was keen on learning new things since childhood. He did his MBBS from KG Medical College, Lucknow in 1968.

He started practising heart surgery under the guidance of Dr. Frank Spencer at the New York University. He is the founder of the Escorts Heart Institute and Research Centre and was also its Chief Cardiothoracic and Vascular Surgeon.

In 1969, he got married to Madhu Trehan, sister of founder of leading news magazine 'India Today', Arun Poorie. The couple has two daughters.

Naresh Trehan's major contribution has been in the realms of cardiovascular and cardiothoracic surgery. He is the founder of Medanta, which is a multi-super specialty institute that not only offers good medical facilities but also boasts of cutting-edge surgical technologies and superlative healthcare service.

He was conferred with many awards including the **Padma Shri** and the **Padma Bhushan** for his contributions in the field of surgery and medicine.

Trehan also led a team and examined social activist, Anna Hazare during his famous 13-day long fast at the Ramlila Maidan against corruption.

Trivia

Trehan was unceremoniously dropped from the Escorts Hospital by the Fortis Management after it was discovered he was involved in irregular practices and trying to run the hospital as a one-man show.

WILLIAM OSLER

Born on July 12, 1849, Sir William Osler was one of the 'Big Four' founding professors at Johns Hopkins Hospital as the first Professor of Medicine and founder of the Medical Service there. (The "Big Four" were William Osler, Professor of Medicine; William Stewart Halsted, Professor of Surgery; Howard A. Kelly, Professor of Gynaecology; and William H. Welch, Professor of Pathology.) Osler created the first residency program for specialty training of physicians and he was the first to bring medical students out of the lecture hall for bedside clinical training.

He has been called the "Father of modern medicine". Osler was a pathologist, physician, educator, bibliophile, historian, author and renowned practical joker.

William Osler was born in Bond Head, Canada West (now Ontario) and raised after 1857 in Dundas, Ontario. He was called William after William of Orange, who won the Battle of the Boyne on July 12, 1690.

TRIVIA

Perhaps Osler's greatest contribution to medicine was to insist that students learn from seeing and talking to patients and the establishment of the medical residency. This latter idea spread across the English-speaking world and remains in place today in most teaching hospitals.

Quote

"The young doctor should look about early for an avocation, a pastime that will take him away from patients, pills and potions..."

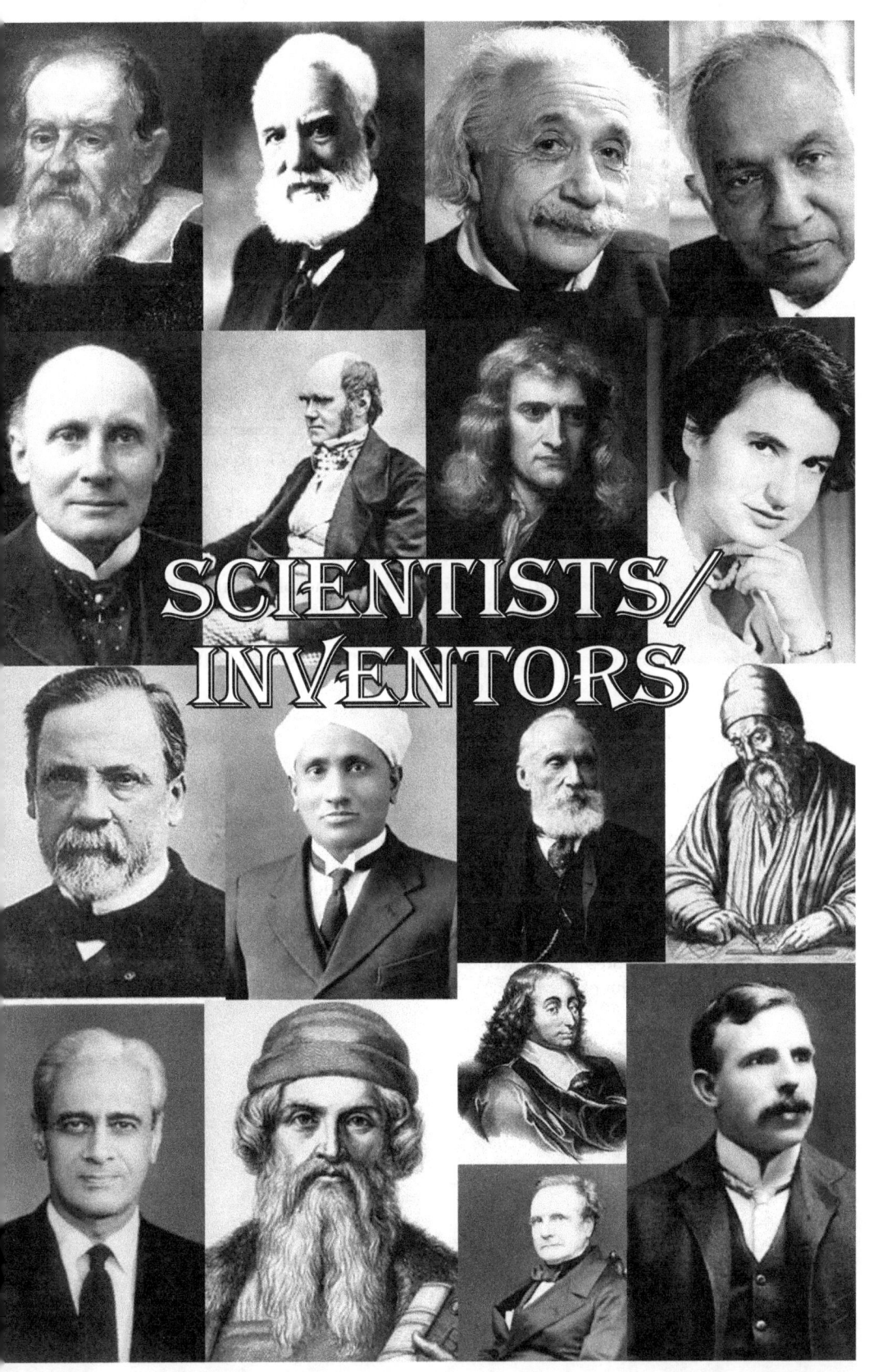

SCIENTISTS/
INVENTORS

ALBERT EINSTEIN

Albert Einstein was born on March 14, 1879 in Ulm, Germany. As a child, he was always fascinated by science and its powers.

Known to the world as a genius, Einstein has carried out researches that became the basis for many equipments that we use on a day to day basis, like television, automatic doors, remote controlled devices, etc.

As a child, he also had a passion for music and played the violin and piano. This passion stayed with him even when he grew up.

He spent his childhood moving from Germany to Italy and later to Switzerland from where he graduated from the High School in 1896.

In 1905, he worked as a patent clerk in Bern, Switzerland. It was then that he published four of his most popular research papers and earned his doctoral degree. These papers included his Special Theory of Relativity and his famous equation $E=mc^2$.

Later in 1915, he came up with his *General Theory of Relativity*. He received the **Nobel Prize in Physics** in 1921 for it.

In 1933, he moved to the United States and became a professor at the Institute of Advanced Study in Princeton, New Jersey.

Einstein's researches and important works include Relativity, Special Theory of Relativity, General Theory of Relativity, Investigations on Theory of Brownian Movement and The Evolution of Physics.

Among his non-scientific works include: About Zionism, Why War?, My Philosophy and Out of My Later Years are the most popular.

Trivia
Albert Einstein could not speak fluently until the age of nine.

Quote
"A person who never made a mistake never tried anything new."

ALEXANDER GRAHAM BELL

Born in Edinburgh, Scotland on March 3, 1847, Alexander Graham Bell was an inventor and a scientist. His father was Alexander Melville Bell, who was a leading authority in speech correction. Bell was mainly educated at home. However, he spent two years in Edinburgh Royal High School and also attended a few lectures at the Edinburgh University.

Bell began his career in 1864 as a teacher at the Elgin's Western House Academy. Later, he moved to London and became his father's assistant. Like his other brothers, who died of tuberculosis, Bell's health began to deteriorate. The family decided to move to Canada in 1870. Soon after they settled in Southern Ontario, Bell's health began to improve.

Bell gave lectures on visible speech, which is a method of teaching speech to the deaf. He was invited to give a series of speeches in the United States in 1871. He then opened a school for teachers of the deaf in Boston and in 1873 became professor of vocal physiology at the city's university.

He has the credit of giving the *first telephone* to the world. After a series of experiments with several acoustical devices, Bell produced the first intelligible telephonic transmission with a message to his assistant, Thomas Watson, on June 5, 1875. Bell patented his telephone on March 3, 1876 after he came to know that electrical engineer, Elisha Gray was also working on a similar project. He formed the Bell Telephone Company in 1877. The telephone was an instant success.

Trivia

His invention of telephone was widely accepted and within three years, there were around 30,000 telephones in use around the world. Elisha Gray later claimed the invention of the telephone but lost the long legal battle in the Supreme Court.

ALFRED NORTH WHITEHEAD

Alfred North Whitehead Born on February 15, 1861 in Ramsgate, Kent, England. He was an English mathematician who later became a philosopher. He wrote on algebra, logic, foundations of mathematics, philosophy of science, physics, metaphysics, and education. Whitehead supervised the doctoral dissertations of Bertrand Russell and Willard Van Orman Quine, thus influencing logic and virtually all of analytic philosophy. He co-authored the epochal Principia Mathematica with Russell.

In 1880, Whitehead matriculated at the Trinity College, Cambridge, where he was the fourth wrangler and gained his BA in 1884. Elected 'a fellow of Trinity' in 1884, Whitehead would teach and write mathematics at the college until 1910, spending the 1890s writing *A Treatise on Universal Algebra* (1898) and the 1900s collaborating with his former pupil, Russell, on the first edition of *Principia Mathematica*.

In 1890, Whitehead married Evelyn Wade, an Irish woman reared in France; they had a daughter and two sons. One son died in action while serving in the Royal Flying Corps during the World War I. Meanwhile, Russell spent much of 1918 in prison because of his pacifist activities. Although Whitehead visited his co-author in prison, he did not take his pacifism seriously, while Russell sneered at Whitehead's later speculative *Platonism* and *panpsychism*. After the war, Russell and Whitehead seldom interacted and he did not contribute to the 1925 second edition of *Principia Mathematica*.

He died in 1947 in Cambridge and there was no funeral; the body was cremated.

Trivia

He was the President of the Aristotelian Society from 1922 to 1923.

Quote

"Almost all new ideas have a certain aspect of foolishness when they are first produced."

APJ Abdul Kalam

Popularly known as the People's President, APJ Abdul Kalam is an Aerospace engineer by profession. He was born on October 15, 1931 in Tamil Nadu. He was the **11th President of India** and served from 2002 to 2007.

Before his term as the President, Kalam worked as an aeronautical engineer with Defence Research and Development Organisation (DRDO) and the Indian Space Research Organisation (ISRO).

Known as the **Missile Man of India** for his work on development of ballistic missile and space rocket technology, he is highly respected as a scientist and as an engineer. He is a man of vision, buzzing with ideas aiming at the development of the country.

Abdul Kalam started his career as a newspaper vendor and grew up in an intimate relationship with nature in his house at Rameshwaram.

Kalam played a crucial technical and political role in India's Pokhran-II nuclear test in 1998, the first since the original nuclear test in 1974. He was involved in the development of India's first **Indigenous Satellite Launch Vehicle (SLV-III)**.

He is a professor at Anna University in Chennai and serves as visiting faculty at many other academic and research institutions across India.

APJ Abdul Kalam has written several inspirational books, most notably his autobiography, 'Wings of Fire' and 'Guiding Souls: Dialogues on the Purpose of Life'.

He has been conferred with the **Padma Bhushan**, the **Padma Vibhushan** and the prestigious **Bharat Ratna**.

Trivia

APJ Abdul Kalam's full name is Avul Pakir Jainulabdeen Abdul Kalam. A poll conducted by a news channel named him 'India's Best President'. With the death of R Venkataraman on January 27, 2009, Kalam became the only surviving former President of India.

BLAISE PASCAL

Blaise Pascal, (June 19, 1623 – August 19, 1662) was a French mathematician, inventor, physicist, a writer and Catholic philosopher.

Pascal's earliest work was in the natural and applied sciences. He made important contributions to the study of fluids and also clarified the concepts of *pressure* and *vacuum.*

While still a teenager in 1642, he started some pioneering work on calculating machines. After three years of effort and 50 prototypes, he invented the *mechanical calculator.* He built twenty of Pascaline machines in the following ten years.

Being a mathematician of the first order, he helped to create two major new areas of research. Pascal wrote a significant treatise on the subject of projective geometry when he was 16 and later corresponded with 'Pierre de Fermat' on *probability theory.* It strongly influenced the development of modern economics and social science.

He refuted Aristotle's followers in 1646 who insisted that nature abhors a vacuum. Before being accepted, his results caused many disputes.

In late 1654, he had his 'second conversion', abandoned his scientific work and devoted himself to philosophy and theology.

Two of his most famous works are – *The Lettres provinciales* and the *Pensées.* Between 1658 and 1659, he wrote on the cycloid and its use in calculating the volume of solids.

He died at the age of 39 in 1662 after he suffered from bad health for a long time.

Trivia

An early Pascaline is on display at the Musée des Arts et Métiers, Paris.

CHARLES BABBAGE

Charles Babbage was born in London, England on December 26, 1791. He was an English mathematician, philosopher, inventor and mechanical engineer who originated the *concept of a programmable computer*.

He suffered from many childhood illnesses, which forced his family to send him to a school for special care.

A period at the Academy at Forty Hills in Middlesex began the process and created his interest in Mathematics. Babbage enjoyed reading many of the major works in maths and showed a solid understanding of what theories and ideas had validity.

He set up a society to critique the works of the French mathematician, 'Lacroix', on the subject of *differential and integral calculus*. Later, Babbage was asked to set up an Analytical Society that was composed of Cambridge undergraduates. The works of this group were serious publications in this period but many of the leading maths scholars expressed praise for the contribution of Babbage.

He completed his schooling and started to write papers on various subjects for the Royal Society of London, who honoured him with an invitation to join and the role of Vice-President.

Later, Babbage became interested in Astronomy and the equipment used to study the heavens. This was the time when Charles got the idea for a 'mechanical calculation device'. Babbage then invented the *Difference Machine* to create 'logarithmic tables'.

Quote

"The whole of the developments and operations of analysis are now capable of being executed by machinery. ... As soon as an Analytical Engine exists, it will necessarily guide the future course of science."

CHARLES DARWIN

Charles Darwin was born on February 12, 1809 at the Mount House, Shrews bury. His father was a doctor. Darwin's mother died when he was eight years old.

Charles Darwin went to Editing University to study medicine but left after two years and then went to the Cambridge University. After leaving the Cambridge University in 1831, he signed up to sail as a naturalist on a ship called the *Beagle* without pay.

He reached Australia in January 1836. After sailing through Merits, South Africa and the Atlantic, Darwin arrived in Shrewsbury.

He wrote several books about his voyage. The first book he wrote was 'Journal of Researches'.

He is credited with many known books. He wrote about Coral Reefs and Geographical Observations on South America.

Darwin noticed in 1838 that all animals are competing with each other to survive and the developed theory later came to be known as the 'survival of the fittest'.

Charles Darwin married his cousin, Emma Wedged in January 1839. The couple had ten children.

His monumental work, 'The Origin of Species', was published in 1859. Proving to be a bestseller, it also caused a controversy.

Charles Darwin published ten books after 1859. His last book was on earthworms and was published in October 1881.

Darwin died of a heart attack on April 19, 1882.

Trivia

Believing that the species of animals could change, Charles Darrin disagreed with Charles Yell's book called the 'Principles of Geology'. In 1837, Darwin began to write notes about his theory called 'The Transmission of Species'.

C.V. Raman

Sir Chandrasekhara Venkata Raman (November 7, 1888 – November 21, 1970) was an Indian physicist, whose work was influential in the growth of science in the world. He was the recipient of the **'Nobel Prize'** for Physics in 1930 for the discovery that when light traverses a transparent material, some of the light that is deflected changes in wavelength. This phenomenon is now called the *Raman scattering* and is the result of the 'Raman Effect'.

Venkata Raman, a Tamil Brahmin, was born at Thiruvanaikaval, near Tiruchirappalli, Madras Presidency to R. Chandrasekhara Iyer and Parvati Ammal (Saptarshi Parvati).

He was the second of their eight children. At an early age, Raman moved to the city of Vizag, Andhra Pradesh. He studied in St Aloysius Anglo-Indian High School. His father was a lecturer in Mathematics and Physics.

In 1941 he was awarded the 'Franklin Medal'. In 1954 he was awarded the **'Bharat Ratna'**. He was also awarded the 'Lenin Peace Prize' in 1957.

Trivia

Raman was honoured with a large number of honorary doctorates and memberships of scientific societies. He was elected a Fellow of the Royal Society early in his career (1924) and knighted in 1929.

India celebrates the 'National Science Day' on February 28 of every year to commemorate the discovery of the Raman Effect in 1928.

ERNEST RUTHERFORD

Ernest Rutherford (August 30, 1871 – October 19, 1937) New Zealand-born British chemist and physicist who became the father of nuclear physics.

In the beginning, he discovered the concept of radioactive half-life. He proved that radioactivity involved the transmutation of one chemical element to another and also differentiated and named the 'alpha' and 'beta' radiation.

This work is the basis for the **Nobel Prize** in Chemistry that he was awarded in 1908 'for his investigations into the disintegration of the elements and the chemistry of radioactive substances'.

Rutherford did his most famous works after he had moved to the United Kingdom in 1907 and was already a **Nobel laureate**.

He theorised that atoms have their positive charge concentrated in a very small nucleus in 1911. Thereby, he pioneered the 'Rutherford model' of the atom through his discovery and interpretation of Rutherford scattering in his gold foil experiment.

He has to his credits - first 'splitting the atom' in 1917 in a nuclear reaction between nitrogen and alpha particles. During the nuclear reaction, he also discovered and named the proton. This led to the first experiment to split the nucleus in a fully controlled manner, performed by two students working under his direction, John Cockcroft and Ernest Walton, in 1932.

He was honoured by being interred with the greatest scientists of the United Kingdom, near Sir Isaac Newton's tomb in Westminster Abbey after his death in 1937.

Trivia

The chemical element Rutherfordium was named after him in 1997.

EUCLID

Born in about 365 BC in Alexandria, Egypt, Euclid Platonic was one of the famous mathematicians.

He taught at Ptolemy's university at Alexandria.

Europe's Elements was a work on elementary geometry. He exceeded other works of its time, which are now known only by indirect reference.

Mathematics of the earlier time dealt only with concrete problems, such as areas and volumes. But mathematics had become an intellectual occupation for philosophers and scientists by the time of Euclid.

Europe's Elements include postulates, definitions and axioms, the famous fifth, or parallel, postulate that one and only one line can be drawn through a point parallel to a given line.

The postulates are divided into 13 books. The first six are on geometry, three on number theory, book 10 is on *Eudoxus's theory of irrational numbers*. Books from 11 to 13 are on *solid geometry*.

Euclid's elements were published in 300 BC. Since then, many mathematicians tried to prove the fifth postulate from Europe's other axioms and other postulates.

Girls Sac cheri attempted a proof by contradiction or reduction absurdly, to show that the fifth postulate is false in the early 18th century.

Proof by contradiction is a powerful method of mathematical reasoning often used today.

More than one thousand editions of work have been published since the first printed version in 1482. He has many important works to his credit including *Phenomena, Data, On Divisions of Figures, Surface Loci, Optics, Prisms* and *Comics*.

Trivia

It is not known for certain whether Euclid was really a creative mathematician or was simply good at collecting and editing the work of others.

FRANCIS BACON

Francis Bacon (January 22, 1561 – April 9, 1626) was an English philosopher, lawyer, scientist, jurist, statesman, author and pioneer of the scientific method.

He had served as Attorney General and Lord Chancellor of England. He remained extremely influential through his works although his political career ended in disgrace. He was influential, especially as philosophical advocate and practitioner of the scientific method during the scientific revolution.

Called the 'father of empiricism', Bacon's works established and popularised inductive methodologies for scientific inquiry, often called the *Baconian method.*

His demand for a planned procedure of investigating all things marked a new turn in the rhetorical and theoretical framework for science. His dedication probably led to his death, bringing him into a rare historical group of scientists who were killed by their own experiments.

He died of pneumonia. He contracted pneumonia, while he was studying the effects of freezing on the preservation of meat.

Bacon was knighted in 1603 and created both the *Baron Verulam* in 1618 and the *Viscount St Alban* in 1621. Both peerages became extinct upon his death as he died without heirs.

Trivia

In 1623, Bacon expressed his aspirations and ideals in New Atlantis. Released in 1627, this novel was his creation of an ideal land, where 'generosity and enlightenment, dignity and splendour, piety and public spirit' were the commonly held qualities of the inhabitants of Bensalem.

GALILEO GALILEI

Italian physicist, mathematician, astronomer, and philosopher, Galileo Galilei was born on February 15, 1564.

He is often refered to as the 'Father of Modern Observational Astronomy', 'Father of Modern Physics' and the 'Father of Modern Science'.

Commonly known as 'Galileo', he played a major role in the Scientific Revolution.

His achievements include improvements to the telescope and consequent astronomical observations in addition to the support for Copernicanism. According to physicist Stephen Hawking, Galileo Galilei was responsible for the birth of modern science.

Galileo's major contributions to observational astronomy include the telescopic confirmation of the phases of Venus, the observation and analysis of sunspots and the discovery of the four largest satellites of Jupiter. The satellites are named after him as the *Galilean moons* in his honour.

Galileo also worked in applied science and technology, inventing an improved military compass and other instruments.

He died after he suffered fever and heart palpitations in 1642 at the age of 77.

Galileo's heliocentrism was controversial within his lifetime, when most subscribed to either Geocentrism or the Tychonic system. He was opposed by astronomers, who doubted his theory due to the absence of an observed stellar parallax.

After investigations by the Roman Inquisition in 1615, they concluded that it could only be supported as a possibility, not as an established fact. Galileo was tried and was put under house arrest. It was during this time that he wrote one of his finest works, *Two New Sciences*.

Trivia

Three of Galileo's fingers and a tooth were removed from his mortal remains, while he was being reburied in the main body of basilica at a monument constructed in his honour. The middle finger is currently on exhibition at the Muse Galileo in Italy.

HJ Bhabha

Homi Jehangir Bhabha, popularly known as Homi Bhabha was born on October 30, 1909. He was a famous Indian atomic scientist.

In Independent India, Bhabha, with the support of Jawaharlal Nehru, laid the foundation of a scientific establishment and created two premier institutions – Tata Institute of Fundamental Research and Bhabha Atomic Research Centre.

Homi Bhabha was also the first chairman of India's Atomic Energy Commission.

Born to a rich Parsi family in Mumbai, he went to Cambridge University after he graduated from the Elphinstone College and the Royal Institute of Science.

During the 1930s, he worked with Niels Bohr on the studies that led to the quantum theory and also with Walter Heitler on the cascade theory of electron showers.

Bhabha returned to India in 1939 due to the outbreak of Second World War and set up the Cosmic Ray Research Unit at the Indian Institute of Science in Bangalore (Bengaluru) under CV Raman in 1939.

Apart from being a great scientist, Homi Bhabha, was also a skilled administrator. Indian scientists worked on the development of atomic energy under his guidance. The first atomic reactor in Asia went into operation at Trombay, near Bombay, in 1956.

Bhabha was also Chairman of the first United Nations Conference on the Peaceful Uses of Atomic Energy, held in Geneva in 1955.

Homi Bhabha authored many articles on quantum theory and cosmic rays. He died in an aeroplane crash in Switzerland on January 24, 1966.

He was also conferred with the **Padma Bhushan** in 1954.

Trivia

He is also known as the 'Father of Indian nuclear program'.

HARISH CHANDRA

Harish Chandra (October 11, 1923 – October 16, 1983) was an Indian mathematician, who did fundamental work in the representation theory, especially the *Harmonic analysis on semisimple Lie groups.*

Harish Chandra was born in Kanpur in the then British India. He was educated at BNSD College in Kanpur and at the University of Allahabad. After receiving his Masters degree in Physics in 1943, he moved to the Indian Institute of Science, Bangalore for further studies in theoretical physics and worked with HJ Bhabha. In 1945, he moved to the University of Cambridge and worked as a research student under Paul Dirac. He attended lectures by Wolfgang Pauli, while at Cambridge. During one of them, he pointed out a mistake in Paul's work. The two became lifelong friends. During this time, he became increasingly interested in mathematics. He obtained his PhD in 1947 at Cambridge.

He was influenced by the mathematicians, Hermann Weyl and Claude Chevalley. He was at the Columbia University and worked on representations of semisimple Lie groups from 1950 to 1963.

He also established, as his special area, the study of the discrete series representations of semisimple Lie groups, which are analogues of the Peter–Weyl theory in the non-compact case.

Trivia

He is also known for his works with Armand Borel on the theory of arithmetic groups and for papers on finite group analogues. He enunciated a philosophy of cusp forms, a precursor of the Langlands philosophy.

Isaac Newton

Isaac Newton was born on December 25, 1642. He was an English physicist, mathematician, astronomer, natural philosopher, alchemist, and theologian and has been "considered by many to be the greatest and most influential scientist, who ever lived. He was most famous for his three laws of *motion*, but was also known for other major discoveries in maths and science.

He compiled most of his works into a masterpiece of science called the *Principia*. Newton was known to be arrogant, so his book was written almost exclusively for the elite and the rich.

Some people claim that only 50 people in history have been able to understand his style of writing. Despite his arrogance, he truly was a father in the field of science. At the age of 18, he had devised a new system of mathematics called the *Calculus*.

He developed three laws which resulted in a new way of understanding motion. All of this happened at his farm while the Black Plague swept across England. In the *Principia*, Newton claimed to have "discovered" gravity when an apple fell on his head. But, many now believe that this was just a story told by Newton, and that in real life, he discovered gravity through thinking a not seeing.

He died on March 20, 1727 at Kensington, England.

Trivia

'Newton's Gravitational Theory' was not inspired by a Falling Apple.

Quote

"This most beautiful system, [The Universe] could only proceed from the dominion of an intelligent and powerful Being."

ISAMBARD KINGDOM BRUNEL

Isambard Kingdom Brunel (April 9, 1806 – September 15, 1859) was a British civil engineer, who built bridges and dockyards including the construction of the first major British railway – *the Great Western Railway.*

Brunel also has a lot other things to his credit, a series of steamships, including the first propeller-driven transatlantic steamship, numerous important bridges and tunnels. His designs revolutionised modern engineering and public transport. Not each of his experiments were successful but Brunel's projects often contained innovative solutions to long-standing engineering problems.

Brunel achieved many engineering 'firsts'. This included assisting in the building of the first tunnel under a navigable river and development of SS Great Britain. SS Great Britain is the first propeller-driven ocean-going iron ship. It was, at the time (1843), also the largest ship ever built.

Brunel set the standard for a very well-built railway, which necessitated expensive construction techniques, new bridges and viaducts, and the two-mile-long Box Tunnel. One controversial feature was the wide gauge – a 'broad gauge' of 2,140 mm, instead of what was later to be known as 'standard gauge' of 1,435 mm. The wider gauge added to passenger comfort but made construction much more expensive. It also caused difficulties when it had to interconnect with other railways using the narrower gauge. Therefore, according to the Railway Regulation (Gauge) Act 1846, the gauge was changed to standard gauge throughout the GWR network.

Trivia

Brunel was placed second in a BBC public poll to determine the '100 Greatest Britons' in 2002. In 2006, the bicentenary of his birth, a major programme of events celebrated his life and work under the name, Brunel 200.

JOHANNES GUTENBERG

Born in 1398, Johannes Gutenberg was a German inventor of a method of printing from the movable type.

He started experimenting with printing by 1438. In 1440, Gutenberg invented a *printing press* process that remained the principal means of printing until the late 20th century.

His method of printing from movable type allowed, for the first time, the mass production of printed books. It also included the use of metal moulds and alloys, a special press and oil-based inks.

Gutenberg's printing technology rapidly spread across Europe and quickly replaced most of the handwritten manuscript methods of book production throughout the world.

'Woodblock printing', 'engraving' and 'rubrication' continued to be used to supplement Gutenberg's printing process.

His first major work using his printing methods was the *Gutenberg Bible* between 1450 and 1455.

The entire *Gutenberg Bible* is likely to fetch an estimated 100 million dollars if it is made available on the world market. An original individual leaf can fetch around $100,000.

Gutenberg's work is material in the world. Johann Gutenberg died in Mainz, Germany on 1468. The inventor could not make profits from his inventions and died in poverty.

Trivia

His full name was Johannes Gensfleisch zur Laden zum Gutenberg.

LORD HOWARD FLOREY

Sir Howard Walter Florey was born on September 24, 1898 at Adelaide, South Australia. Florey was educated at St. Peter's Collegiate School, following which he went on to the Adelaide University.

Florey was awarded the Rhodes Scholarship to the Magdalen College, Oxford. He then went to Cambridge as a John Lucas Walker's Student.

He visited the US on a Rockefeller Travelling Fellowship for a year in 1925, returning in 1926 to a Fellowship at Gonville and Caius College. Florey also held the Freedom Research Fellowship at the London Hospital.

He was appointed as Huddersfi eld Lecturer in Special Pathology at Cambridge in 1927. In 1931, he succeeded to the Chair of Pathology at the University of Sheffi eld.

After he left Sheffi eld in 1935, he became Professor of Pathology and a Fellow of Lincoln College.

During World War II, he was appointed the Honorary Consultant in Pathology to the Army and he became the Nuffi eld Visiting Professor to Australia and New Zealand in 1944.

He was made an Honorary Fellow of Gonville and Caius College, Cambridge in 1946 and an Honorary Fellow of Magdalen College, Oxford in 1952. He was also made the Provost of The Queen's College, Oxford in 1962.

Trivia

His best-known work began in 1938 when he conducted a systematic investigation of the properties of naturally occurring anti-bacterial substances. Lysozyme, an antibacterial substance, was their original interest, but their interest moved to substances now known as antibiotics. The work on penicillin was a result of this interest.

LORD KELVIN

Popularly known as Lord Kelvin, William Thomson (June 26, 1824 – December 17, 1907) was a physicist and engineer.

In 1832, Kelvin's father, James Thomson was appointed as the Professor of Mathematics at Glasgow. Therefore, the family moved to Glasgow in October 1833. He did important work in the mathematical analysis of electricity and formulation of the first and second laws of *thermodynamics* at the University of Glasgow.

Lord Kelvin did a lot to unify the emerging discipline of physics in its modern form. He also had a career as an electric telegraph engineer and inventor. These were the works that propelled him into the public eye and ensured his fame, wealth and honour.

He was knighted by Queen Victoria, becoming Sir William Thomson for his work on the Transatlantic Telegraph Project.

Lord Kelvin had extensive maritime interests and was most noted for his work on the *mariner's compass*.

He married childhood sweetheart, Margaret Crum in September 1852. Margaret did not keep well after their marriage, which became a distraction for William Thomson for the next seventeen years.

Lord Kelvin has the credit for realising that there was a lower limit to temperature, an absolute zero. Absolute temperatures are stated in units of Kelvin in his honour.

In honour of his achievements in thermodynamics, he adopted the title, 'Baron Kelvin of Largs' and is therefore often described as Lord Kelvin.

He was the first British scientist to be elevated to the 'House of Lords'.

Trivia

The Hunterian Museum at the University of Glasgow has a permanent exhibition on Lord Kelvin's work including many of his original papers, instruments and other artifacts.

LOUIS PASTEUR

Born on December 27, 1822, Louis Pasteur was a French chemist and microbiologist. Remembered for his remarkable breakthroughs in the causes and preventions of diseases, his discoveries reduced mortality from puerperal fever.

He created the *first vaccine* for rabies and anthrax. His experiments supported the *germ theory of disease.*

Best known to people for inventing the process called *pasteurisation*, he is regarded as one of the three main founders of microbiology, together with Ferdinand Cohn and Robert Koch.

Louis grew up in the town of Arbois and gained degrees in Mathematical Sciences before entering an elite college, École Normale Supérieure.

After serving briefly as a professor of physics at Dijon Lycée in 1848, he became the professor of chemistry at the University of Strasbourg. At the University of Strasbourg, he met and courted Marie Laurent in 1849. They were married on May 29, 1849. The couple had five children. Out of his five children, only two survived till adulthood, the other three died of typhoid. These tragedies inspired Pasteur to try to find cures for diseases, such as *typhoid.*

Pasteur also made many discoveries in the field of chemistry, the most notable one being the molecular basis for the asymmetry of certain crystals.

He died on September 28, 1895. His body lies beneath the Institute Pasteur in Paris in a spectacular vault cover.

Trivia

In 1995, the centennial of the death of Louis Pasteur, the New York Times ran an article titled, 'Pasteur's Deception'. After reading Pasteur's lab notes thoroughly, the science historian, Gerald L Geison declared that Pasteur had given a misleading account of the preparation of the anthrax vaccine used in the experiment at Pouilly-le-Fort.

NEIL ARMSTRONG

Being the first person to set foot upon Moon, Neil Armstrong is a well-known name. Born on August 5, 1930, Neil Alden Armstrong is an American former astronaut, aerospace engineer, test pilot, university professor, United States Naval Aviator.

Before becoming an astronaut, Armstrong was in the United States Navy and served in the Korean War. He served as a test pilot at the National Advisory Committee for Aeronautics (NACA) High-Speed Flight Station, now known as the Dryden Flight Research Centre after the war. There he flew over 900 flights in a variety of aircraft.

As a research pilot, Armstrong served as project pilot on the F-101 Voodoo, F-100 Super Sabre A and C variants, and the Lockheed F-104, A Starfighter. He also flew the Bell X-5, Bell X-1B, F-105 Thunderchief, North American X-15, KC-135 Stratotanker, F-106 Delta Dart, B-47 Stratojet, and one of eight elite pilots paraglider research vehicle program (Paresev).

He graduated from Purdue University and University of Southern California.

Armstrong joined the NASA Astronaut Corps in 1962. His first spaceflight was the NASA Gemini 8 mission in 1966, for which he was the command pilot. He became one of the first US civilian to fly in space.

Armstrong was awarded the **Presidential Medal of Freedom** by Richard Nixon along with Collins and Aldrin on this mission.

Trivia

He was also awarded the **Congressional Space Medal of Honour** by President Jimmy Carter in 1978.

ROSALIND FRANKLIN

By 1953, everyone knew about DNA and its role as genetic material but what was unknown was how the molecule looked like and how it performed the function. It was Rosalind Elsie Franklin who deciphered the well-known *double helical structure of the molecule* in 1953.

Rosalind Franklin was born on July 25, 1920 and died at an early age of 37 due to cancer on April 16, 1958. She was a British biophysicist and X-ray crystallographer, who made critical contributions to the understanding of the fine molecular structures of DNA, RNA, viruses, coal and graphite.

The individuals most commonly associated with this remarkable accomplishment are *James Watson* and *Francis Crick.*

She discovered that DNA could crystallise into two different forms – *A form and B form.* Rosalind Franklin worked on the DNA molecule from 1951 until 1953. She took photographs of the B version of the molecule using x-ray crystallography.

She also provided the first DNA crystals pure enough to yield interpretable diffraction patterns. Franklin discovered that the sugar-phosphate backbone of DNA lies outside the molecule and not inside as was previously thought. She discovered the helical structure of DNA has two strands and not three as proposed in other theories.

Franklin did not marry nor have children.

Trivia

Finch University of Health Sciences/The Chicago Medical School changed its name to the Rosalind Franklin University of Medicine and Science in 2004, to honour her role in science and medicine.

SIR ALEXANDER FLEMING

Sir Alexander Fleming was born on August 6, 1881 at Lochfield, Scotland. He was a Scottish biologist and pharmacologist.

He wrote many articles on bacteriology, immunology and chemotherapy.

His best-known discoveries are the discovery of the enzyme, *lysozyme* in 1923 and the antibiotic substance, penicillin from the mould, *Penicillium notatum* in 1928. He shared the **Nobel Prize in Physiology or Medicine** in 1945 with Howard Florey and Ernst Boris Chain.

The active ingredient Penicillin in the *Penicillium notatum* turned out to be an infection-fighting agent of enormous potency.

It was the most efficacious life-saving drug in the world. Penicillin could alter the treatment of bacterial infections forever. By the middle of the century, Fleming's discovery had spawned a hug pharmaceutical industry churning out synthetic penicillin that would conquer some of mankind's most ancient scourges.

In 1955, Fleming died at his home in London of a heart attack. He was buried at St Paul's Cathedral.

Trivia

The Time magazine named Fleming one of the 100 Most Important People of the 20th Century for his discovery of penicillin in 1999.

Quote

"I have been trying to point out that in our lives, chance may have an astonishing influence and, if I may offer advice to the young laboratory worker, it would be this – never to neglect an extraordinary appearance or happening."

S CHANDRASEKHAR

Born on October 19, 1910, Subrahmanyan Chandrasekhar was an India-born American astrophysicist and mathematician. Better known as Chandra, Subrahmanyan Chandrasekhar worked on the *origins and structures of stars*, earning an important place in the world of science.

The Nobel Prize-winning physicist's most celebrated work concerns the radiation of energy from stars, particularly *The white dwarf stars.*

Chandra received his early education at home, beginning at the age of five. After his schooling, he studied Physics as his subject in college. As soon as he completed his studies from the Trinity College in Cambridge, England, he turned to Atsrophysics as a research student. In 1931, he worked with the physicist, Max Born.

He left for Copenhagen, Denmark, to devote more of his energies to pure Physics in 1932. He studied the stellar structure, including the theory of white dwarfs during the years, 1929 to 1939 and subsequently, focused on *stellar dynamics* from 1939 to 1943.

Then, he studied the mathematical theory of black holes during the period of 1971 to 1983 and worked on the theory of colliding gravitational waves during the late 1980s.

He was awarded the **Nobel Prize in Physics** in 1983 for his studies on the physical processes which were important to the structure and evolution of stars.

Chandra died in Chicago on August 21, 1995, at the age of 82. Chandra strove to acquire knowledge and understanding throughout his life.

Trivia

The Nobel Prize-winning Indian physicist, Sir CV Raman was Chandra's uncle.

SATISH DHAWAN

Born on September 25, 1920 in Srinagar, Satish Dhawan was an Indian rocket scientist. Considered to be the Father of Experimental Fluid Dynamics Research in India by the Indian scientific community, he was one of the most eminent researchers in the field of *turbulence and boundary layers.*

He succeeded the founder of the Indian Space Programme, Vikram Sarabhai as Chairman of the Indian Space Research Organisation (ISRO) in 1972.

He was also chosen as the Space Commission and Secretary to the Government in the Department of Space. He also directed the Indian Space Programme through a period of extraordinary growth and spectacular achievement.

Satish Dhawan carried out pioneering experiments in rural education, remote sensing and satellite communications. His efforts led to operational systems like IRS – the Indian Remote Sensing satellite, INSAT- a telecommunications satellite and the Polar Satellite Launch Vehicle (PSLV).

He was a popular professor at the Indian Institute of Science (IISc), located in Bangalore (Bengaluru). He is credited for setting up the first supersonic wind tunnel in India at IISc.

He died on January 3, 2002, after which the Indian satellite launch centre at Sriharikota was renamed as the Satish Dhawan Space Centre.

Trivia

Dhawan has been conferred with many awards including the Padma Vibhushan and the Indira Gandhi Award for National Integration.

THE WRIGHT BROTHERS

The Wright Brothers, **Wilbur** and **Orville Wright,** Perhaps the most influential brothers in history, were the sons of a bishop of the United Brethren in Christ Milton Wright.

Wilbur was born on April 16, 1867 in Millville, Indiana, while Orville was born on August 19, 1871 in Dayton, Ohio.

The two were inseparable until the death of Wilbur in 1912. Their personalities were perfectly complementary to each other providing what the other lacked. While, Orville was full of ideas and enthusiasm, Wilbur was more mature in his judgements and more likely to see a project through.

In their early years, Orville and Wilbur helped their father, who edited a journal called the 'Religious Telescope'. Later, they began a publication of a four-page weekly newspaper, 'West Side News'.

In 1829, they started a bicycle repair shop and a factory, and started making aerial experiments with kites and gliders in 1896.

After having failed many flight experiments, the Wrights thought that it would be better to control a plane by moving its wings.

In 1900, they made their first flight to Kitty Hawk, North Carolina and set up a camp there. They confirmed their data by making thousands of flights in two years and then were determined to apply power to their machine.

Soon, they made a 12 horsepower engine, weighing 750 pounds. It proved to be capable of travelling 31 miles per hour.

Both of them made many record-breaking flights near Le Mans and France. Wilbur died on May 30, 1912 and Orville died on January 30, 1948.

Trivia

Orville lived quietly in Dayton after Wilbur's death, conducting experiments on mechanical problems of interest to him.

THOMAS EDISON

Thomas Edison was born on February 11, 1847 in Milan, US. Born in a small town in the Midwest, in Ohio, young Thomas was a restless student whose mind often wondered as the teacher gave lessons. But, it was his mother that would educate him at home.

He invented *the phonograph, the incandescent electric lightbulb, the alkaline storage battery* among other things. He held more than 900 patents and laid the foundation for the 'modern electric age'.

It would not be until Thomas Edison and his new wife moved to New Jersey that his career would really unfold. There, he unveiled his automatic repeater that would revolutionise the telegraph world. He also displayed his *phonograph*, the first device of its kind to record and play back sound. The invention so frightened the crowd that they believed him to be a sorcerer. With better design and longer-lasting records, the phonograph became a huge hit at home and abroad – especially in England.

He went on to form the 'Edison Electric Light Company' in New York City. The small company provided the first lights to lower Manhattan, New York. Thomas Edison's dream was to provide every American household with affordable electric power. He continued working on his inventions, even designing phone speakers that were used through the latter 20th century.

He died on 18th October 1931, West Orange, New Jersey, USA with complications of diabetes.

Trivia
He was a member of the Academy of Motion Picture Arts & Sciences (AMPAS).

Quote
"Anything that won't sell, I don't want to invent. Its sale is proof of utility, and utility is success."

WILLIAM OSLER

Born on July 12, 1849, Sir William Osler was a physician. He was one of the 'Big Four' founding professors at Johns Hopkins Hospital as the first Professor of Medicine and founder of the Medical Service there.

Usually addressed as Sir William Osler, William created the *first residency program for specialty training of physicians*. He was the first to bring medical students out of the lecture hall for clinical training.

Popularly known as the 'Father of Modern Medicine', Osler was a physician, pathologist, bibliophile, educator, historian and an author.

William Osler was born in Bond Head, Ontario, and brought up in the Canada West. He was called William after William of Orange, who won the Battle of the Boyne on July 12, 1690.

Trivia

Osler's greatest contribution to medicine was to insist that students learn from talking to patients and the establishment of the medical residency. This idea spread across the world and has remained in place today in most of the teaching hospitals.

Quote

"The young doctor should look about early for an avocation, a pastime that will take him away from patients, pills and potions..."

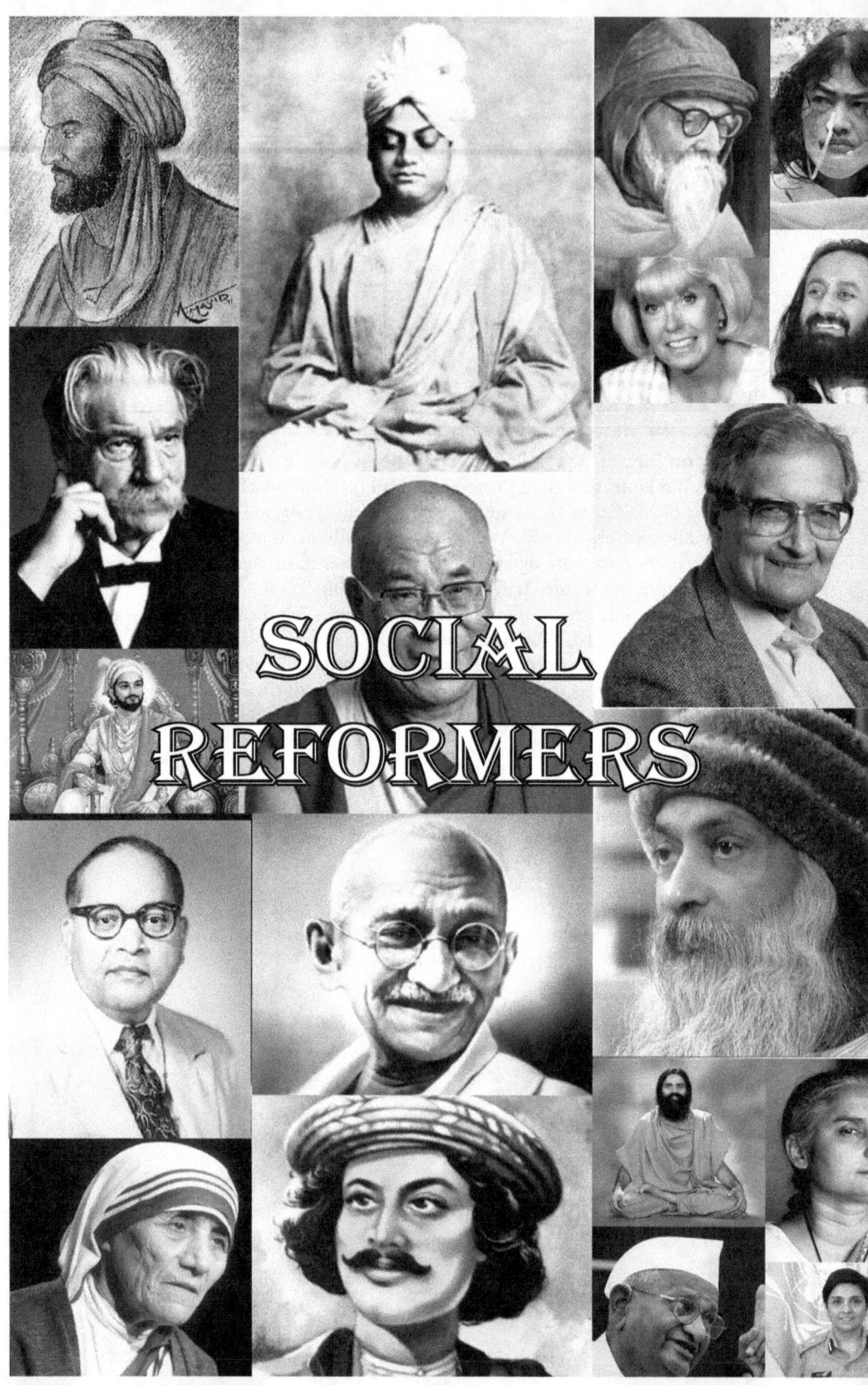

SOCIAL REFORMERS

ACHARYA VINOBA BHAVE

Born on September 11, 1895, Acharya Vinoba Bhave was considered as Mahatma Gandhi's spiritual successor. Vinobha Bhave's original name was Vinayak Narahari Bhave and was born in a Brahmin family in Maharashtra.

His 'Bhoodan' (Gift of the Land) Movement started on April 18, 1951 and attracted the attention of the world.

Vinoba Bhave was well-read in the writings of Maharashtra's saints and philosophers and was also deeply interested in Mathematics.

In 1916, while he was on his way to Mumbai to appear for the intermediate examination, he took a detour and reached Varanasi. He was motivated by his desire to attain the imperishable. He studied ancient Sanskrit texts in Varanasi.

After exchange of few letters between Bhave and Mahatma Gandhi, Vinoba Bhave went and met Gandhiji on June 7, 1916 which changed the course of Bhave's life. He developed a deep bond with Gandhiji and participated in the activities at Gandhi's ashram with keen interest.

Vinoba Bhave was asked by Gandhiji to take charge of the ashram at Wardha in 1921. In 1923, he brought out the *Maharashtra Dharma*, a monthly in Marathi, which had his essays on the Upanishads.

In 1940, Bhave was chosen by Gandhi to be the first Individual *Satyagrahi.* Vinoba Bhave also participated in the 'Quit India Movement'.

After independence, he started the social reform movements, such as Bhoodan Movement and Sarvodaya Movement.

He died on November 15, 1982 after refusing food and medicine few days earlier. He was *posthumously* honoured with the **Bharat Ratna** in 1984.

Trivia

He observed a *year of silence* from December 25, 1974 to December 25, 1975 and in 1976, undertook a fast to stop the slaughter of cows.

ALBERT SCHWEITZER

Albert Schweitzer (January 14, 1875 – September 4, 1965) was an Allocation theologian, philosopher, organist, physician and a medical missionary.

Born in Kaysersberg in the province of Alsace-Lorraine, Schweitzer challenged both the secular view of Jesus as depicted by historical-critical methodology as well as the traditional Christian view.

Schweitzer received the **Nobel Peace Prize in 1952** for his philosophy of 'Reverence for Life'. This philosophy was expressed in many ways, most famously in founding and sustaining the Albert Schweitzer Hospital in Gavin, the then Lambaste. As a music scholar and organist, he studied the music of German composer, Joann Sebastian Bach. He influenced the Organ Reform Movement.

Schweitzer's quest was to discover a universal ethical philosophy and make it directly available to all of humanity.

He established his reputation also as a *New Testament scholar* with other theological studies including 'The Psychiatric Study of Jesus' and his two studies of the apostle Paul, 'Paul and his Interpreters' and 'The Mysticism of Paul, the Apostle'.

Trivia

The publication of 'The Quest for the Historical Jesus' effectively put a stop for decades to work on the Historical Jesus as a sub-discipline of New Testament studies. This work resumed, however, with the development of the so-called 'Second Quest'.

AMARTYA SEN

Born on November 3, 1933, Amartya Sen is an Indian economist who was awarded the 1998 **Nobel Prize** in Economic Sciences for his contributions to welfare economics and social choice theory.

He is also known for his interest in the problems of society's poorest members. Amartya Sen is best known for his work on the causes of famine, which led to the development of practical solutions for preventing or limiting the effects of food shortage.

Currently the Professor of Thomas W Lamont University and Professor of Economics and Philosophy at the Harvard University, he is also a senior fellow at the Harvard Society of Fellows. He is also a distinguished fellow of All Souls College, Oxford and a Fellow of Trinity College, Cambridge. Sen is the first Indian and the first Asian academic to head an Oxbridge College.

Amartya Sen's books have been translated into more than 30 languages over a period of 40 years. Sen is a trustee of Economists for Peace and Security.

The *Time* magazine listed him under '60 years of Asian Heroes' in 2006 and in 2010 included him in their '100 most influential persons in the world'.

Trivia

He has not only been into lists of the Time magazine but has also featured in the lists of New Statesman. The New Statesman listed him in their 2010 edition of the 'World's 50 Most Influential People Who Matter'.

ANNA HAZARE

Born on June 15, 1937, Kisan Baburao Hazare, popularly known as 'Anna Hazare' is an Indian social activist and a prominent leader in the 'Indian Anti-corruption Movement', 2011.

He joined the Indian Army in 1963 and served for 15 years.

From a determined soldier to a social reformer and a Right to Information crusader, Anna Hazare's journey of four decades has been unprecedented in terms of a non-violent yet effective campaign.

Recently, Hazare launched an Anti-corruption Movement for passing a stronger *Jan Lokpal* (Ombudsman) Bill in the Indian Parliament.

The differences among the civil society and Team Anna over various issues including inclusion of the Prime Minister, higher judiciary and the acts of the MPs under the purview of the draft Lokpal bill led to the movement.

Anna Hazare began his indefinite strike on April 5, 2011, which ended on April 9, 2011, giving a deadline of August 15 to pass the Bill. After the government failed to meet the deadline, he began his next indefinite hunger strike on August 16, which lasted for 13 days.

Thousands gathered at the Ramlila ground during the 13-day strike to support the anti-crusader.

Anna Hazare contributed tremendously for the development of his native village, *Ralegan Siddhi*. He opened grain banks, promoted education and milk production as a secondary occupation.

Trivia

He was awarded the third-highest civilian award by the Government of India, the Padma Bhushan in 1992 for his efforts in establishing Ralegan Siddhi as an ideal model for others.

B.R. AMBEDKAR

Bhimrao Ramji Ambedkar, usually called B.R. Ambedkar, was born on April 14, 1891. He is also known as *Babasaheb* and was an Indian jurist, orator, political leader, thinker, philosopher, anthropologist, historian, prolific writer, economist, scholar, editor, a revolutionary and one of the founding fathers of independent India.

Ambedkar was born into a poor Mahar family and spent his whole life fighting against social discrimination.

He converted to Buddhism and is also credited with providing a spark for the conversion of many untouchables to Theravada Buddhism.

Ambedkar was also the Chairman of the Drafting Committee of Indian Constitution. He was *posthumously* awarded the **Bharat Ratna** in 1990.

Ambedkar became one of the first so-called outcastes to obtain a college education in India. He gained reputation as a scholar and practised law for a few years. Later, he also campaigned for advocating political rights and social freedom for India's so-called untouchables by publishing journals.

Ambedkar is regarded as a *Bodhisattva* by some Indian Buddhists, though he never claimed himself to be a Bodhisattva.

He died on December 6, 1956.

Trivia

As he was educated by the Baroda State, he was bound to serve the state. He was appointed as the Military Secretary to the Gaekwad of Baroda. However, he had to quit within a short time. This fiasco was described by Ambedkar in his autobiography.

BETTY WILLIAMS

Born on May 24, 1943 in the city of Belfast in Northern Ireland, Betty Williams is a co-recipient with Mairead Corrigan of the **Nobel Peace Prize** in 1976 for her work as a co-founder of Community of Peace People. Community of Peace People is an organisation dedicated to promoting a peaceful resolution to The Troubles in Northern Ireland.

She was working as a receptionist and raising the two children she had with Ralph Williams at the time she was conferred with the **Nobel Prize**. After the couple divorced, she married James Perkins in 1982, and lived with him in the United States.

She toured and lectured extensively. She heads the 'Global Children's Foundation' and is also the President of the World Centre of Compassion for Children International. Williams is the Chair of Institute for Asian Democracy in Washington DC and also a distinguished visiting professor at the Nova South-eastern University.

Williams was one of the founders of the **Nobel Women's Initiative** along with the Nobel Peace Laureates Mairead Corrigan Maguire, Wangari Maathi, Shirin Ebadi, Jody Williams and Rigoberta Menchu Tum.

It is the goal of the Nobel Women's Initiative to strengthen works being done in support of women's rights around the world.

Trivia

Six women representing North America and South America, the Middle East and Africa decided to bring together their experiences in a united effort for peace, justice and equality.

Quote

"There's no use talking about the problem unless you talk about the solution."

Dalai Lama

His holiness, the 14th Dalai Lama, born as Tenzin Gyatso, is Tibet's head of state as well as the spiritual leader of the Tibetan people.

The Dalai Lama was born in Taktser, Qinghai, and was selected as the rebirth of the 13th Dalai Lama, two years later, although he was only formally recognised as the 14th on the November 17, 1950, at the age of 15.

He inherited control over a government controlling area roughly corresponding to the Tibet Autonomous Region just as the nascent People's Republic of China wished to reassert central control over it. There is a dispute over whether the respective governments reached an agreement for a joint Communist-Lamaist administration.

His Holiness assumed full power of Tibet in November 1950. He completed his 'Doctorate of Buddhist Philosophy' in 1959, the same year when China attacked Tibet, after which he escaped to Dharamsala, India, from where he has since then led the Tibetan government in exile.

On December 10, 1989, His Holiness accepted the Nobel Peace Prize *'on behalf of the oppressed everywhere and all those, who struggle for freedom and work for world peace and the people of Tibet'*. In his acceptance statement, he declared, 'This prize reaffirms our conviction that with truth, courage, and determination as our weapons, Tibet will be liberated. Our struggle must remain non-violent and free of hatred'.

Trivia
Tenzin was awarded the Christmas Humphreys Award from the Buddhist Society of the United Kingdom on May 28, 2004.

Quote
"Be kind whenever possible. It is always possible."

IROM SHARMILA CHANU

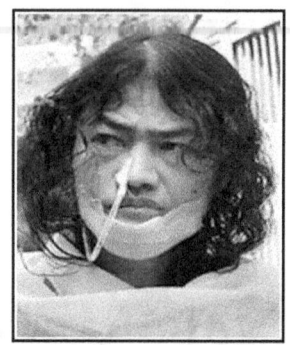

Born on March 14, 1972, Irom Sharmila Chanu is also known as the *Iron Lady of Manipur* or 'Menghoubi'.

She is a civil rights activist, a political activist, and a poet. She is called 'the world's longest hunger striker' as she has refused food and water since November 3, 2000.

She is on a hunger strike repealing the Indian government to withdraw the AFSPA (Armed Forces Special Power Act) from Manipur. Ten innocent people were mowed down by security forces in a village near Imphal Malom in November 2000. The perpetrators were protected under the AFSPA, which allowed the soldiers to indefinitely detain, shoot or even kill any citizen on suspicion of being a rebel.

The government arrested her and force-fed her through nasal tubes.

She has been arrested several times since she began her fast on charges of 'attempt to commit suicide' and released after the completion of a year's sentence since Section 309 of the IPC says a person who attempts to commit suicide is punishable with simple imprisonment for a term.

Veteran Gandhian, Anna Hazare also invited Sharmila to join his recent agitation against corruption.

Trivia

Sharmila was nominated to **Nobel Peace Prize** in 2005 by a Guwahati-based woman's organisation, the North-East Network.

KIRAN BEDI

India's first and highest ranking woman police officer Kiran Bedi joined the Indian Police Service in 1972 and retired in 2007.

Her expertise includes more than 35 years of creative and reformative policing and prison management. Born on June 9, 1949, Kiran Bedi held the post of 'Director General' at the Bureau of Police Research and Development before she voluntarily retired from the IPS.

Bedi has worked as the 'Police Advisor to the Secretary General of the United Nations' in the Department of Peacekeeping Operations and has represented India at the United Nations. She has received the **President's Gallantry Award** by the President of India in 1979.

She is the founder of two NGOs – *Navjyoti* and *India Vision Foundation* – which reach out to thousands of underserved children, women and men in the sectors of education, environment, vocational skills, counselling and healthcare to the urban and rural poor.

She is consistently voted one of the most admired women in India.

Since she retired from active police duty, Bedi has become an international activist on drug abuse, crime prevention, police and prison reform, corruption, women's issues and human welfare. Currently, she has been an active participant in the 'India Against Corruption Movement' – led by social activist, Anna Hazare. The movement compelled the government to pass a unanimous resolution in the Parliament, accepting three key demands of the *Janlokpal* Bill drafted by Team Anna.

Trivia

A non-fiction feature film on Bedi's life, titled *Yes, Madam* Sir has won accolades at several international film festivals. She is also an Asian tennis champion.

MEDHA PATKAR

A well-known social activist in India, popularly known for her *Narmada Bachao Andolan*, Medha Patkar was born on December 1, 1954 in Mumbai. She was born to and raised by politically and socially active parents, Indu and Vasant Khanolkar.

Prior to becoming a social reformer, she completed her MA in Social Work from the Tata Institute of Social Sciences (TISS). She left PhD in the middle and got actively involved in the agitations conducted by Tribals and peasants of Maharashtra, Madhya Pradesh and Gujarat. This led to the formation of the organisation, Narmada Bachao Andolan.

She started a hunger strike on March 28, 2006 to protest against the decision of the authorities to raise the height of the Narmada Dam. She ended her 20 day fast on April 17, 2006, after the Supreme Court refused the Narmada Bachao Aandolan's appeal to stop the construction of the dam and gave the dam construction a conditional go ahead.

Medha Patkar was arrested by the police at Singur in West Bengal on December 2, 2006 for her active involvement in the protest against getting the hold of the farmland. She was detained because the police officers thought that she might provoke people that might lead to law and order problem.

Medha Patkar has faced a lot of criticism. She has been criticised of being a hate-monger and of using anti-Gujarati sentiments to advance her cause of the Narmada Dam. The Madhya Pradesh Government also alleged the Narmada Bachao Andolan of receiving foreign funds and using them for unclear purposes. They claimed that the money obtained was being used by the organisation to hamper the rehabilitation process.

Trivia

Medha Patkar received the 1999 MA Thomas National Human Rights Award from the Vigil India Movement. She was also a Commissioner to the World Commission on Dams.

MOHANDAS KARAMCHAND GANDHI

Mohandas Karamchand Gandhi (October 2, 1869 – January 30, 1948) was the pre-eminent political and ideological leader of India during the Indian Independence Movement.

A pioneer of *satyagraha*, or resistance to tyranny through Mass Civil Disobedience – a philosophy firmly founded upon *ahimsa*, or total non-violence – Gandhi led India to independence and inspired movements for civil rights and freedom across the world.

Gandhi is often referred to as the *Mahatma* or the "Great Soul," an honorific first applied to him by Rabindranath Tagore. In India, he is also called *Bapu* and officially honoured as the **Father of the Nation**. His birthday, October 2, is commemorated in India as *Gandhi Jayanti*, a national holiday, and worldwide as the 'International Day of Non-Violence'.

Gandhi first employed non-violent civil disobedience as an expatriate lawyer in South Africa, in the resident Indian community's struggle for civil rights.

After his return to India in 1915, he set about organising peasants, farmers, and urban labourers in protesting excessive land-tax and discrimination. Assuming leadership of the Indian National Congress in 1921, Gandhi led nationwide campaigns for easing poverty, expanding women's rights, building religious and ethnic amity, ending untouchability, increasing economic self-reliance, but above all for achieving *Swaraj* – the independence of India from foreign domination. Gandhi famously led Indians in protesting the British-imposed salt tax with the 400 km (250 miles) *Dandi Salt March* in 1930, and later in calling for the British to 'Quit India' in 1942.

Trivia
He was imprisoned for many years, on many occasions, in both South Africa and India.

MOTHER TERESA

The image of a short woman in a white sari with blue border with kindness in her eyes and the will to help in her heart, reminds of Mother Teresa (August 26, 1910 – September 5, 1997).

Born in Skopje, the Republic of Macedonia, to well-to-do parents, Mother Teresa always knew in her heart that she was born to serve the poor. At the age of 18, she was given permission to join a group of nuns in Ireland. After a few months of training in Dublin, she travelled to Kolkata, accepted the vows of a nun, and took the name, Teresa.

Touched by the poverty around her in Calcutta (Kolkata), while teaching at St. Mary's High School for Girls, she left the school and started working in the slums of Calcutta and opened an open-air school for children. Soon, many volunteers joined her and many funded the good cause. She soon started 'The Missionaries of Charity'.

Today, the institution has many well trained doctors, nurses and social workers working to help the poor and the victims of natural catastrophes like floods, famine, epidemics, etc. It has also got many branches worldwide. In a time, when leprosy stricken people were a common sight around Calcutta, and people wouldn't even look at the lepers, Mother Teresa hugged them, changed their bandages, and took care of them.

She also started a *lepers' colony* called 'Shanti'. She was awarded the **Nobel Peace Prize** for her sacrificial work towards those in need.

Trivia

Mother Teresa's real name was Agnes Gonxha Bojaxhiu. Agnes Bojaxhiu was her family name and Gonxha, her middle name. Gonxha means 'flower bud' in Albania and people often called her by this name.

Quote

"Being unwanted, unloved, uncared for, forgotten by everybody, I think that is a much greater hunger, a much greater poverty than the person who has nothing to eat."

Nkosi Johnson

Nkosi Johnson (February 4, 1989 – June 1, 2001) was a South African child with HIV/AIDS, who made a powerful and long-lasting impact on public perceptions of the pandemic and its effects before his death at the age of 12.

He was ranked fifth amongst SABC (South African Broadcasting Corporation television channel) Great South Africans. He was the longest-surviving HIV-positive born child at the time of his death.

Nkosi was born to Nonthlanthla Daphne Nkosi in a town of Johannesburg. Nkosi was legally adopted by Gail Johnson, a Johannesburg Public Relations practitioner and was a HIV-positive from birth.

It was when a primary school refused to accept him as a pupil because of his HIV-positive status that the young Nkosi Johnson first came to public attention in 1997. The incident caused a furore at the highest political level–South Africa's Constitution forbids discrimination on the grounds of medical status. The school later reversed its decision.

Nkosi's mother died of HIV/AIDS in the same year he started his school. His own condition steadily worsened over the years. However, he was able to lead a fairly active life at school and at home, with the help of medication and treatment.

Nkosi was the keynote speaker at the 13th International AIDS Conference. He encouraged people living with HIV/AIDS to be open about the disease.

Trivia

Nkosi founded a refuge for HIV positive mothers and their children by the name Nkosi's Haven in Johannesburg.

In November 2005, Nkosi posthumously received the **International Children's Peace Prize**. Nkosi's Haven received a prize of US$100,000 from the Kids Rights Foundation.

OSHO

Born as Chandra Mohan Jain on December 1, 1931, Osho was an Indian mystic, guru, and spiritual teacher who garnered an international following.

He was known as Acharya Rajneesh from the 1960s, as Bhagwan Shree Rajneesh during 1970s and 1980s and as *Osho* from 1989.

He was a professor of philosophy and travelled throughout India in the 1960s as a public speaker.

His outspoken criticism of socialism, Mahatma Gandhi and institutionalised religions made him a controversial figure. He advocated a more open attitude towards sexuality. It was the stance that earned him the sobriquet, 'sex guru' in the Indian and later international press.

Osho settled for a while in Bombay (Mumbai) in 1970. He began initiating disciples, known as *neo-sannyasins* and took on the role of a spiritual teacher.

He reinterpreted writings of religious traditions, mystics and philosophers from across the world.

She established an *ashram* that attracted increasing numbers of Westerners after moving to Poona in 1974. The *ashram* offered therapies derived from the human potential movement to its western audience and made news in India and abroad because of its permissive climate.

Osho left his body on January 19, 1990. Osho's teachings have had a notable impact on western new age thought and their popularity has increased markedly since his death.

Trivia

His syncretic teachings emphasise the importance of awareness, meditation, love, courage, creativity, celebration and humour – qualities that he viewed as being suppressed by adherence to static belief systems, religious traditions and socialisation.

RAJA RAM MOHAN ROY

Born in a famous family of Bengal in 1772, Raja Ram Mohan Roy was a great scholar of Sanskrit, Persian and English and knew Arabic, Latin and Greek.

He was one of the greatest social reformers that India has produced. He was instrumental in eradicating social evils like *Sati*, *Purdah* and *Child Marriage* from the Indian soil and therefore, rightly called the 'Father of Modern India'.

He also advocated equal rights of widows to remarry, rights for women, and right of women to property but his fight to eradicate Sati is a landmark in Indian history.

Having a rational and scientific approach, he believed in the principle of human dignity and social equality. He read the Hindu scriptures and other books of other religions.

He joined the service of the East India Company in 1805 and gradually rose to high offices.

He, along with Dwarkanath Tagore and others, founded the Brahmo Sabha in 1828, which engendered the Brahmo Samaj, which was an influential Indian socio-religious reform movement during the "Bengal Renaissance".

Roy wrote a book in Persian the 'Gift of Monotheists' in 1809. He preached that 'God in one' and believed in universal brotherhood. In one of his books, 'Precepts of Jesus', published in 1820, he tried to clear the difference between the moral and philosophic message of the 'New Testament'.

Raja Ram Mohan Roy died at Bristol in England in 1833 due to meningitis.

Trivia

Roy married thrice in his lifetime. His third wife, Uma devi outlived him. Mughal emperor Akbar shah II conferred on him the title of 'Raja'.

Shivaji Raje Bhosle

Popularly known as Chhatrapati Shivaji Maharaj, Shivaji Raje Bhosle was born on February 19, 1630 was a Maratha aristocrat of the Bhosle clan who founded the Maratha Empire.

Shivaji led a resistance to free the Maratha kingdom from the Sultanate of Bijapur and establish *Hindavi Swarajya* (self-rule of Hindu people).

He created an independent Maratha kingdom with Vedant Raigad as its capital and successfully fought against the Mughals to defend his kingdom. He was crowned as *Chhatrapati* (sovereign) of the Maratha kingdom in 1674.

He established a progressive civil rule with the help of well-regulated and disciplined military and well-structured administrative organisations. The prevalent practices of destruction of religious monuments, treating women as spoils of war, slavery and forceful religious conversions were firmly opposed under his administration.

He also innovated rules of military engagement, pioneering the *ganimi kava* (guerrilla tactics) or 'Shiva sutra', which leveraged strategic factors like speed, geography, surprise and focused pinpoint attacks to defeat his larger and more powerful enemies.

He died on April 3, 1680.

Trivia

Shivaji was an able administrator, who established a government that included modern concepts such as foreign affairs (Dabir), cabinet (Ashtapradhan mandal) and internal intelligence. Shivaji established an effective civil and military administration.

SRI SRI RAVI SHANKAR

Born on May 13, 1956 in Tamil Nadu, Sri Sri Ravi Shankar is a renowned Indian spiritual leader, who is a popular figure not just in India but across the world.

He is the founder of the famous 'Art of Living Foundation' that has made an incredible contribution in changing the lives of people.

Being a child with precocious mind, he could recite the verses of *Bhagavad Gita* at the age of four. He obtained the Advanced degree in Modern Physics at the age of 17. Later, he received the Honorary Doctorate from the Kuvempu University in Karnataka.

Later in 1982, Shri Shri Ravishankar went into ten days of silence and turned into an enlightened master. After this period, he started serving the society by making them learn the art of living life.

'Art of living' and Sri Sri Ravishankar are two names that go hand in hand with each other.

Sudarshan Kriya is the main component of the art of living course taught by Sri Sri Ravishankar. It is basically the technique of breathing and consists of various cycles of breath – long, medium and short. It involves several *asanas* and exercises.

He has received a number of awards for the excellent work performed by him including the 'Global Humanitarian Award', in 2005 'Guru Mahatmya Award', 'Phoenix Award' and others.

A noted humanitarian leader, his programs have provided assistance to people from a wide range of backgrounds – survivors of terror attacks and war, victims of natural disasters, children from marginalised population and communities in conflict, among others.

Trivia

In 2010, Shankar was named by the Forbes magazine as the fifth most influential person in India.

SWAMI RAMDEV

Swami Ramdev, also known as Baba Ramdev, is particularly known for his efforts in popularising Yoga. Popularly known as *Yoga Guru*, Ramdev is one of the founders of the 'Divya Yoga Mandir Trust' that aims to popularise Yoga.

Born on January 11, 1965 in Alipur as 'Ramkrishan Yadav, Ramdev' attended school till the eight[th] grade and then joined in a Yogic monastery or the *Gurukul.* He then entered into *Sanyas.* Eventually, he went to Jind district to join the *Kalva gurukul.* Later, he started imparting free yoga training in villages across Haryana.

Before settling in Haridwar, he had travelled through the Himalayas where he discovered many medicinal plants which he uses in treating his patients.

In 1995, while training to be a Swami, Ramdev spent many years undertaking a thorough study of ancient Indian scriptures.

Ramdev has taught several aspects of traditional Indian scriptures, such as the *Mahabhashya, the Ashtadhyayee,* and the *Upanishads.* He has helped establish *Gurukuls* and institutions in India. These institutions provide a comprehensive facility that promotes the practice of *Ayurveda.*

He also set up the 'Patanjali Yog Peeth Trust' in 2006. The Trust has acquired a Scottish island for £2 million to set up a wellness centre.

Baba Ramdev launched a nationwide protest against corruption and the issue of black money on June 4, 2011. However, the police raided the Ramlila ground at midnight. The crackdown was widely criticised by Ramdev and the opposition parties.

Trivia

A well-respected teaching and research institute for Science and Technology, the KITT University awarded Ramdev with an Honorary Doctorate degree for his efforts at popularising Yoga.

SWAMI VIVEKANANDA

Swami Vivekananda was born to Viswanath Dutta and Bhuvaneswari Devi on January 12, 1863 in Shimla Pally of Kolkata, West Bengal. This precocious child started meditating at a very early age. Even as a child, he was an all rounder. One of the most inspiring personalities of India, who did a lot to make India a better place to live in, within a short span of time, Vivekananda achieved a lot and went a long way in serving humans. He was the principal disciple of Sri Ramakrishna Paramahamsa.

The *Ramakrishna Mission* was founded by Swami Vivekananda, on the 1st of May in the year 1897. The Ramakrishna Mission is actively involved in the missionary as well as altruistic works, such as disaster relief. The disciples that are serving the mission consist of both monastic and householder. Its headquarters are based near Kolkata, India.

He compiled a number of books on the four Yogas, namely the *Raja Yoga, Karma Yoga, Bhakti Yoga* and the *Jnana Yoga*. His best works include the letters written by him. He maintained a very simple style of writing, so that the laymen, are able to understand his each and every word. He was not just actively involved in writing, but also was a great singer and composed several songs.

On July 4, 1902, at a young age of 39, this great man headed his way for heaven.

Trivia

Before turning into a monastic, Vivekananda was called by the name Narendranath Dutta.

SPORTSPERSONS

ANDRE AGASSI

A ndre Kirk Agassi was born on April 29, 1970 in Las Vegas to Emmanuel Mike Aghassian and Betty. He is a retired American professional tennis player. At the age of 13, he went to Nick Bollettieri's Tennis Academy in Florida, where he was coached for free. He had a natural talent for the game.

Agassi turned professional at the age of 16. By the end of the year, he was ranked no 91. In 1987, he won the singles title in the Sul American Open in Itaparica and ended ranked world no 25. After winning several tournaments in 1988, his year end ranking was world No 3. The Association of Tennis Professionals and the Tennis Magazine named him as the Most Improved Player of the Year, 1988.

He reached his first Grand Slam Final in 1990 at the French Open. In the same year, Agassi won the *Davis Cup*, a victory for America after eight years, and won his only Tennis Masters Cup. He played in Wimbledon in 1991. He won the 'Wimbledon' title in 1992 and was the BBC Overseas Sports Personality of the Year.

Agassi won the Australian Open in 1995, the first appearance in the event. He reached the world no 1 ranking in April 1995. At the Olympic Games, Agassi won the men's singles gold medal in Atlanta. In 1999, he became only the fifth male player to have won all four grand slam titles during his career. He was also the first male player in history to have won all four grand slam titles on three different surfaces. Agassi was also the first male player to win the Career Golden Slam.

In 2006, while in Wimbledon Agassi announced his retirement. He has earned more US$ 30 million in his career and more than US$ 25 million a year in endorsements.

Agassi married actress Brooke Shields on April 19, 1997 and the couple filed for divorce less than two years later. Agassi and Steffi Graf married in 2001. They have two children and live in Las Vegas area. In 2005, the Tennis magazine named him the seventh greatest male player and the 12th greatest player overall for the period, 1965 through 2005. In 2011, Agassi was inducted into the International Tennis Hall of Fame at a ceremony in Newport, Rhode Island.

ANNA KOURNIKOVA

Anna Kournikova was born on June 7, 1981 in Moscow, Russia. She is a Russian retired professional tennis player. Her beauty and celebrity status made her one of the best known tennis stars worldwide.

Her father began teaching her how to play tennis at the age of seven. She played her first tennis competition when she was a teenager. For her looks, Anna started to be known as the 'Britney Spears of Tennis'.

During the Paris Indoors of 1998, her fastest serve was clocked at 111.2 mph. Anna's talent for playing tennis got her noticed not just for tennis competitions, but for TV as well.

She got a small, but noticeable part in a comedy film, *Me, Myself & Irene* in 2000 when she was 19 years old. She also appeared in Enrique Iglesias's music video, 'Escape'.

She sustained an injury to her lower back and worked as an on-site reporter for the US networks coverage of the US Open in September 2003. Anna retired from professional tennis due to chronic lower back trouble, in March 2004. Though, she has never won a WTA singles title, she did win two Australian Open doubles titles with Martina Hingis.

She continues to be the most searched athlete on the Internet through 2008 even though she had retired from the professional tennis circuit, years back.

Kournikova's forte always was doubles. She attained the position of World No. 1 player in doubles during her professional tenis career.

Trivia

Anna Kournikova was voted the Sexiest Woman in the World in FHM's 100 Sexiest Girls poll for 2002.

BRIAN LARA

Born on May 2, 1969, Brian Charles Lara is a former West Indian international cricket player. One of his elder sisters, Agnes Cyrus got him enrolled in the local Harvard Coaching Clinic at the age of six for weekly coaching sessions. Lara had a very early education in correct batting technique.

Generally regarded as one of the greatest batsmen of all time, Lara made both his Test and ODI debut in 1990 against Pakistan.

Brian Lara retired from International Cricket in The World Cup 2007 played in West Indies.

The attractive left-hander owns two most prestigious records in cricket - highest individual score with 400 not out in Tests and highest individual score with 501 not out in first class cricket.

He broke the test world record of 365 against England in Antigua, 1994.

He became test cricket's leading run scorer of all time in November 2005, passing the 11,174 total of former Australian captain, Allan Border. Lara scored 226 in that innings against the Australians.

Although Test Cricket was always his first choice, Lara still finished with 10,405 runs in One-Day Internationals.

Lara has played for the team in five Cricket World Cups in 1992, 1996, 1999, 2003 and 2007.

Trivia

Nicknamed 'The Prince of Port-of-Spain' or simply 'The Prince', Brian Lara married journalist and model, Leasel Rovedas and has a daughter.

DIEGO MARADONA

Diego Armando Maradona was born on October 30, 1960. He is a retired Argentine football player. He was born in Lanus and raised in Villa Fiorito near Buenos Aires. Maradona was playing in his neighbourhood club at the age of ten when he was spotted by a talent scout. He played for the Los Cebollitas, junior team of Buenos Aires.

Maradona made his professional debut in 1976 with Argentinos Juniors. He was transferred to the Boca Juniors in 1981. In 1982, he was transferred to Barcelona in Spain after the 1982 World Cup. Barcelona won the 'Copa Del Ray' in 1983. He was then transferred to Napoli in 1984.

Led by Maradona, Napoli reached its most successful era in its history. They won Serie A Italian Championships, Coppa Italia in 1987, the UEFA Cup in 1989 and the Italian Super Cup in 1990. He was banned for 15 months after failing a drug test for cocaine and left Napoli.

Maradona's first World Cup was in 1982. He captained the Argentine national team to victory in the 1986 World Cup. During the quarter final against England his second goal was voted by FIFA as the greatest goal in the history of World Cup. The goal was voted Goal of the Century in 2002 online poll conducted by FIFA. In a tribute to Maradona, the Azteca Stadium authorities built a statue of him scoring the Goal of the Century and placed it at the entrance of the stadium.

In 1990, Argentina reached the finals but lost to West Germany. Maradona published his autobiography, 'Yo Soy El Diego' (I am The Diego). In 2000, Maradona finished top of the poll conducted by FIFA, making him the 'Player of the Century'. Maradona has also won polls for Best Goal Ever Scored in a World Cup and All-Time Ultimate World Cup Team. The Argentine Juniors named their stadium after Maradona in 2003.

Maradona became the host of a talk-variety show on Argentine television, *La Noche del 10* ("The Night of the Number 10) in 2005.

Serbian filmmaker, Emir Kusturica made a documentary, *Maradona* on the player's life. Maradona was appointed the 'Goodwill Ambassador' of IIMSAM. In 2010, Maradona was chosen No. 1 in the Greatest 10 World Cup players of all time by the *Times*, a London based paper.

DON BRADMAN

Generally regarded as the greatest cricketer ever to play the game, Sir Donald George Bradman was born on August 27, 1908. He was an Australian cricketer, widely acknowledged as the greatest batsman of all time.

Often referred as 'The Don', Don Bradman averaged 99.94 runs per innings during his illustrious career.

Bradman's meteoric rise from bush cricket to the Australian Test team took just over two years. He had set many records for high scoring, some of which still stand, even before the age of 22 and became Australia's sporting idol.

Bradman consistently scored at a level that made him 'worth three batsmen to Australia' during a 20-year playing career.

As a captain and administrator, Bradman was committed to attacking, entertaining cricket. The focus of attention on his individual performances strained relationships with some teammates, administrators and journalists.

Following an enforced break, due to the Second World War, he made a great comeback, captaining an Australian team known as 'The Invincibles' on a record-breaking unbeaten tour of England.

In 2001, Australian Prime Minister John Howard called him the 'greatest living Australian'. Bradman's image has appeared on postage stamps and coins. He was the first living Australian to have a museum dedicated to his life. On November 19, 2009, Sir Donald Bradman was inducted into the ICC Cricket Hall of Fame.

He died on February 25, 2001.

Trivia

The post office box of the Australian Broadcasting Commission is 9994, which is a homage to Bradman's Test batting average of 99.94.

EVONNE GOOLAGONG CAWLEY

Born on July 31, 1951, Evonne Fay Goolagong Cawley is a former World No. 1 Australian female tennis player.

She was one of the world's leading players in the 1970s and early 1980s. She won 14 Grand Slam titles – seven in singles, six in women's doubles and one in mixed doubles.

Born in Griffith, New South Wales in an Aboriginal family, Goolagong grew up in the small country town of Barellan.

Although Aboriginal people faced widespread discrimination in rural Australia at that time, she was able to play tennis in Barellan from childhood. The credit of Goolagong playing tennis goes to Bill Kurtzman, who saw her peering through the fence at the local courts and encouraged her to come in and play.

The proprietor of a tennis school in Sydney, Vic Edwards travelled to the country in 1967 to take a look at the young Evonne and immediately saw her potential. After Edwards persuaded her parents to allow Evonne to move to Sydney, she attended Willoughby Girls High School. She completed her School Certificate in 1968 and was coached by Edwards, and lived in his household.

Goolagong spent some time as the touring professional at the Hilton Head Racquet Club in South Carolina before returning to Australia.

Goolagong was a member of the Board of the Australian Sports Commission from 1995 to 1997 and has held the position of Sports Ambassador to Aboriginal and Torres Strait Islander Communities since 1997.

Goolagong was appointed Captain of the Australian Fed Cup team in 2002. In 2003, she won the International Olympic Committee's 2003 Women and Sports Trophy.

Trivia

Goolagong runs an annual 'Goolagong National Development Camp', with the aim of facilitating Aboriginal children playing competitive tennis.

JACKIE ROBINSON

Jackie Robinson (January 31, 1919 – October 24, 1972) was the first black major league player of baseball of modern era. Robinson broke the baseball colour line when he debuted with the Brooklyn Dodgers in 1947.

As the first black man to play in the major leagues since the 1880s, he was instrumental in bringing an end to racial segregation in professional baseball. The racial segregation had relegated black players to the Negro leagues for six decades.

The example of his character and unquestionable talent challenged the traditional basis of segregation, which then marked many other aspects of American life, and contributed significantly to the Civil Rights Movement.

In addition to his cultural impact, Robinson had an exceptional baseball career. Over ten seasons, he played in six World Series and contributed to the Dodgers' 1955 World Championship.

He was selected for six consecutive All-Star Games from 1949 to 1954, was the recipient of the inaugural MLB Rookie of the Year Award in 1947, and won the National League Most Valuable Player Award in 1949 – the first black player so honoured. Robinson was inducted into the Baseball Hall of Fame in 1962. In 1997, Major League Baseball retired his uniform number, 42, across all major league teams.

Trivia

Robinson was also known for his pursuits outside the baseball diamond. He was the first black television analyst in the Major League Baseball, and the first black vice-president of a major American corporation.

KAPIL DEV

Kapil Dev Ramlal Nikhanj better known as Kapil Dev is a former Indian cricketer and said to be one of the all time greatest all-rounders to have existed in the world of Cricket.

Born on January 6, 1959 in Chandigarh, Kapil Dev began his Cricket career in Domestic Cricket from the Haryana team, with a match played against Punjab team in November 1975.

Kapil gave best performance of his initial times in a match against Bengal, in which he took seven wickets giving only 20 runs within nine overs in the second innings.

He debuted in the Test Cricket in 1978 against Pakistan and played his first One-Day International (ODI) on October 1, 1978 against Pakistan.

Kapil scored a huge 175 runs off 138 balls against a crucial match against Zimbabwe during the 1983 World Cup. India won the match by 31 runs and went on to win its first World Cup Trophy, the other being the recent one earlier in 2011. The innings played by Kapil Dev is regarded as one of the Top 10 ODI Batting Performances of all times by the Wisden magazine.

Kapil Dev played 131 Test matches and played 225 ODI matches throughout his career. He served as the Coach of the Indian Cricket team from October 1999 to August 2000 but resigned after match fixing allegations were imposed upon him.

He was captain when India won the world cup in 1983. He was titled as the Indian Cricketer of the Century in 2002 by Wisden.

Trivia

He has won the prestigious **Arjuna Award**, the **Padma Shri** and the **Padma Bhushan**.

MICHAEL JORDAN

Michael Jeffrey Jordan is a former American professional basketball player. He was born in Brookyln, New York on February 17, 1963. As a kid, Michael Jordan was more interested in playing baseball rather than basketball but he soon started to play basketball to try and follow the footsteps of his elder brother, Larry, whom he idolised growing up.

He decided to enter the National Basketball Association (NBA) draft after winning the Naismith College Player of the Year Award in 1984.

Jordan's individual accomplishments include ten All-NBA First Team designations, five MVP awards, ten scoring titles, fourteen NBA All-Star Game appearances, nine All-Defensive First Team honors, three All-Star Game MVP awards, three steals titles, six NBA Finals MVP awards and the 1988 NBA Defensive Player of the Year Award.

In 1993, tragedy struck Jordan's seemingly perfect life. On July 23, 1993, his father James was murdered off Interstate 95 in North Carolina. Two locals had robbed him, shot him in the chest and threw his body in a swamp.

Three months later, in 1993, he announced his retirement. In 1994, he played baseball for Chicago White Sox, though the season didn't go that well.

He retired for good following the 2002-03 seasons and was subsequently dismissed as President of the Washington Wizards.

Trivia

His leaping ability, illustrated by performing slam dunks from the free throw line in slam dunk contests, earned him the nicknames, 'Air Jordan' and 'His Airness'.

Quote

"I've missed more than 9000 shots in my career. I've lost almost 300 games. 26 times. I've been trusted to take the game winning shot and missed. I've failed over and over and over again in my life. And that is why I succeed."

Muhammad Ali

Born on January 17, 1942, Muhammad Ali is a former American professional boxer, a philanthropist and a social activist. Considered a cultural icon, Ali was both idolised and vilified.

Originally known as Cassius Clay, Ali changed his name after joining the 'Nation of Islam' in 1964, subsequently converting to 'Sunni Islam' in 1975, and more recently to Sufism.

At the age of 12, Ali discovered his talent for boxing through an odd twist of fate.

In 1967, three years after Ali had won the 'World Heavyweight Championship', he was publicly vilified for his refusal to be conscripted into the US military. The decision, he said, was based on his religious beliefs.

Though Ali cleared his name after a lengthy court battle. The boxing association took away his title and also suspended him from the sport for three and a half years.

He came back in the ring in 1970 and knocked out Jerry Quarry in October in Atlanta. Ali fought the reigning heavyweight champion George Foreman in 1974 and became the heavyweight champion of the world.

In 1981, Ali fought his last bout, losing his heavyweight title to Trevor Berbick.

In his retirement, Ali has devoted much of his time to philanthropy.

Trivia

He opened the 'Muhammad Ali Centre' in his hometown, Louisville, in 2005. He also received the 'Presidential Medal of Freedom' from President George W. Bush.

OLIVER "THE TITAN" KAHN

Oliver Rolf Kahn was born on June 15, 1969. He is a former German football goalkeeper. He was born in Karlsruhe and is of Latvian descent. He started his career in the Karlsruhe SC Junior team at the age of six. Before becoming a goalkeeper, he played as an outfield player. In 1987, he made his league debut in a home victory.

In 1994-95, Bayern Munich signed him. He was established as the starting goalkeeper. Oliver played his first game in Germany's national team where Bayern defeated Bordeaux in the 1996 UEFA Cup final. Bayern also won the 'German League Cup' and Oliver was named 'German Goalkeeper of the Year'.

In 1999, he was named the 'World Goalkeeper of the Year' by the International Federation of Football History and Statistics. In the 2001 Champions League title against Valentia he was named 'Man of the Match' and he received a 'UEFA Fair Play' Award for the match.

In 2002, Oliver received the squad's captaincy. The team lost in the finals of the 2002 FIFA World Cup. The FIFA Technical Support group awarded him the 'Lev yashin' Award for the best goalkeeper of the tournament and he also became the first goalkeeper in football history to win the Golden Ball for the best individual performance. He maintained his number one spot for the 2004 UEFA European Football Championship.

In a play-off match in 2006, he made his last appearance for Germany. In the following match, he announced his retirement from the German national team. Through his career, he won 89 caps for Germany, 49 as team captain.

In 2004, he joined the ZDF sports team as an analyst for the German National Team's games. He was also a part of the jury of a China Central television reality show to find China's best young goalkeeper. He was in several television commercials. In 2008, his wax figure was inaugurated in the 'Berlin branch of Madame Tussauds'. He is nicknamed "The Titan" due to his formidable presence and influence he showed during his professional career.

PELÉ

Also known by the name of **The Black Pearl**, Pelé was born on October 23, 1940 in Tres Coracoes, Minas Gerais,Brazil.

Simply he was, and for many people still is, the greatest football player of the world. Not a single thing was impossible for him: he won *three* World Cups with his National Team of Brazil (Sweden 1958, Chile 1962, Mexico 1970).

He scored more than 1200 goals during his long career (more than 1300 official matches). He also won many national Leagues and Continental Cup ("Copa Libertadores"), with his team, the Santos Futebol Clube (of Brazilian 'São Paulo' State).

In the Sixties he was nicknamed "O Rei" (The King) and in the Seventies 95 people out of 100 knew his name. ("Wow, man, you're popular!" said Robert Redford, some years ago, after seeing Pelé give dozens of autographs in New York, while he was not asked for one). In the late, 1960's, when he and his team, Santos, went to Nigeria to play a few friendly matches, the ongoing civil war stopped for the duration of his visit.

He finished his career in the New York Cosmos, in 1977. Now he is a United Nation's Ambassador and has been also Minister for Sports in his country, but for the people who saw him make magics with his right foot, he is, now and forever, the greatest footballer in the world, and the one and only "King".

Trivia

He is the only player to have won *three* FIFA World Cup titles (1958, 1962, 1970).

Quote

"Enthusiasm is everything. It must be taut and vibrating like a guitar string."

P.T. USHA

P.T. Usha was born on June 27, 1964. She is an Indian athlete from the state of Kerala. PT Usha has been associated with Indian athletics since 1979. She is regarded as one of the greatest athletes India has ever produced and is often called the 'Queen of Indian track and field'. She is nicknamed *Payyoli Express*. Currently she runs the 'Usha School of Athletics' at Koyilandy in Kerala.

P.T. Usha was born in the village of Payyoli, Kozhikode District, Kerala. In 1976, the Kerala State Government started a Sports School for women, and Usha was chosen to represent her district.

In the 10th Asian Games held at Seoul in 1986, PT Usha won four gold and one silver medals in the track and field events. Here she created new Asian Games records in all the events she participated.

She won five golds at the '6th Asian Track and Field Championship' at Jakarta in 1985. Her six medals at the same meet is a record for a single athlete in a single international meet. Usha has won 101 international medals so far. She is employed as an officer in the Southern Railways. In 1985, she was conferred the **Padma Shri** and the **Arjuna Award**.

Trivia

P.T. Usha's full name is Pilavullakandi Thekkeparambil Usha.

RAHUL DRAVID

Rahul Sharad Dravid, born on January 11, 1973, is an Indian cricketer. He has been a regular member of the Indian Cricket Team since 1996. He was appointed as the captain of the Indian cricket team in October 2005 and resigned from the post in September 2007. Dravid was honoured as one of the top-five Wisden Cricketers of the Year in 2000. Dravid was also awarded the 'ICC Player of the Year' and the 'Test Player of the Year' at the inaugural awards ceremony held in 2004. Dravid also holds the record of having taken the most number of catches in Test cricket.

On August 7, 2011 after getting a surprise call to play in ODI series against England, he declared his retirement from One Day Internationals and T20s.

Popularly hailed as 'The Wall of Indian Cricket', Dravid is regarded by many to be one of the greatest batsmen in the history of the game.

Dravid holds multiple cricketing records. He is the second Indian batsman, after Sachin Tendulkar, and the third international player to reach 12,000 runs in Test cricket. On February 14, 2007, he became the sixth player overall and the third Indian (after Sachin Tendulkar and Sourav Ganguly), to score 10,000 runs in ODI cricket in the cricketing history.

He is the first and only batsman to score a century in all ten Test playing nations. With more than 200 catches, Dravid currently holds the world record for the most number of catches in Test cricket.

Trivia

Dravid has been involved in more than 80 century partnerships with 18 different partners and has been involved in 19 century partnerships with Sachin Tendulkar – a world record.

RONALDO

Commonly known as Ronaldo, Ronaldo Luís Nazário de Lima is a retired Brazilian footballer who last played for Corinthians.

Born on September 18, 1976, Ronaldo is widely considered to be the greatest 'pure' striker in the history of the modern game, and by some accounts, in the history of football.

He has been one of the most prolific scorers in the world in the late 1990s and the early 2000s. He won his first 'Ballon d'Or' (the Golden Ball) as the European Footballer of the Year in 1997 at the age of 21 and the second one at the age of 26.

Additionally, he and French footballer Zinedine Zidane are the only two men to have won the FIFA Player of the Year Award three times.

He was named as one of the best starting eleven of all-time by France Football and was named to the FIFA 100 – a list of the greatest footballers compiled by fellow countryman Pelé – in 2007.

In 2010, he was voted goal.com's 'Player of the Decade' in an online poll, gathering 43.63 percent of all votes. On 23 February 2010, Ronaldo announced that he will retire after the 2011 season, signing a two-year contract extension with the Corinthians at the same time.

Trivia

Ronaldo has played for Brazil in 97 international matches, amassing 62 goals.

SACHIN TENDULKAR

Sachin Ramesh Tendulkar also known as 'The God of Cricket' is regarded as one of the greatest batsmen in the history of cricket.

Tendulkar is the first and only player in Test Cricket to have scored 50 centuries and the first cricketer to score 100 centuries in all International Cricket combined. He holds the world record of 100 centuries (49 ODI & 51 Test Cricket) in international cricket.

Born into a Rajapur Saraswat Brahmin family in Bombay (now Mumbai), his father, Ramesh Tendulkar was a Marathi novelist. He was named 'Sachin' because his father was as great fan of the famous music director, Sachin Dev Burman. Tendulkar's elder brother, 'Ajit' encouraged him to play cricket. When he was young, Sachin would practise for hours in the nets.

At the age of 13, Tendulkar made his debut in club cricket for the Cricket Club of India. When he was just 15 years old, Sachin scored 100 not out in his debut first class match for Bomaby against Gujarat making him the youngest Indian to score a century on first-class debut. After the veteran player, Sunil Manohar Gavaskar, Sachin is the only cricketer to be nicknamed as the 'Little Master'. Sachin is married to a doctor named Anjali, who happens to be the daughter of a Gujarati industrialist.

This great cricketer has been awarded with innumerable honours and appreciations, across the globe. He has been conferrerd with **Padma Vibushan**, India's second highest civilian award in 2008. He is also the recipient of **Rajiv Gandhi Khel Ratna Award**, Indian highest honour given for achievement in sports. Besides this, he was awarded the 'BCCI Cricketer of the Year' award on May 31, 2011 after India won the prestigious World Cup.

Trivia

Sachin Ramesh Tendulkar went to Shradashram Vidyamandir in Mumbai, where he began his cricketing career under his coach, Ramakant Achrekar.

SAINA NEHWAL

Saina Nehwal was born on March 17, 1990. She is an Indian badminton player. Saina was born in Hyderabad, India to Dr. Harvir Singh and Usha Nehwal, both of whom were top badminton players in Haryana, India.

Saina has been the under 19 national champion. She has won the Asian Satellite Badminton tournament twice and is the first player to do so. She became the first Indian women to win a four-star tournament, the Philippines Open in 2006. In 2008, she became the first Indian women to win the World Junior Badminton Championship. She also became the first Indian woman to reach the quarter finals at the Olympic Games. In 2008, she won the Chinese Taipei Open. She was named the 'Most Promising Player' in 2008.

In 2009, she won the BWG Super series and the most prominent badminton series 'Indonesia Open'. She was awarded the **'Arjuna'** Award in 2009 and her coach Gopichand won the **'Dronacharya'** Award at the same time. Saina was also awarded the **Padma Shri** in 2010.

Saina has been awarded the highest national sporting award given to players, **Rajiv Gandhi Khel Ratna Award** in 2010. In the Commonwealth Games held in India, Sania won a gold medal for women's single's badminton event. In December 2010, Saina won the Hong Kong super series.

Saina Nehwal has been voted the third best badminton player of the year 2010 by Badzine, an international badminton magazine. She won the 2010 Indian Open Grand Prix gold. She was ranked world no 3 in women's single's badminton rankings and in July 2010 she reached the world ranking no 2.

Saina managed to win the 'Swiss Open Grand Prix' in March 2011. After that she hasn't managed a win in any of the championships she played in which were Indian Open Super Series, Malaysian Open Grand Prix Gold tournament, 2011 BWF Double Star Surdiman Cup, Thailand Open GP Gold, Singapore Open Super Series and Indonesian Open Super Series Premiere.

SUNIL GAVASKAR

Born on July 10, 1949, Sunil Gavaskar is a former Indian batsman. His record of 34 Test centuries took 20 years to be broken by Sachin Tendulkar in 2005.

The record-setting batsman has been a national hero to cricket fans. His spectacular career began with a bang with scoring 774 runs against West Indies in 1971.

He was the first batsman to score 10,000 runs in Test Cricket.

He was the greatest Test scorer with the highest number of centuries to his credit during his times.

He has served as a captain of the Indian cricket team for a long time. However, the team did not fare well during his captaincy. He led the team in 47 Test matches, out of which, the team won nine, eight were lost and 30 were drawn.

Under his captaincy, the Indian team won 14 ODI matches, lost 21 and two went without any result out of the 37 ODI matches.

Gavaskar played his last Test match against Pakistan in March 1987 and scored 117 runs. His last ODI match was against England in November 1987 in which he scored just four runs.

He dominated the Indian cricket and became famous for his meticulous approach as well as his distinctive headgear.

He became a commentator and columnist after he retired in 1988.

Trivia

Sunil Manohar Gavaskar has been conferred with **Padma Bhushan**. He has written four books on cricket and an autobiography, titled 'Sunny days'. A Test Cricket Series between India and Australia has been jointly named after him and the Australian Cricketer, Allan Border as the 'Border-Gavaskar Trophy'.

TIGER WOODS

Eldrick Tont 'Tiger' Woods was born on December 30, 1975. He is an American professional golfer whose achievements to date rank him among the most successful golfers of all time.

Formerly the World No 1, Tigre Woods is the highest-paid professional athlete in the world, having earned an estimated US$90.5 million from winnings and endorsements in 2010.

Woods has won 14 professional major golf championships, the second highest of any male player and 71 PGA Tour events. He is the third all time behind Sam Snead and Nicklaus.

He has more career PGA Tour wins and career major wins than any other active golfer. He is the youngest player to achieve the career Grand Slam and the youngest and fastest to win 50 tournaments on tour.

Woods is the second golfer, after Jack Nicklaus, to have achieved a career Grand Slam three times.

Woods has won 16 World Golf Championships. Additionally, he has won at least one of those events in each of the first 11 years after they began in 1999.

He married Elin Nordegren in 2004 and the couple had two children before they announced divorce in 2010. The media reports accused Woods of having an extra marital affair.

His multiple infidelities were revealed by over a dozen women, through many worldwide media sources.

He has been awarded **PGA Player of the Year**, a record **ten times**, the **Byron Nelson Award** for lowest adjusted scoring average a record about **eight times**.

Trivia

On December 11, 2009, Woods announced he would take an indefinite leave from professional golf to focus on his marriage after he admitted infidelity and returned to Golf on April 8, 2010.

USAIN ST. LEO BOLT

U sain St. Leo Bolt, the Fastest Man on Earth born on August 21, 1986, is a Jamaican sprinter and a five-time World and three-time Olympic gold medallist. He is the world record and Olympic record holder in the 100 metres, the 200 metres and the 4×100 metres relay. He is the *reigning Olympic champion* in these three events.

Bolt won a 200 m gold medal at the 2002 World Junior Championships, making him the competition's youngest-ever gold medallist. In 2004, at the CARIFTA Games, he became the first junior sprinter to run the 200 m in under 20 seconds with a time of 19.93 s, breaking the previous world junior record held by Roy Martin by two-tenths of a second. He turned professional in 2004, and although he competed at the 2004 Summer Olympics, he missed most of the next two seasons due to injuries. In 2007, he broke Don Quarrie's 200 m Jamaican record with a run of 19.75 s.

His 2008 season began with his first world record performance – a 100 m world record of 9.72 s – and culminated in world and Olympic records in both the 100 m and 200 m events at the 2008 Beijing Summer Olympics. He ran 9.69 s for the 100 m and 19.30 s in the 200 m, and also set a 4×100 m relay record of 37.10 s with the Jamaican team.

Trivia

His 2009 record breaking margin over 100 m is the highest since the start of digital time measurements. His achievements in sprinting have earned him the media nickname, "Lightning Bolt", and awards including the IAAF World Athlete of the Year, Track & Field Athlete of the Year, and Laureus Sportsman of the Year.

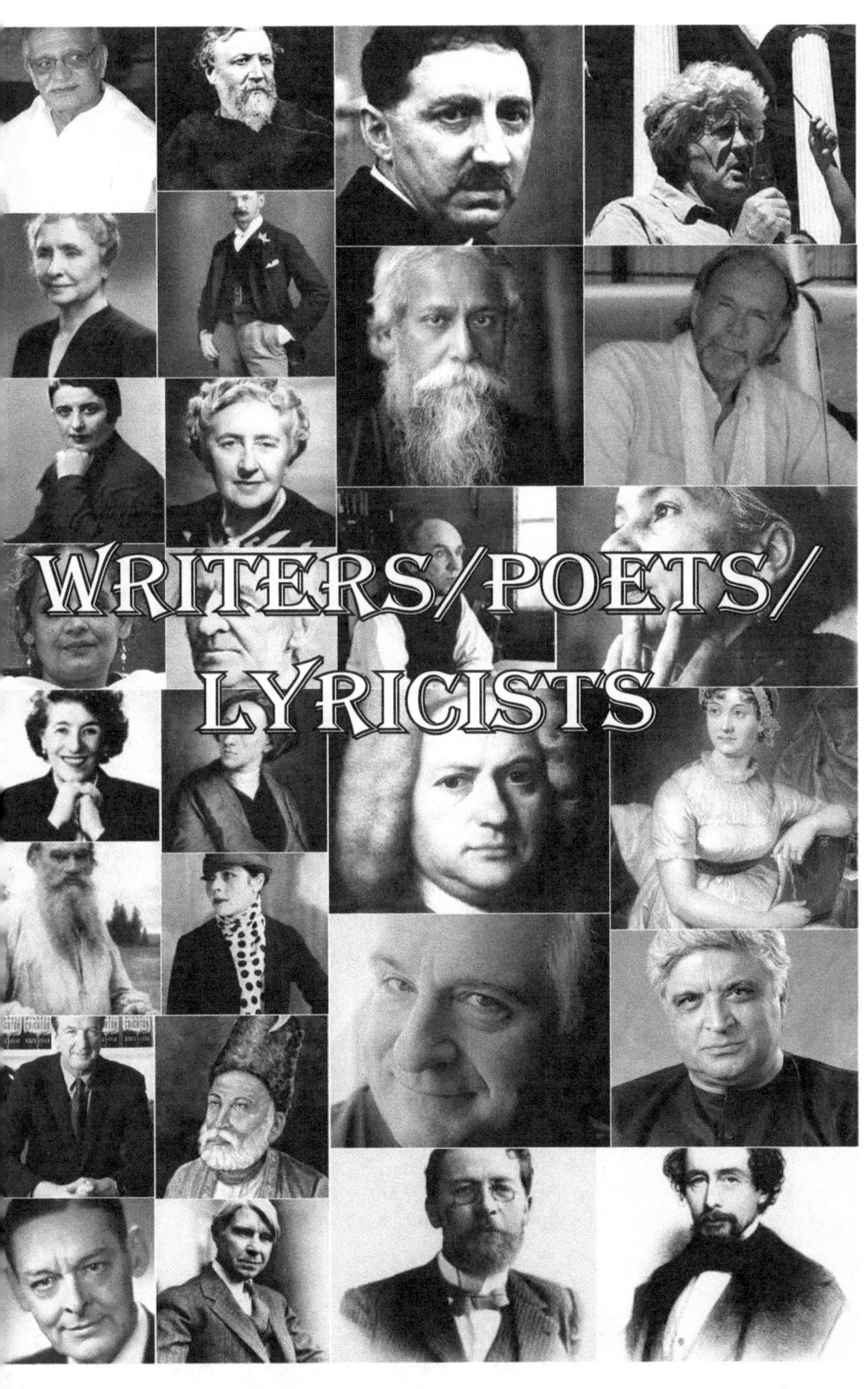

WRITERS/POETS/
LYRICISTS

AGATHA CHRISTIE

Dame Agatha Christie was born on September 15, 1890. She was a British crime writer of novels, short stories and plays. She also wrote romances under the name, Mary Westmacott.

Agatha Chritsie was born in Torquay, Devon, England. While she never received any formal schooling, she did not lack an education. Her father taught her mathematics via story problems, and the family played question-and-answer games. Agatha made up stories from a very early age and invented a number of imaginary friends and paracosms.

During the First World War, she worked at a hospital as a nurse. She later worked at a hospital pharmacy, a job that influenced her work, as many of the murders in her books are carried out with poison.

Despite a turbulent courtship, on Christmas Eve 1914, Agatha married Archibald Christie, an aviator in the Royal Flying Corps. The couple had one daughter, Rosalind Hicks. The Christies divorced in 1928. In 1930, Christie married an archaeologist. Their marriage was especially happy in the early years and remained so until Christie's death in 1976.

Agatha Christie's first novel, *The Mysterious Affair at Styles* was published in 1920 and introduced the long-running character detective, Hercule Poirot appeared in 33 of Christie's novels and 54 short stories. Her other well-known character, Miss Marple, was introduced in *The Tuesday Night Club* in 1927 (short story) and was based on women like Christie's grandmother and her cronies.

Christie wrote two novels, *Curtain*, and *Sleeping Murder*, intended as the last cases of these two great detectives, Hercule Poirot and Jane Marple. Both books were sealed in a bank vault for over thirty years and were released for publication by Christie only at the end of her life. These publications came on the heels of the success of the film version of *Murder on the Orient Express* in 1974.

Agatha Christie was revered as a **master of suspense**, plotting, and characterisation by most of her contemporaries.

Christie has been portrayed on a number of occasions in film and television. Several biographical programs have been made, such as the

2004 BBC television programme entitled *Agatha Christie: A Life in Pictures*, in which she is portrayed by Olivia Williams, Anna Massey, and Bonnie Wright. Christie has also been parodied on screen, such as in the film, *Murder by Indecision*, which featured the character, "Agatha Crispy".

In 2004, the Japanese broadcasting company Nippon Hōsō Kyōkai turned Poirot and Marple into animated characters in the anime series, Agatha Christie's Great Detectives Poirot and Marple, introducing Mabel West and her duck Oliver as new characters.

Agatha Christie died on January 12, 1976.

Trivia

At one point in her successful career, Agatha Christie actually owned eight different houses. Many of these were used as the houses in many of her novels, such as: Taken at the Flood, Dead Man's Folly, Five Little Pigs, Crooked House, etc.

Quote

"Crime is terribly revealing. Try and vary your methods as you will, your tastes, your habits, your atitude of mind and your soul is revealed by your actions."

ALEXANDER POPE

Alexander Pope was born on May 21, 1688 in Plough Court, Lombard Street, London to parents Alexander Pope Senior and Edith. He was an English poet. Alexander Pope was taught to read by his aunt, and went to Twyford School in about 1698/99. He mostly educated himself by reading the works of classical writers, such as the satirists, Horace and Juvenal, the epic poets, Homer and Virgil, as well as English authors, such as Geoffrey Chaucer, William Shakespeare and John Dryden. He also studied many languages and came into contact with figures from the London Literary Society. He died on May 30, 1744.

In 1709, *Pope's Pastorals* was published in the sixth part of Tonson's Poetical Miscellanies. Followed by *An Essay on Criticism*, published in May 1711, both were equally well received. Pope became friends with Tory writers, John Gay, Jonathan Swift, Thomas Parnell and John Arbuthnot, and together formed the satirical Scriblerus Club around 1711. In March 1713, *Windsor Forest* was published to great acclaim.

Pope's next poem, *The Rape of the Lock*, first published in 1712, with a revised version published in 1714 is sometimes considered Pope's most popular poem.

Alexander Pope contributed to Addison's play, *Cato*, as well as writing for *The Guardian* and *The Spectator*.

In 1731, Pope published his "Epistle to Burlington", on the subject of architecture, the first of four poems which would later be grouped under the title, *Moral Essays*. Pope wrote *An Essay on Man* (1733), then the *Imitations of Horace* followed (1733–38). Pope also added a wholly original poem, *An Epistle to Doctor Arbuthnot*, as an introduction to the "Imitations". After 1738, Pope wrote little.

ANITA DESAI

Anita Desai Mazumdar was born on June 24, 1937. She is an Indian novelist and professor. She was born to D. N. Mazumdar and Toni Nime in Mussoorie, India. She studied in Queen Mary's Higher Secondary School in Delhi. She began to write at the age of seven and published her first story when she was nine. She has received a B.A. in English Literature from the Miranda House of the University of Delhi. In 1958, she married Ashwin Desai.

Anita Desai's first novel, *Cry, The Peacock* was published in 1963. Her other novels are *Clear Light of Day* (1980), *In Custody* (1984) which was shortlisted for the **Booker Prize**.

In 1993, she became the creative writing teacher at the Massachusetts Institute of Technology. Her latest novel is *The Zigzag Way* (2004). She has taught at the Mount Holyoke College, the Baruch College and the Smith College. She is a Fellow of the Royal Society of Literature, the American Academy of Arts and Letters, and of Girton College, Cambridge University. She also writes for the *New York Review of Books*.

In Custody was made into a film by the Merchant Ivory Productions in 1993. It was directed by Ismail Merchant, and the screenplay by Shahrukh Husain. It won the 1994 President of India Gold Medal for Best Picture and stars Shashi Kapoor, Shabana Azmi and Om Puri.

Anita Desai has been shortlisted for the **Booker Prize for Fiction** for her novels, *Clear Light of Day*, *In Custody* and *Fasting, Feasting*. She has won the Sahitya Academy Award and Winifred Holtby Memorial Prize for *Fire on the Mountain* and Guardian's children fiction prize for *The Village by the Sea*.

She has also won the Neil Gunn Prize, Alberto Moravia Prize for Literature (Italy) and the Benson Medal of Royal Society of Literature.

ANTON CHEKHOV

Born on January 29, 1860, Anton Pavlovich Chekhov, popularly known as Anton Chekhov was a Russian physician, dramatist and author. He is considered to be among the greatest writers of short stories in history.

While a student, Chekhov published numerous short stories and humorous sketches under a pseudonym. While he was serving as a doctor, he kept writing and had success with his first books, and his first play 'Ivanov'.

Gradually, Chekhov decreased his medical practice in favour of writing. He created his own style based on brevity, objectivity, originality and compassion.

He avoided stereotyping and instructive political messages in favour of cool comic irony.

His career as a dramatist produced four classics and his best short stories are held in high esteem. Chekhov had at first written stories only for financial gain, but as his artistic ambition grew, he made formal innovations which have influenced the evolution of the modern short story.

He died on July 15, 1904 in Badenweiler, Germany due to complications of lung tuberculosis.

Trivia

His drama, Uncle Vanya performed at the Donmar Warehouse, was awarded the 2003 Laurence Olivier Theatre Award for Best Revival of 2002.

Quote

"Medicine is my lawful wife," he once said, "and literature is my mistress."

ARUNDHATI ROY

Born on November 24, 1961, Arundhati Roy is an Indian novelist, activist and a world citizen. She won the **Booker Prize** in 1997 for her first novel, *The God of Small Things.*

Roy was born in Shillong, Meghalaya and spent her childhood in Aymanam in Kerala. She came to Delhi at the age of Sixteen and embarked on a homeless lifestyle. She stayed in a small hut with a tin roof.

After she won the Booker Prize, she has concentrated her writing on political issues including – *India's Nuclear Weapons, the Narmada Dam project, Dabhol Power Company* activities in India.

In response to India's testing of nuclear weapons in Pokhran, Roy wrote *The End of Imagination.* In her collection, *The Cost of Living,* she also crusaded against India's massive hydroelectric dam projects in Maharashtra, Madhya Pradesh and Gujarat.

Roy has devoted herself solely to non-fiction and politics, publishing two more collections of essays. She has also worked for social causes.

She was awarded the 'Sydney Peace Prize' in May 2004 for her work in social campaigns.

She took part in the 'World Tribunal' on Iraq in June 2005. She was awarded the **Sahitya Akademi Award** for her collection of essays, 'The Algebra of Infinite Justice' in 2006, but declined to accept it.

She has been in many controversies due to her comments and articles on several issues.

Most recently, in August 2011, Roy accused Anna Hazare in a newspaper article of being non-secular.

Trivia

She studied architecture at the Delhi School of Architecture, where she met her first husband, the architect, Gerard Da Cunha.

AYN RAND

Russian-American novelist, philosopher, playwright, and screenwriter Ayn Rand was born on January 20, 1905.

She has been known for developing a philosophical system, she called 'Objectivism' until her death on March 6, 1982 .

Born and educated in Russia, Rand moved to the Uinted States in 1926. She worked as a screenwriter in Hollywood and had a play produced on Broadway in 1935.

After two initially unsuccessful early novels, she achieved fame with her 1943 novel, *The Fountainhead.* She published her philosophical novel, *Atlas Shrugged* in 1957.

Rand is known for her these two best-selling novels, *The Fountainhead* and *Atlas Shrugged.*

Afterwards, she turned to non-fiction to promote her philosophy, publishing her own magazines and releasing several collections of essays until her death in 1982.

Rand advocated reason as the only means of acquiring knowledge and rejected all forms of faith and religion. In politics, she opposed all forms of collectivism and statism, instead supporting *laissez-faire capitalism*, which she believed was the only social system that protected individual rights.

She was sharply critical of most other philosophers and philosophical traditions.

Trivia

The reception for Rand's fiction from literary critics was largely negative and most academics have ignored or rejected her philosophy. However, she continues to have a popular following and her political ideas have been quite influential. The Objectivist Movement attempts to spread her ideas, both to the public and in academic settings.

CARL SANDBURG

Carl Sandburg (January 6, 1878 – July 22, 1967) was an American writer and editor. He was best known for his poetry.

Sandburg won **three Pulitzer Prizes** – two for his poetry and another for biography of Abraham Lincoln. Much of Carl Sandburg's poetry, such as 'Chicago', focussed on Chicago, where he spent his time as a reporter for the *Chicago Daily News* and the *Day Book*.

One of his most famous descriptions of the city is as 'Hog Butcher for the World/Tool Maker, Stacked of Wheat/Player with Railroads and the Nation's Freight Handler, Stormy, Husky, Brawling, City of the Big Shoulders'.

Sandburg is also remembered by generations of children for his series of whimsical, sometimes melancholy stories, *Rooting Stories*, which he originally created for his own daughters. These stories were an inspiration from Sandburg's desire for 'American fairy tales' to match the American childhood. He felt that the European stories involved royalty and knights that were inappropriate. Sandburg populated his stories with trains, skyscrapers, corn fairies and the 'Five Marvelous Pretzel'.

He is known for his biography of Abraham Lincoln (Abraham Lincoln: The War Years). He recorded excerpts from the biography and some of Lincoln's speeches for Goodman Records in New York City in May 1957. Sandburg was awarded a **Grammy Award** in 1959 for best performance – Documentary Or Spoken Word (Other Than Comedy) for his recording of Aaron Copeland's Lincoln Portrait with the New York Philharmonic.

Trivia

Sandburg's home in Flat Rock, Henderson Count in North Carolina, is preserved by the National Park Service as theCarl Sandburg Home National Historic Site.

CHARLES DICKENS

Charles John Huffam Dickens, usually called Charles Dickens, was born on February 7, 1812. He was an English novelist, the greatest of the Victorian period.

Charles was bon to John and Elizabeth Dickens. His father used to work as a clerk in the Navy-Pay office. Having a poor head for finances, he found himself imprisoned for debt in 1824. His wife and children, except Charles, joined him in the Marshalsea Prison. Charles was put to work at Warren's Blacking Factory.

He attended a school in London from 1824 to 1827. He later became a reporter and started writing for a newspaper.

Many of his writings were originally published serially, in monthly instalments or parts. Dickens often created the episodes as they were being serialised. This practice kept the public looking forward to the next instalment.

The first series of *Sketches by Boz* was published in 1836. Later, Dickens was hired to write short texts to accompany a series of humorous sporting illustrations by a popular artist, *Robert Seymour*.

Then, Dickens altered the initial conception of *The Pickwick Papers*, which became a novel and was a huge success. After its success, he embarked on a full-time career as novelist.

Some of his other works include *Master Humphrey's Clock*, *The Old Curiosity Shop*, *The Chimes*, *The Cricket* and the *Hearth*.

Dickens' work has been highly praised for its realism, comedy and mastery of prose, unique personalities and concern for social reform by famous writers.

He suffered a mild stroke in 1869 and another on June 8, 1870. He died on June 9, 1870.

Trivia

Dickens enjoyed a wider popularity and fame than any previous author during his lifetime.

DJUNA BARNES

Djuna Barnes (June 12, 1892 – June 18, 1982) was an American writer and played an important part in the development of the 20th century English language modernist writing.

She was one of the key figures in 1920s and 1930s Bohemian Paris after filling a similar role in the Greenwich Village of the teens.

In 1912, Barnes enrolled as a student at the Pratt Institute and the Art Students League in 1915. She began her writing career as a reporter and illustrator for the *Brooklyn Eagle*.

Barnes wrote mostly featured articles and interviews. She first published her poetry in 1915 as a collection of 'rhythms and drawings' entitled, *The Book of Repulsive Women*. Three of her plays were produced by the Provincetown Players, four years later.

In 1923, Barnes published a collection of lyrical poems, stories, drawings, and one-act plays which she entitled, *A Book*.

Barnes's novel, *Ryder* published in 1928 draws heavily on her childhood experiences in Cornwall-on-Hudson.

Her novel, *Nightwood* became a cult work of modern fiction, helped by an introduction by TS Eliot and stands out today for its portrayal of lesbian themes and its distinctive writing style.

Some of the other works include, *The Antiphon* (1958) and *Creatures in an Alphabet* (1982), etc.

Trivia

Since Barnes's death, interest in her work has grown amid the publishers and readers, and many of her books are back in print.

DOUGLAS NOEL ADAMS

Douglas Noel Adams (March 11, 1952 – May 11, 2001) was an English writer and dramatist. He is best known as the author of *The Hitchhiker's Guide to the Galaxy* which started life in 1978 as a BBC radio comedy before developing into a 'trilogy' of five books that sold over 15 million copies in his lifetime, a television series, several stage plays, comics, a computer game, and in 2005, a feature film. Adams's contribution to the British radio is commemorated in **The Radio Academy's Hall of Fame**.

Adams became known as an advocate for environmental and conservation causes and also as a lover of fast cars, cameras, and the Apple Macintosh. He was a staunch atheist, famously imagining a sentient puddle who wakes up one morning and thinks, "This is an interesting world I find myself in – an interesting hole I find myself in – fits me rather neatly, doesn't it? In fact, it fits me staggeringly well, must have been made to have me in it!"

Biologist Richard Dawkins dedicated his book, *The God Delusion,* to Adams, writing on his death that, 'science has lost a friend, literature has lost a luminary, the mountain gorilla and the black rhino have lost a gallant defender.'

Trivia

A posthumous collection of his work, including an unfinished novel, was published as *The Salmon of Doubt* in 2002. Adams also wrote Dirk Gently's *Holistic Detective Agency* (1987) and *The Long Dark Tea-Time of the Soul* (1988), and co-wrote *The Meaning of Liff* (1983), *Last Chance to See* (1990), and three stories for the television series, Doctor Who.

E.M. FORSTER

Edward Morgan Forster (January 1, 1879 – June 7, 1970) was an English novelist, short story writer, essayist and a liberalist.

Best known for his ironic and well-plotted novels examining class difference, Forster's humanistic impulse towards understanding and sympathy may be aptly summed up in the epigraph to his 1910 novel, *Howards End: 'Only connect'*.

After having attended the Tonbridge School in Kent, Forster went to King's College, Cambridge between 1897 and 1901. After leaving the University, he visited Egypt, Germany and India with the classicist Goldsworthy Lowes Dickinson in 1914.

He had five novels published in his lifetime. His first novel was *Where Angels Fear to Tread* (1905), *The Longest Journey* (1907), *A Room with a View* (1908), *Howards End* (1910), *A Passage to India* (1924).

He was in India in the early 1920s and *The Hill of Devi* is his non-fictional account of the trip. After returning from India, he completed his last novel, *A Passage to India* in 1924, for which he won the **James Tait Black Memorial Prize** for fiction.

Forster became a successful broadcaster on the BBC Radio in the 1930s and 1940s.

Forster is noted for his use of symbolism as a technique in his novels. He has been criticised for his attachment to mysticism. One example of his symbolism is the 'wych elm tree' in *Howards End* and 'Mrs Moore' in *A Passage to India* has a mystical link with the past and a striking ability to connect with people from beyond their own circles.

Trivia

His name was officially registered as Henry Morgan Forster but at his baptism, he was accidentally named Edward Morgan Forster.

ENID BLYTON

Enid Blyton (August 11, 1897 – November 28, 1968) was an English children's writer also known as 'Mary Pollock'.

She was noted for numerous series of books based on recurring characters and designed for different age groups. Her books have enjoyed huge success in many parts of the world, and have sold over 600 million copies.

One of the most widely known characters is *Noddy*, intended for early years readers. Her main work is the genre of young readers' novels in which children have their own adventures with minimal adult help.

Series of such books by her include – *The Famous Five* (21 novels, 1942–1963), the *Five Find-Outers and Dog*, (15 novels, 1943–1961) as well as *The Secret Seven* (15 novels, 1949–1963).

Enid announced her marriage to Hugh Alexander Pollock, who was the editor of the book department in the publishing firm of George Newnes in 1924. The couple had two children.

Her work basically involved children's adventure stories and fantasy and sometimes, magic. Her books were and still are enormously popular throughout the Commonwealth – as translations in the former Yugoslavia, Japan; as adaptations in Arabic; and across most of the globe. Her work has been translated into nearly *90 languages.*

She has an estimated **800 books** to her credit over roughly 40 years. 'Chorion Limited of London' now owns and handles the intellectual properties and character brands of *Blyton's Noddy* and the well-known series of the *Famous Five.*

Trivia

As a child, Enid Blyton faced some medical problems that brought her very close to death.

GULZAR

Sampooran Singh Kalra was born on August 18, 1936. Popularly known by his pen name Gulzar, he is an Indian poet, lyricist and director. He primarily writes in Hindi-Urdu and has also written in Punjabi including several dialects of Hindi, such as *Braj Bhasha, Khariboli, Haryanvi* and *Marwari.*

Gulzar was awarded the 'Padma Bhushan' in 2004 for his contribution to the arts and the 'Sahitya Akademi Award' in 2002.

In 2009, he won the 'Academy Award' for the Best Original Song for 'Jai Ho' in the film, *Slumdog Millionaire* (2008). On January 31, 2010, the same song won him a **Grammy Award** in the category of Grammy Award for Best Song Written for a Motion Picture, Television or Other Visual Media.

Gulzar's poetry is partly published in three compilations: *Chand Pukhraaj Ka, Raat Pashminey Ki* and *Pandrah Paanch Pachattar* (15-05-75).His short stories are published in *Raavi-paar* (Dustkhat in Pakistan) and 'Dhuan'.

As a lyricist, Gulzar is best known for his association with the music directors, Rahul Dev Burman, A. R. Rahman and Vishal Bhardwaj. He has also worked with other leading Bollywood music directors including Sachin Dev Burman, Salil Chowdhury, Hemant Kumar, Madan Mohan and Shankar–Ehsaan–Loy.

Trivia
His biography is written by his daughter, Meghna Gulzar.

Quote
"Music has a natural place in our lives. Music fills our spaces naturally. It will always be dear to us."

HELEN KELLER

An author, political activist and lecturer, Helen Keller was the first deaf and blind person to be a graduate. Her life is an example of how perseverance can overcome obstacles.

Helen Keller was born on June 27, 1880 in Tuscumbia, Alabama.

When she was one year and seven months old, she suffered from fever, assumed to be scarlet fever that left her deaf and blind. She was recommended to the Perkins Institute for the Blind in Boston by Alexander Graham Bell.

She met her teacher, Anne Sullivan in the Perkins Institute. Sullivan discovered a unique way to teach Helen words and their meanings. She once held Helen's hand under the flowing water. As the water fell on her hand, Sullivan wrote the alphabets of the word, 'water' one by one on her arm. Helen tried to grasp every motion felt on her arm and realised that the substance falling on her hand was called 'water'.

Sullivan's teaching abilities and Helen's will to learn helped her to pass examinations, learn five languages and write twelve books, including her autobiography, 'The Story of My Life'.

She was involved in campaigns for women's rights at her college level, which laid the foundation for her as a socialist. Helen also wrote articles for 'The Masses', a socialist journal. She devoted her life and travelled around the world to raise funds for the *American Foundation of the Blind*.

Helen Keller died in Westport, Connecticut, on June 1, 1968.

Trivia

Helen had a protruding left eye, due to which she was usually photographed in profile. Both her eyes were later replaced with glass eyes for 'medical and cosmetic' reasons.

Quote

"I can see, and that is why I can be happy, in what you call the dark, but which to me is golden. I can see a God-made world, not a man-made world."

JANE AUSTEN

Jane Austen (December 16, 1775 – July 18, 1817) was an English novelist whose works of romantic fiction, set among the landed gentry, earned her a place as one of the most widely read writers in English literature, her realism and biting social commentary cementing her historical importance among scholars and critics.

She was educated primarily by her father and elder brothers as well as through her own reading. The steadfast support of her family was critical to her development as a professional writer.

Her artistic apprenticeship lasted from her teenage years, until she was about 35 years old. During this period, she experimented with various literary forms, including the epistolary novel which she tried, then abandoned and wrote, and extensively revised three major novels. She also began a fourth one.

From 1811 until 1816, many of her books were released including *Sense and Sensibility* (1811), *Pride and Prejudice* (1813), *Mansfield Park* (1814) and *Emma* (1816), she achieved success as a great writer.

She wrote two additional novels, *Northanger Abbey* and *Persuasion*, both published posthumously in 1818, and began a third, which was eventually titled *Sanditon*, but died before completing it.

Trivia

Biographical information concerning Jane Austen is 'famously scarce', according to one biographer. Only some personal and family letters remain as her sister, Cassandra, burnt 'the greater part' of the ones she kept and censored those she did not destroy.

JAVED AKHTAR

Javed Akhtar was born on January 17, 1945 in Gwalior. He is a poet, lyricist and scriptwriter from India. Some of his most successful work was done in the late 1970s and 1980s with Salim Khan. The script-writing duo Salim-Javed is credited with many good and long-lasting songs. Both of them delivered some beautiful hits like *Zanjeer, Deewar, Haathi Mere Saathi, Don* and many more.

Javed Akhtar continues to be a prominent figure in Bollywood and is one of the most popular lyricists in the industry. His original name was Jadoo, taken from a line in a poem written by his father – 'Lamha, lamha kisi jadoo ka fasana hoga'. He was given an official name of Javed.

Javed Akhtar has also won about seven 'Filmfare' awards. He has been conferred with **Padma Shri** and **Padma Bhushan**.

A multi-talented personality, Javed Akhtar continues to get rave reviews and awards for his works. His first collection of Urdu poems was released in the year, 1995. It was also released as an album and sold many CDs.

The famous artist, M.F. Hussain is said to have painted around 16 canvases inspired from Javed Akhtar's poems.

He not only excels as a poet but also as a scriptwriter and lyricist.

Trivia

After the success of 'Don', it was remade in Tamil as 'Billa' starring Rajinikanth, but the story writers were the same, Salim–Javed, in it and they made a few changes in the script, here and there.

Quote

"We put women on a pedestal. So we do not consider them to be human beings."

Jerome Klapka Jerome

Jerome Klapka Jerome (May 2, 1859 – June 14, 1927) was an English writer and humorist, best known for the humorous travelogue, *Three Men in a Boat*.

Jerome was born in Caldmore, Walsall, England, and was brought up in poverty in London. He attended St Marylebone Grammar School.

Jerome was the fourth child of Jerome Clapp, an iron monger and lay preacher who dabbled in architecture, and Marguerite Jones. Jerome K Jerome was registered, like his father's amended name, as Jerome Clapp Jerome, and the Klapka appears to be a later variation.

Owing to bad investments in the local mining industry, the family suffered poverty, and debt collectors often visited. This was an experience of Jerome's life, which he has described vividly in his autobiography, *My Life and Times*.

His other works include the essay collections, 'Idle Thoughts of an Idle Fellow' and 'Second Thoughts of an Idle Fellow'. Several other novels are credited in his name including *Three Men on the Bummel* is a sequel to *Three Men in a Boat*.

Trivia

The young Jerome wished to go into politics or be a man of letters but the death of his father at the age of 13 and his mother at the age of 15, forced him to quit his studies and find work to support himself. He was employed at the London and North-Western Railway, initially collecting coal that fell along the railway, remaining there for about four years.

JONATHAN SWIFT

Jonathan Swift (November 30, 1667 – October 19, 1745) was an Anglo-Irish satirist, political pamphleteer, essayist and poet. Born in Dublin, Ireland, Swift began his education at the age of six. Later, he graduated from the Trinity College in 1686.

After the political turmoil during the Glorious Revolution, Swift came to England and became secretary to Sir William Temple, a diplomat and man of letters.

It was the period between 1696 and 1699 that Swift composed most of his first great work – *A Tale of a Tub*, a prose satire on the religious extremes represented by Roman Catholicism and Calvinism and *The Battle of the Books* in 1697. In 1699, Swift travelled to Ireland as chaplain and secretary to the Earl of Berkeley.

He is remembered for works, such as *Gulliver's Travels*, *A Journal to Stella*, *A Modest Proposal*, *Drapier's Letters*, *The Battle of the Books* and *An Argument Against Abolishing Christianity*.

Swift originally published all of his works under pseudonyms – such as Lemuel Gulliver, Isaac Bickerstaff, MB Drapier – or anonymously. He is also known for being a master of two styles of satire – the 'Horatian' and the 'Juvenalian styles'.

Swift's final trip to England took place in 1727. He published five volumes of 'Swift-Pope Miscellanies' between 1727 and 1736. Swift's ghastly 'A Beautiful Young Nymph Going to Bed' was published in 1731.

By 1735, his Meniere's disease became more acute, resulting in periods of dizziness and nausea.

After a prolonged illness, Swift died on October 19, 1745.

LEO TOLSTOY

Lev Nikolayevich Tolstoy (September 9, 1828 – November 20, 1910) was a Russian writer. He primarily wrote novels and short stories.

Later in life, he also wrote plays and essays. Two of his most famous works – the novels, *War and Peace* and *Anna Karenina* – are acknowledged as a pinnacle of realistic fiction.

Leo Tolstoy studied languages and law at the Kazan University for three years. Being dissatisfied with the school, he left Kazan without a degree, returned to his estate and educated himself independently.

Considered to be one of the world's greatest novelists, Tolstoy is equally known for his complicated persona and for his extreme moralistic views, which he adopted after a moral crisis and spiritual awakening in the 1870s. After this period, he also became noted as a moral thinker and social reformer.

His literal interpretation of the ethical teachings of Jesus caused him, in later life, to become a fervent Christian anarchist. His ideas on non-violent resistance are expressed in works, such as *The Kingdom of God Is Within You.* They had a profound impact on pivotal twentieth-century figures, such as Mahatma Gandhi and Martin Luther King, Jr.

He died of pneumonia at the age of 82.

Trivia

He was probably the first writer to have groupies. Towards the end of his life, there were nearly one hundred fans living in and around his home so that they could experience his greatness firsthand.

Quote

"Love is life. All, everything that I understand, I understand only because I love. Everything is, everything exists, only because I love. Everything is united by it alone. Love is God, and to die means that I, a particle of love, shall return to the general and eternal source."

MICHAEL CRICHTON

Born on October 23, 1942, John Michael Crichton was an American best-selling author, producer, director, and screenwriter, best known for his work in the science fiction, medical fiction, and thriller genres. He was best known as Michael Crichton.

His books have sold over 150 million copies worldwide and many have been adapted into films.

In 1994, Crichton became the only creative artist ever to have works simultaneously charting at number one in television, film, and book sales with *ER, Jurassic Park*, and *Disclosure*, respectively.

His novels exemplify the techno-thriller genre of literature, often exploring technology and failures of human interaction with it, especially resulting in catastrophes with biotechnology.

Many of his history novels have medical or scientific underpinnings, reflecting his medical training and science background. He was the author of *Rising Sun, The Andromeda Strain, Jurassic Park, Congo, Sphere, Travels, Disclosure, Airframe, Timeline, The Lost World, Prey, State of Fear* and *Next* which were some of his well-known books. 'Next' was the last book published before his death in 2008.

Pirate Latitudes was published on November 24, 2009, 20 days after his death. An unfinished techno-thriller, *Micro* was published in November 2011.

Trivia

Amazon is a graphical text adventure game created by Michael Crichton and produced by John Wells under the Trillium Corp. It sold more than 100,000 copies, making it a significant commercial success at the time. It featured plot elements similar to those later used in Congo.

MICHAEL LEUNIG

Michael Leunig, born on June 2, 1945, typically referred to as Leunig, is an Australian poet, cartoonist and cultural commentator.

Some of his best-known works include 'The Adventures of Vasco Pyjama' and the 'Curly Flats' series. Leunig was born in East Melbourne, Victoria. He went to Maribyrnong High School before entering an arts degree at the Monash University.

He then enrolled at the Swinburne Film and Television School and began his cartoon career.

Leunig's first marriage to Pamela ended in divorce. He married Helga in 1992. The couple had four children – Gus on Guy Fawkes Day, 1973; Sunny on Valentine's Day 1975; Minna on Australia Day 1992 and Felix on the Christmas Day, 1995.

Leunig's first cartoons appeared in the Monash University student newspaper in the late 1960s. He was conscripted in the Vietnam War call-up but registered as a conscientious objector. He was rejected on health grounds when it was revealed that he was deaf in one ear.

His work appeared in the satirical magazine, 'Nation Review', 'Woman's Day', 'London's Oz magazine' and also various newspapers in the early 1970s.

Other newspapers that Leunig worked for are the: 'Fairfax Press', 'The Sydney Morning Herald' and 'The Age (Melbourne)'. He has focused mainly on political commentary in the recent years.

Leunig was declared an Australian Living Treasure by the National Trust of Australia in 1999.

Trivia

The Australian Broadcasting Corporation has also provided airtime to Leunig to discuss his views on a range of political and philosophical issues.

MIRZA GHALIB

One of the best-known Urdu poets of all times, Mirza Ghalib is a name synonymous with Urdu poetry. Popularly known as Ghalib, Mirza Asadullah Baig Khan was born on December 27, 1796.

He wrote several 'ghazals' during his lifetime, which have since been interpreted and sung in many different ways.

Born in Agra, his father died in a battle when Ghalib was five years old. He was, then, looked after by his uncle, who also died when Ghalib was ten years old.

The death of his father and uncle during his early youth left Ghalib with no male-dominant figures. He then moved to Delhi.

There are no known records of Ghalib's formal education, although it was known that friends in Delhi were some of the most intelligent minds of the time.

He was married into a family of nobles, at the age of thirteen around 1810. He had seven children, none of whom survived.

Ghalib's fame came to him posthumously. He had himself had said during his lifetime that though his age ignored his greatness, his work would be recognised by later generations.

He also is arguably the most 'written about' among the Urdu poets.

The first complete English translation of Ghalib's love poems (ghazals) was written by Dr. Sarfaraz K Niazi, titled 'Love Sonnets of Ghalib', which was published in India and Pakistan.

Ghalib died in Delhi on February 15, 1869.

Trivia

Ghalib never worked as such for his livelihood and lived on state patronage, credit or generosity of his friends.

RABINDRANATH TAGORE

Rabindranath Tagore was born in the Jorasanko mansion in Calcutta (Kolkata) on May 7, 1861 to Debendranath Tagore and Sarada Devi.

Author of *Gitanjali* and its 'profoundly sensitive, fresh and beautiful verse', he became the first non-European Nobel laureate by earning the 1913 Nobel Prize in Literature. In translation, his poetry was viewed as spiritual and mercurial; his seemingly mesmeric persona, floccose locks, and empyreal garb garnered him a prophet-like aura in the West.

His 'elegant prose and magical poetry' remain largely unknown outside Bengal.

As a humanist, universalist, internationalist and strident anti-nationalist, he denounced the Raj and advocated for independence from Britain.

As an exponent of the Bengal Renaissance, he advanced a vast canon that comprised paintings, sketches and doodles, hundreds of texts, and some two thousand songs; his legacy endures also in the institution he founded, the Visva-Bharati University.

He started writing poetry at an age of 8. At the age of 16, he cheekily released his first substantial poems under the pseudonym, *Bhanusingha* (Sun Lion), his novels, stories, songs, dance-dramas, and essays spoke to topics – political and personal.

Gitanjali (Song Offerings), *Gora* (Fair-Faced), and *Ghare-Baire* (The Home and the World) are his best-known works, and his verse, short stories and novels were acclaimed for their lyricism, colloquialism, naturalism and unnatural contemplation. He penned two national anthems: the Republic of India's 'Jana Gana Mana' and Bangladesh's 'Amar Shonar Bangla'.

Trivia

He established the Bolpur Bramhacharya Ashram at Shantiniketan, a school based on the pattern of old Indian Ashram.

Quote

"I slept and dreamt that life was joy. I awoke and saw that life was service. I acted and behold, service was joy."

RALPH WALDO EMERSON

Ralph Waldo Emerson (May 25, 1803 – April 27, 1882) was an American essayist, lecturer and poet. He led the Transcendentalist Movement of the mid-19th century.

He was seen as a champion of individualism and a prescient critic of the countervailing pressures of the society. He disseminated his thoughts through dozens of published essays and more than 1,500 public lectures across the United States.

In his 1836 essay, *Nature*, Emerson formulated and expressed the philosophy of Transcendentalism, gradually moving away from the religious and social beliefs of his contemporaries.

Following this ground-breaking work, he gave a speech titled, *The American Scholar* in 1837, which Oliver Wendell Holmes Sr. considered to be America's 'Intellectual Declaration of Independence'.

Emerson's first two collections of essays – Essays: First Series and Essays: Second Series were published respectively in 1841 and 1844. They represent the core of his thinking, and include well-known essays, such as *The Over-Soul*, *Self-Reliance*, *The Poet*, *Circles* and the *Experience*.

Emerson wrote on a number of subjects, developing certain ideas such as freedom, individuality, the ability for humankind to realise almost anything and the relationship between the soul and the surrounding world. Emerson's 'Nature' was more philosophical than naturalistic, 'Philosophically considered, the universe is composed of Nature and the Soul'.

Trivia

Emerson's essays remain among the linchpins of American thinking and his work has greatly influenced the thinkers, writers and poets that have followed him.

RICHARD DAVID BACH

Born on June 23, 1936 in Oak Park, Illinois, Richard David Bach is an American writer. Widely known as the author of the hugely popular 1970s best-sellers, he has books like *Jonathan Livingston Seagull*, *Illusions: The Adventures of a Reluctant Messiah* to his credit.

His books advocate his philosophy that our apparent physical limits and mortality are merely appearance. Bach claims to be a direct descendant of Johann Sebastian Bach.

Richard is known for his love for flying and his books related to air flight and flying in a metaphorical context. He has pursued flying as a hobby since the age of 17.

Most of his books have been semi-autobiographical, where he used actual or fictionalised events from his life to illustrate his philosophy.

He has authored numerous works of fictions and non-fictions, including *Illusions*, *Jonathan Livingston Seagull*, *One and Out of My Mind*, etc.

He has also served in the United States Navy Reserve, later in the New Jersey Air National Guard's 108th Fighter Wing, 141st Fighter Squadron (USAF) as an F-84F pilot.

He has also worked as a technical writer for Douglas Aircraft and contributing editor for the Flying magazine.

Most of his books involve flight in some way, from the early stories which are straightforwardly about flying aircraft to *Stranger to the Ground*, his first book, to his later works, in which he used flight as a philosophical metaphor.

Trivia

In 1973, the book was turned into a movie, Jonathan Livingston Seagull, produced by Paramount Pictures Corporation.

ROBERT BROWNING

Robert Browning was born on May 7, 1812 in Camberwell, London. He was an English poet and playwright. His mastery of dramatic verse, especially dramatic monologues made him one of the foremost Victorian poets.

Browning was an extremely bright child and a voracious reader. He learned Greek, Latin, French and Italian by the time he was fourteen years old. He attended the University of London in 1828. In the 1830s, he tried to write verse drama for stage several times and realised that his talent lies in taking a single character.

He started writing poems during the same time. Some of his earlier works were *Paracelsus* (1835) and *Sordello* (1840).

He met the poet, Elizabeth Barrett in 1845. Although she was an invalid and very much under the control of a domineering father, they got married in 1846 and later eloped to Italy.

Barrett had been a more popular poet than Browning during their lifetimes. Some of his other works include *Collected Poems* (1862) and *Dramatis Personae* (1863). *The Ring and the Book* (1868-9), based on an 'old yellow book', which told of a Roman murder and trial, finally won him popularity.

The late 1860s were the peak of his career. Browning's influence continued to grow and finally led to the founding of the *Browning Society* in 1881. He died in 1889, on the same day when his final volume of verse, *Asolando*, was published.

Trivia

Elizabeth Barrett's love for Browning was demonstrated in the 'Sonnets from the Portuguese', and to her, he dedicated 'Men and Women' that contains his best poetry.

THOMAS MERTON

Thomas Merton was born on January 31, 1915 in Prades, Pyrénées-Orientales, France, to Owen Merton, a New Zealand painter, active in Europe and the United States, and Ruth Jenkins, an American Quaker and artist.

He was basically an Anglo-American Catholic **writer and mystic**. A Trappist monk of the Abbey of Gethsemani, he was a poet, a social activist and a student of comparative religion. He came to be known as Father Louis after he was ordained to the priesthood in 1949.

Thomas Merton wrote over 70 books, mostly on social justice spirituality, and a quiet pacifism, as well as scores of essays and reviews. His best-selling autobiography, *The Seven Storey Mountain*, sent scores of disillusioned World War II veterans, students, and even teenagers assembling at monasteries across the United States.

His autobiography was also featured in *National Review's* list of the 100 best non-fiction books of the century.

Merton was a keen proponent of interfaith understanding. He pioneered dialogue with prominent Asian spiritual figures, including the Japanese writer, DT Suzuki, the Dalai Lama and the Vietnamese monk, Thich Nhat Hanh.

He was baptised in the Church of England, in accordance with his father's wishes. However, his father was often absent during Merton's upbringing.

Merton died in an accident on December 10, 1968, when he reached out to an electric fan while taking bath and was accidently electrocuted.

Trivia
Merton's influence has grown since his death and he is widely recognised as an important 20th-century Catholic mystic and thinker.

TS ELIOT

Thomas Stearns, 'T S' Eliot (September 26, 1888 – January 4, 1965) was a playwright, literary critic and the most important English-language poet of the 20th century.

The poem that brought him fame was *The Love Song of J Alfred Prufrock*. Regarded as a masterpiece of the modernist movement, he started writing the poem in 1910 and it was published in Chicago in 1915.

This was followed with what have become some of the best-known poems in the English language, including *Gerontion*, *The Waste Land*, *The Hollow Men*, *Ash Wednesday*, and *Four Quartets*.

He is also known for his seven plays, the most important being *Murder in the Cathedral*.

He was awarded the **Nobel Prize in Literature** in 1948.

Eliot died of emphysema in London on January 4, 1965 after prolonged illness due to his heavy smoking. In accordance with Eliot's wishes, his ashes were taken to St Michael's Church in East Coker, the village from which his ancestors had emigrated to America.

Trivia

Although he was born an American, he moved to The United Kingdom in 1914 at the age of 25 and was naturalised as a British subject in 1927 at the age of 39.

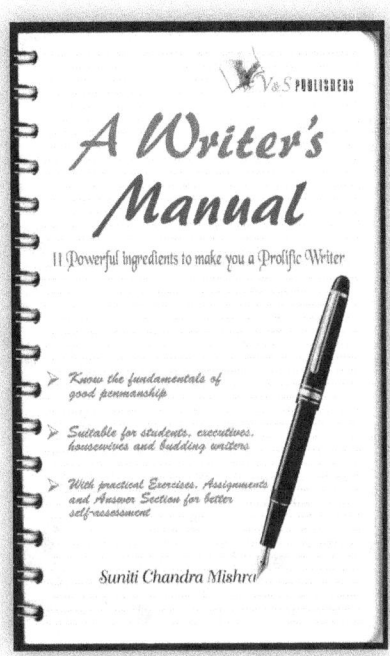

A Writer's Manual

Author: Suniti Chandra Mishra
Format: Paperback
Language: English
Page: 168
Price: ₹ 195
Publisher: V&S PUBLISHERS

It is a unique book dedicated to all those individuals who have a burning desire in their heart to write profitably. The author discusses 11 powerful ingredients that will help one become a prolific writer. The instructions that the author has shared, will greatly influence the reader's writing quality and is meant to make his road to success as a writer less jerky.

A Youngsters' Guide to PERSONALITY DEVELOPMENT

Author: S.P. Sharma
Format: Paperback
Language: English
Page: 120
Price: ₹ 110
Publisher: V&S PUBLISHERS

In a world marked by competition, personality is the key to success – whether it is social, business, personal or political arena. Interview for IAS or an MNC, meeting with the parents of your prospective bride, addressing a public rally, or delivering a speech in an international conference...

Out of SYLLABUS

Author: V. Rajesh
Format: Paperback
Language: English
Page: 96
Price: ₹ 120
Publisher: V&S PUBLISHERS

It is easy to skip a question during an exam if it is "Out of Syllabus" but what do you do if you are faced with a situation in life for which you were not given any input? Can you run away from the situation using the "Out of Syllabus" excuse?

251 STUDY SECRETS

Author: B.K. Narayan & Preeti Narayan
Format: Paperback
Language: English
Page: 133
Price: ₹ 150
Publisher: V&S PUBLISHERS

Forget that there are no short cuts to remember fast. Innumerable ideas exist that really work. Start using them to read fast, learn quickly and score high in exams!

Inspirational Quotes and Thoughts

Author: G.C. Beri
Format: Paperback
Language: English
Page: 132
Price: ₹ 80
Publisher: V&S PUBLISHERS

This book contains as many as 460 inspiring quotes classified in well defined 19 groups. To one who is feeling depressed and confused, this book 'Inspirational Quotes and Thoughts' would bring him out of that disturbed mental state.

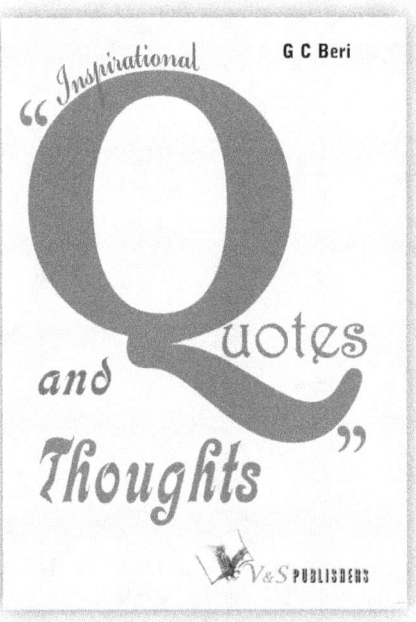

Become Proficient in Speaking and Writing GOOD ENGLISH

Author: Archana Mathur
Format: Paperback
Language: English
Page: 148
Price: ₹ 120
Publisher: V&S PUBLISHERS

Learn sophisticated style of English writing and speaking correctly. Polish your communication skills by using effective and altractive words readers as well as listeners prefer.

GREATEST CRAFTS & PROJECTS

Author: Vikas Khatri
Format: Paperback
Language: English
Page: 120
Price: ₹ 100
Publisher: V&S PUBLISHERS

54 cool and awesome projects, crafts, experiments and more for kids!!! Greatest Crafts and Projects for Children is packed with 54 experiments ranging from outdoor projects to gifts and party favours to holiday decor to projects that promote learning through play; with step-by-step instructions to guide children for successful completion of each project.

Drawing & Painting Course

Author: A.H. Hashmi
Format: Paperback
Language: English
Page: 124
Price: ₹ 150
Publisher: V&S PUBLISHERS

Children have always been attracted towards bright colours, various shapes and diverse objects that they see around them. Nature fascinates them. The beautiful birds, animals, flowers and trees fire their imagination; and they want to capture it on paper. But how, for all are not artists. This book tells you...

Also available in Hindi

Mind Benders Brain Teasers & Puzzle Conundrums

Author: Vikas Khatri
Format: Paperback
Language: English
Page: 152
Price: ₹ 110
Publisher: V&S PUBLISHERS

- Enjoy mental workouts?
- Use maths occasionally?
- Like numerical brain teasers?
- Accept intellectual challenges?
- Dabble in solving puzzles?
- Love solving Riddles?

If you answer "YES" to any of these questions, then this is the right book for you! If you want to test your logical skills and have fun, then read this collection of brain teasers and mind benders and check out how smart you are!!

ENVIRONMENT QUIZ BOOK

Author: Manasvi Vohra
Format: Paperback
Language: English
Page: 144
Price: ₹ 110
Publisher: V&S PUBLISHERS

The study of environment includes physical and biological sciences like Ecology, Botany, Zoology, Physics, Chemistry, Geography, etc. To test your knowledge about the environment around us, **Environment Quiz Book** is an ideal companion.

SUDOKU
SUDOKU NEXT

Author: Sahil Gupta
Format: Paperback
Language: English
Page: 96
Price: ₹ 60
Publisher: V&S PUBLISHERS

Sudoku means "single number". Popular all over the world, it is a logic based number placement puzzle. Solving the puzzles help sharpen reasoning ability of the brain.

GREATEST WONDERS OF THE WORLD

Author: Vikas Khatri
Format: Paperback
Language: English
Page: 128
Price: ₹ 100
Publisher: V&S PUBLISHERS

The Earth is indeed an extraordinary planet. It has infinite variety of life. The land itself is fabricated marvellously with wonders. The book distils outstanding marvels that have allured curiosity of people throughout the ages.

Nobel PEACE PRIZE WINNERS

Author: Vikas Khatri
Format: Paperback
Language: English
Page: 168
Price: ₹ 120
Publisher: V&S PUBLISHERS

Awarded by Nobel Peace Committee annually Nobel Peace Prize has been awarded to 101 individuals and 20 organisations since the award of first prize in 1901 till 2011. Learn about those wo worked for the nobel Cause.

FAMOUS INDIANS OF THE 20TH CENTURY

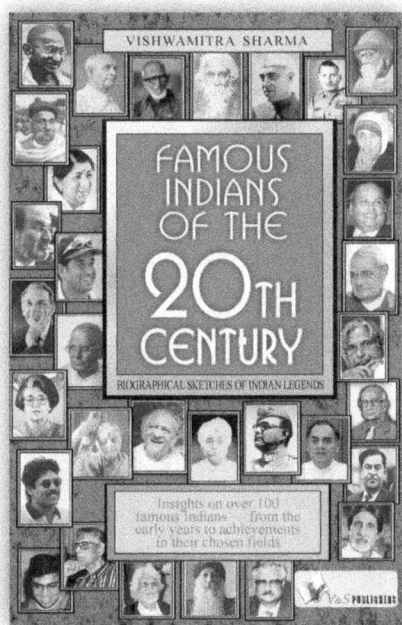

Author: Vishwamitra Sharma
Format: Paperback
Language: English
Page: 228
Price: ₹ 135
Publisher: V&S PUBLISHERS

For people of all age groups, reading about the lives and times of great Indians is always inspiring and uplifting. This book presents high points on the lives of more than 100 famous Indians of the 20th century. The names include Mahatma Gandhi, Jawahar Lal Nehru, Rajendra Prasad, Indira Gandhi, JRD Tata, Subash Chandra Bose, Mother Teresa, etc.